Cowboy Truth

Cowboy Justice Association
Book Three

By Olivia Jaymes

www.OliviaJaymes.com

COWBOY TRUTH
Copyright © 2014 by Olivia Jaymes
Print Edition
E-Book ISBN: 978-0-9899833-4-1
Print Book ISBN: 978-0-9899833-5-8

Cover art by Sloan Winters

ALL RIGHTS RESERVED: The unauthorized reproduction or distribution of this copyrighted work is illegal. Criminal copyright infringement is investigated by the FBI and is punishable by up to 5 years in federal prison and a fine of $250,000.

All characters and events in this book are fictitious. Any resemblance to actual persons living or dead is strictly coincidental.

Dedication

To all the good girls out there who like bad boys.
This one's for you.

Chapter One

Sheriff Logan Wright sat back in his chair, a smile playing on his lips, and let his gaze linger on the two generous curves struggling for escape from the tight blue dress. Charlene Decker's cleavage was looking good tonight. She was wriggling on the dance floor, her boobs bouncing up and down against what was assuredly a complex structure of hooks, elastic, and wire. God bless the engineer that had designed that damn thing. He'd had his hands full.

Logan chuckled and took another draw from his beer. He'd had his own hands full of Charlene's bounty on more than one occasion and had enjoyed it immensely. The way she was eyeing him tonight, he might be in for a repeat performance.

The wedding reception, held in a large tent on the grounds of the Bryson estate, was in full swing and it was a good night for a party. August was still warm, even in Montana, and everyone was in high spirits. The bride and groom were leading a line of people doing the "bunny hop" and Charlene was right in there with them. Logan was one of the groomsmen for his friend Lyle's wedding, and while he loved Lyle like a brother, the last fucking thing Logan wanted to do was hop around a dance floor looking like a crazed clown jumping out of a jack in the box.

A man had to have some damn dignity in this world.

The bridesmaid Logan had been paired with during the wedding apparently felt the same. Ava Hayworth was sitting on the opposite side of the dance floor plucking at the petals of a flower in her bouquet of roses. She was alone at the table, and zealously avoided eye contact with any of the guests or staff. Unlike most women who were alone, she didn't seem glum or sad. Instead, she had an air of peace and contentment around her as if the loud music and partying weren't happening inches away.

"How come you aren't out on the dance floor?" Wade Bryson, oldest brother of the groom and Logan's best childhood friend, slid into the chair next to his. Wade's face was flushed from either dancing or drink. Maybe a touch of both. "Charlene has her eye on you."

Wade elbowed Logan and grinned widely. Wade loved Logan's sex life more than Logan did. As a happily married man with three wild kids, Wade hadn't had sex with anyone but Nancy since high school, so he lived vicariously through Logan.

He pointed the bottle toward the dance floor where everyone was now doing a passable rendition of the "chicken dance." "I think I'll pass. Poultry and rabbits are things I eat, not things I do to entertain the good citizens of Corville."

It felt like the entire town was here tonight, the crush of bodies overwhelming to a man who liked his solitude. Logan knew every person's name and of course they all knew him.

Warts and all.

"Then go ask Ava to dance, will you? Mary paired her with you because she thought you'd be a gentleman and take care of her tonight. You don't want the bride pissed at you, do you?"

No, Logan did not. Mary, Lyle's bride, was okay in small doses, but had the temperament of a bubbling volcano made for the science fair. You never knew when it was going to erupt and spew all over everything and everyone. Logan had made a habit of staying out of her kill zone.

"I danced with her once." He didn't know why he was being such a dick about Ava tonight. She was a nice kid and easy to look at with her golden brown curls and hazel eyes. The pink dress she was wearing was a godawful mess of satin, lace, and ruffles, but she probably had a decent figure underneath it. She wasn't glamorous, but she was cute and non-demanding. In fact, she'd abandoned him after the first dance, muttering something about checking on the bride.

"Once?" Wade scoffed. At that moment, he looked exactly like his father, real estate developer extraordinaire Bill Bryson. Hell, all three of the Bryson boys looked just like their daddy, dark hair and eyes. "Dance with her again. The DJ's putting on a slow one."

Logan sighed and set down the beer bottle. "Fine. She didn't step all over my boots earlier. After this dance though, I'm out of here."

Wade shook his head. "You can't leave before they cut the cake and all that shit. You were in the wedding, man."

For the dozenth time in the last week, Logan wished he hadn't agreed to be a groomsman. Things like these had expectations, guidelines, and fuck it, rules. He wasn't a huge fan of any of those things, preferring to navigate life with his instincts. Even as a cop Logan followed his gut, eschewing traditional police practices and regulations. So far it hadn't let him down.

Standing up, he eyed the woman in question from a safe distance. It wasn't that he didn't want to dance with Ava. He liked her fine. She was, however, well educated. A college graduate of

English or something like that. She wrote books for a living. Logan had scraped through high school by the skin of his teeth. He simply didn't know what to talk to her about. Their one dance earlier had been awkward to say the least.

"Dance with her. Make sure she has a good time. If Mary thinks her sister isn't having fun, heaven help us all." Wade dashed off toward the main house without another word.

He walked across the dance floor, side stepping slowly swaying couples and came to a halt in front of Ava. She looked up at him with eyes wide as if she couldn't believe he dared to cross over to her. Although he couldn't remember a woman turning him down for anything from extra gravy on his mashed potatoes at the diner to rip-roaring, raunchy sex, this little miss just might refuse to dance with him. He opened his mouth to ask her but his sleeve was grabbed and tugged. He turned to see Charlene there – all hair, boobs, and teeth.

"C'mon, Logan." Unfortunately, her voice didn't match the outwardly sensual appearance. Her tone was high and girlish and always made Logan want to put something hard in her mouth to keep her quiet. "Come dance with me."

"Not now, Charlene." Logan gently extricated his elbow from her claw-like fingers with their long, red nails. "I'm dancing with Ava first."

Charlene pouted, her lip gloss shiny under the cheesy disco ball hanging from the center of the tent. "I guess I can wait. You're worth it." She fluttered her eyelashes for effect, but Logan didn't rise to the bait. It almost wasn't fun chasing women anymore when they made it so damn easy.

Logan turned back to Ava and she was already shaking her head. "Go ahead with Charlene. I'm fine here."

"No, let's dance." Logan eyed the stubborn miss. Her chin was lifted and there were green sparks of rebellion in her eyes. "I'll dance with Charlene afterward."

Charlene hovered a few feet away watching the byplay with interest. Nothing this town loved more than some juicy gossip. Logan getting his ass handed to him by a little bit of a thing would be news indeed. He had to admit she piqued his interest. He wasn't used to women ignoring him.

Ava bit into her full lower lip and shook her head again. "No, go ahead. Really, it's okay."

Logan sighed and leaned forward, his hand resting on the arm of her chair, their faces inches from one another. From this position, he could see her shocked expression and smell the floral fragrance of her perfume. It was a soft, pleasant aroma that wrapped around him, reminding him of the Montana prairie in the spring.

"I don't want your sister pissed at me. Dance." He kept his voice soft but unyielding.

Shock gave way to amusement and she smiled, dimples appearing in her cheeks. "Hurricane Mary is on your case, huh? I'll take pity on you, Sheriff. But watch those big cowboy boots."

He bit back his usual rejoinder about how his big boots matched another part of his anatomy. He wasn't looking to get Miss Goody Two-Shoes between the sheets tonight. She was the original good girl. Everyone knew that. Ava was the kind of girl who went to church socials, volunteered for the elderly, and sure as shit wore white cotton panties underneath that pink nightmare of a dress.

He placed his hand under her elbow and led her onto the small dance floor. The lights were low and he pulled her into his arms as another slow song started up. They moved slowly to the baleful strains, and Logan searched his mind for small talk.

"I read your last book," he heard himself saying. "I liked it."

She looked up, craning her head back. She was a tiny thing, barely up to his shoulder. Her face was wreathed in an honest-to-god genuine smile. It made his stomach do funny things and he immediately, ruthlessly, pushed the feeling away. "Really? Logan, that's so sweet. I didn't even know you read my books."

Sweet? Logan Wright had never been described as sweet. Horny. Wild. Laid back. Yep, he'd been called all of that. And a few things he'd probably never heard about. At least by the fathers in town.

"I've read all of them."

Now why the fuck did he admit that? It made him sound like some pathetic stalker fan or something. He simply liked to read in the winter when it was too fucking cold to do anything else.

"I'm so glad." Her voice was soft but sure. "I'm researching a new one, actually."

"Another murder mystery?" It was easy to talk to her about her writing. She was totally animated at the moment.

"Yes," she nodded eagerly. "A grisly one, of course. Melissa and Mark will really have to work to figure this one out."

Melissa and Mark were Ava's lead characters. Both of them rookie reporters for a local paper. They were friends who spent their free time solving murders.

"A lot of crime in that small town you write about." Her body brushed against him and his throat went dry.

Ava giggled. "I know. You'd think they'd slip into some existential void after seeing so many dead bodies, wouldn't you?"

Logan didn't know what an existential void was, but he'd seen more than his share of dead bodies.

"Seeing a dead body will change a person."

Her brows pulled together. "Are you saying that Melissa and Mark aren't growing enough with what's happened to them in the first six books?"

Logan had no fucking idea.

"All I'm saying is that seeing death leaves its mark."

Ava chewed on her lower lip, her frown growing deeper. "How has it changed you?"

He was not going to have this conversation with her.

"We're not talking about me."

"We are now. I need to understand how this should change Melissa and Mark. I need for them to be believable."

"Does it matter? I'm willing to bet the majority of the American population hasn't seen a dead body except on television."

"What about people who have?" she insisted.

"Then they have more important shit to think about than Melissa and Mark," he countered.

They lapsed back into an uncomfortable silence and he let his gaze wander around the room. Lyle was dancing with his new bride. Aaron, the third Bryson brother, was dancing with Charlene but holding her at arm's length. Aaron was a married man and didn't need his wife's wrath to come down on him.

Ava looked over her shoulder, her gaze following his. "You know those aren't real, right?"

Logan shook his head, not following her for a second. When he realized what she was referring to, his face split into a grin.

"What would you know about Charlene's boobs?"

"I know she went off to Dallas a few years ago to visit her cousins and came back with that rack strapped to her chest." Ava sniffed. "I bet when she lies down, they stick straight up in the air. No way she sleeps on her stomach."

They did stick up in the air, but Logan wasn't going to say shit about it.

"You sound a little jealous." He shouldn't poke and prod at Ava but she'd brought it up first.

Her mouth fell open and her eyes narrowed. "I am not jealous. I don't want anything fake on me. I'm only saying that you should know what you're getting." Her face relaxed into a smile. "You know – truth in advertising."

Logan shrugged. "It's not like she stuffed her bra with toilet paper. Besides, no man I know cares whether they're real or not."

Pressing her lips together, Ava shook her head. "You all think with your penises – that's the problem."

Logan laughed. "Penis? I thought only doctors talked that way. So formal and proper. But what else would I expect? I bet you've never even sworn in your entire life."

Her cheeks turned a becoming pink. "I have. I can swear." She turned and looked all around her before facing him to make sure no one was listening. "Shit. There, are you happy?"

"It sounded so natural, too," he mocked as the song ended. He stepped back and she did the same. They stared at one another for a moment.

"Thank you for the dance." Ava flicked a curl behind her ear. "It was nice seeing you, Logan."

She was dismissing him, and that was fine and dandy. At the rate they were going, he'd get blamed for besmirching her lily white reputation by introducing her to four-letter words and heaven knew what else.

"It was nice seeing you, Ava. Save me a dance at the next wedding."

The rest of the evening passed quickly, and despite a blatant invitation from Charlene, Logan refused her offer of a late-night skinny dip in the nearby lake. He wanted a hot shower and some quality shut eye. He suffered from insomnia and spent many nights wide awake, but he was just tired enough tonight to actually sleep. He wouldn't fuck with the rare mood. Instead he planned to take advantage of it.

He pulled out of the Bryson estate and headed south toward his own small spread on the outskirts of town. Driving down the deserted stretch of highway, Logan began writing out his mental list of things to do the next day. This was one of the reasons he couldn't get to sleep. His mind never fucking rested, constantly working on one puzzle or another.

The beep from his phone broke the silence, and he reached for his cell that he'd tossed carelessly on the passenger seat. He swiped the screen with his thumb.

"Wright." He kept his eyes on the road, not bothering to look at the display. He didn't get telemarketers or strangers calling him enough to worry about such things. People acted these days as if a stranger calling them was a goddamn crime or something. They needed to fucking relax and get a hobby. Not worry about petty shit that was going to shorten your life.

"Logan, turn around and head back to Bryson's. I'll meet you there." It was Logan's deputy Drake James on the other end.

Logan didn't hesitate. Drake wouldn't call unless it was important. Logan turned the SUV with a grunt of frustration. He wouldn't be getting the sleep he was hoping for tonight. A couple of cowboys had probably had one too many and were throwing punches in the barn.

"What's going on?"

Logan heard Drake's indrawn breath. "It's Bill Bryson. He was shot. In the head. I've called the state police and asked for their forensics team."

Tightening his fingers on the steering wheel, Logan swallowed the shock that ran through his body. Instead his thoughts went immediately to Wade, Aaron, and Lyle. They were close to their father and this was going to hit them hard. Logan felt a lump rise in his throat as well. Bill Bryson had never been an easy man to know, but he had always treated Logan decently even when he'd been raising hell with Wade.

"I'll be there in ten." Logan shoved the phone into his pocket.

Hitting the siren and lights, he pressed down on the accelerator. The last time he'd seen the dead body of someone he knew well he had been in the Persian Gulf. It hadn't been a pleasant sight then, and it would be less so this time. He only hoped he could keep his friends from seeing their father's corpse.

No one should have to live with the image of someone shot in the brain. The human mind wasn't built for pictures like that. And the bodies weren't built to withstand the bullets.

It was an ugly, no win combination.

Chapter Two

Ava couldn't see a thing. She stood on her tip-toes and tried to peer around the wall of man standing in the doorway to the game room of the Bryson estate. Dressed in a charcoal gray suit and sporting a badge, he had to be over six feet tall with shoulders just as wide. He looked vaguely familiar and about her age. She had probably gone to school with him but drew a blank on his name. Currently he wasn't budging an inch. When she'd tried to enter the room, he'd gently but firmly held up his hand asking her to step back into the hallway.

According to the buzz in the reception tent, someone had shot Bill Bryson in his own home while guests less than two hundred feet away danced and partied. Ava's sister Mary and her new husband Lyle were understandably upset, although Mary seemed more upset that it had ruined her wedding rather than that her father-in-law was no longer breathing. Ava's sister didn't like it when things didn't go as planned. Consequently, Mary was currently in the reception tent urging her guests to have more cake in some strange attempt at normalcy.

Lyle, on the other hand, was pacing up and down the hallway with his two brothers Aaron and Wade. All three men had grim, bleak expressions and Ava's heart went out to them. She hadn't really known Bill Bryson, but his sons seemed to have grown into fine men. Pillar of the community stuff.

Sheriff Logan Wright appeared at the end of the hall, his face carved from granite. He strode toward the library and brushed past her without a look or word, his attention elsewhere. The man in the doorway stepped back and they both went deeper into the room.

Ava edged into the library hanging back as far as she could in a shadowed area, but still close enough to see Mr. Bryson stretched out on the rug in front of the fireplace. Several lamps had been turned on but it was still hard to see, especially with Logan and the other man blocking a portion of the view. Logan knelt down about a foot away from the body examining the scene.

"No one's moved him, Drake?"

"No. I secured the scene as soon as I heard the ruckus."

Logan scraped a hand down his face and closed his eyes for a moment. "Holy fuck, who would want to do this to Bill? Shit, he and his ancestors practically built this town. This is going to kill Wade."

Everyone knew Logan and Wade were friends and that it went back to childhood.

"Who found him?" Logan's voice was tired and his shoulders stiff.

"Bryson's brother, George. He said—"

Drake was interrupted by Wade, Aaron, and Lyle storming the room. They stomped up to Logan who had turned on his heel at the sound. He put his hand on Wade and Lyle's chests, pressing them back.

"You don't want to come in here. Trust me on this. You don't want to remember Bill this way," he urged, succeeding in pushing them back a few feet. "He wouldn't want you to see him this way."

Aaron stood motionless, a strange look on his face as he stood apart from his two brothers. From the angle he had, he was afforded the perfect view of the back of his father's head.

What was left of it.

Aaron appeared shattered, his skin a ghostly white and his eyes almost unblinking. Logan turned from Lyle and Wade to see the expression on Aaron's face and swore. Logan sighed and ran a hand through his hair.

"I didn't want you to see this."

Ava shivered as the reality of the morbid scene seeped into her brain. This wasn't a whodunnit party or one of the many police training simulations she'd attended. This was the real thing and Bill Bryson wouldn't be getting up from the blood-soaked carpet. He'd be carried away in a coroner's van leaving a grieving family.

She now knew what Logan had been talking about when they were dancing earlier. Seeing death did things to a person. She wouldn't be the same Ava who had walked into this room five minutes ago, and Aaron would most certainly be a changed man.

George Bryson walked into the library, a highball glass in one hand, his features a ghastly color.

"Son of a bitch, will everyone please leave the crime scene?" Logan growled, frustration written in every line of his face.

No one moved. Swaying slightly on his feet, George came right up to Logan. "It was my brother and I'm the one who found him. I have a right to know what's going on. Have you found who did this yet?"

George's voice was almost shrill at the end of his question. It made Ava want to put her hands over her ears, but Logan didn't even seem fazed.

"No, and you are hampering my investigation, George. Deputy Drake, will you please escort the family into the kitchen? I'd like them to wait there so I can get everyone's statement. We also need to clear this room for the state forensics team. They should be here soon, and they won't be happy that their evidence is being destroyed."

Wade grabbed Logan by the arm. "I need to be here." The words were choked and broken.

"You need to be with your wife and brothers," Logan said firmly, placing his own hand on Wade's. "Let me do my job."

He said the last part more gently and Wade nodded, his shoulders hunched. Drake led the three brothers and the uncle from the room, George Bryson still muttering to himself and gulping back the amber liquid in his glass.

Ava let out her breath slowly, realizing she'd been holding it as the scene had unfurled. She'd been shown a more gentle side of Logan Wright. A side she'd never been privy to before, but then she'd never spent much time with him. He'd been four years ahead of her in school before leaving for the military. She'd left for college and eventually settled in Portland these last few years.

Standing in the middle of the room, he slowly seemed to become aware he wasn't alone. His head swiveled and his gaze came to rest on her standing in the shadows. He frowned and pressed his lips flat.

"Are you trying to hide? You're not exactly dressed to blend in, you know." His tone was hard but he didn't appear angry.

Ava shrugged. "I know." Her pink dress clashed with the rich earth tones of the room. It pretty much clashed with everything, if the truth be known. "And I'm not trying to hide. I'm just trying to stay out of your way."

His frown deepened to a scowl. "You need to go into the kitchen so I can get your statement."

His voice was commanding and a part of her thought about moving, but she wanted to stay more.

"I don't have any evidence. I didn't see or hear anything. I only found out from the other guests."

Logan put his hands on his hips and exhaled. "Then what are you doing in here? You need to go back to the party. I've got deputies out there who need to account for everyone at the wedding and what they were doing at the time of the murder."

Ava stepped forward eagerly. "That's exactly what you should do. I can help you with that."

"I have deputies to help me," Logan said flatly. He wasn't being receptive, and it appeared she needed to make things clear to him. She took another step forward.

"I want to help. I know about solving a murder." Ava held her breath as Logan chewed on her offer.

He barked in laughter that didn't sound amused. "What do you know about solving murders?"

"I've solved six of them," she replied indignantly. "One was a real doozy, too. You're lucky that your pool of suspects is contained. It should make solving the case much easier. First, we need to go over the guest list and talk to each person. We can create a map of where they were when Bill Bryson was shot. That will give us a visual look at who had opportunity. Then we can look for motive."

A few men in work overalls came into the room, and Logan held up his hand. "Stop right there. Don't move. I need to talk to these people. Then you and I will finish this conversation."

He turned his back and spoke low to the men. They nodded and began opening what looked like toolkits. Ava had enough crime education to know they were forensic investigators. They would gather and analyze the physical evidence.

Logan finished with the men and walked back to her, placing his hand under her elbow. He leaned down close to her ear.

"Come with me. Don't touch anything. Don't say anything. Just follow."

His grip was tight and she didn't so much follow him as simply try and keep up as his long legs ate up the distance to a bedroom down the hall. He closed the door behind them and spun her around before crossing his arms across his chest.

"Ava, I am trying to be very patient with you tonight." A muscle worked in Logan's square jaw. His blond hair was ruffled and he was getting a faint shadow of a beard. "This isn't one of your books. This is real life. A man is dead and I need to find his killer. Do you understand that?"

He was speaking to her as if she wasn't very bright, and she understood why. Everyone knew she lived inside the stories running through her head. Mary had always been the practical one. Grounded and efficient, although annoyingly superior.

Ava was the opposite. She'd missed more meals than she could count either reading or writing a book. Her house was perpetually messy when she was working on a new story, and her head was filled with characters talking to her and telling their stories. If she hadn't written them down, she would have surely gone mad.

"I do understand." Ava nodded. "I know you think I don't. I just want to help. Let me help you, Logan."

He nodded to the door. "This doesn't bother you? There's a dead body down the hall, Ava. He's not going to hop up and join everyone on the dance floor. Your sister's father-in-law is dead."

His bald statement made her swallow hard. Actually, now that he was mentioning it, her stomach was a little queasy. The smell of copper had hung in the air, assailing her nostrils. The blood spilled on the rug had looked almost black in that light. It was a haunting image that would stay with her whenever she wrote a murder scene.

"I'm okay," she denied. "I've seen lots of crime scene photos in my research."

"Is that what this is? You think this is something for one of your books?" He looked aghast at the idea and she vehemently shook her head.

"No. This isn't for a book. I just really want to help you."

"I am sending you back out to the reception. You are not to interfere with this investigation, do you hear me?" Logan shook a finger at her, his blue eyes icy. He was clearly pissed. "This is not a game. A respected man of this community is dead. I won't let you turn this into some kind of circus for your entertainment."

Ava gritted her teeth. "I would never do that. God, I hope you know me better than that."

His expression softened slightly. "Listen, I know you mean well. You're a good kid and I know you think you can help. But this is the real world, Ava, not one of your books. Now I want you to go join everyone else."

"Fine."

She wasn't going to win this argument tonight. She needed to live through this battle to fight another day. Turning on her high heels, she headed straight for the exit, stopping just as she reached the doorway.

"I'm going to help you, Logan. I'm not sure how, but I will."

"This isn't *Scooby Doo*, Ava. Leave this to the professionals."

On that insulting note, she twisted the doorknob, pushing it open hard and almost knocking a deputy walking down the hall in the face. She muttered an apology and flew toward the back door.

She continued fuming as she headed for the tent to check on her sister. Logan had always been an arrogant SOB, but he'd never been hurtful. In fact, his easy laidback charm was what endeared him to the town. That and the fact that he was a total badass who kept their little burg relatively crime free.

She would find a way to help him. Solving a crime in one of her books was fine, but she knew she could do it for real. She'd been honing these skills her entire life.

Just for a moment like this.

Logan didn't need this shit in his life. He stalked back to the library, his temper simmering. He didn't get angry often. He had a long fuse, but when it was tripped it wasn't a pretty sight. Luckily, tonight he'd managed to hold on and not let it fly on Ava.

She hadn't meant any harm, he kept reminding himself.

She'd only been trying to help, which in and of itself wasn't a bad thing. In fact, it was really sweet. And naive. She simply didn't realize that investigating a murder wasn't like writing one. After all, she'd known the murderer before she wrote the book. It sure as shit probably made things a hell of a lot easier.

Ava needed to turn her attention to making cookies or brownies or whatever the church ladies did when someone died. He wouldn't let her interfere with this investigation. It was too important.

Logan stood outside the kitchen and beckoned to Drake, his deputy.

"Is everything okay? You look pissed," Drake said, leaning against the wall.

Logan rubbed his chin. "I'm not happy, that's for sure. Have you talked to them?"

Drake nodded. "Preliminary stuff from Wade, Aaron, and Lyle. I thought I'd leave George Bryson to you."

"Is he drunk?" Logan asked, already knowing the answer.

"He ain't sober. But drunk? Not really. Although he might have been an hour ago when the murder took place. You thinking his direction?"

Logan shook his head. "Fuck, I don't know. George and Bill had their moments, but murder? Seems extreme."

Drake's eyebrow arched. "Who inherits if Bill's out of the way?"

"The three sons, I assume." Logan shrugged. "George has his own money and business."

"I remember Mrs. Bryson died here in this house under mysterious circumstances." Drake looked around at the opulent luxury surrounding them. "I think I'd put the house on the market."

"Who would be able to afford it?" Logan replied. "Bill built this house for his wife. I don't think it's leaving the family any time soon."

"Just bricks and mortar." Drake didn't look impressed by the display of wealth. "This house feels kind of cold and lifeless if you ask me."

Logan couldn't argue. The home had never felt warm or drawn people in during his memory.

"I'm going to talk to George. Why don't you talk to one of the other deputies and have them get with the bride or the mother of the bride? We need a guest list. And a vendor list as well."

"Will do. Want me back here?" Drake turned to leave.

"Yes." Logan sighed. "It's going to be a long night."

"Want me to have one of the catering staff make you some coffee?" Drake offered.

"If they can. I think we'll be here into the morning."

"I can stay as late as you need." Drake knew that Logan suffered from insomnia. "You should try and get some sleep tonight. Me and the guys can handle this, Logan."

"Sleep won't happen." Logan shook his head. "I already know. The opportunity has passed me by. Besides, this is more than just a murder."

"I'm afraid to ask you what it is. I hope you're not thinking what I think you're thinking."

Drake's voice had a note of warning, but Logan was long past heeding it. He turned to enter the kitchen.

"It's personal. What was done here tonight was very personal."

Chapter Three

"Where are you going, Ava?"

Bruce Hayworth's voice boomed from the family room. Ava had been trying to get out of the house without her father noticing but it was not to be. He seemed to have a sensor underneath the rug by the front door. The minute anyone stepped on it, he was instantly alert, giving the escapee the third degree.

Ava sighed and closed her eyes, praying for patience. It wasn't her father's fault he still thought of her as a teenager. He hadn't evolved much the last fifteen years or so. He didn't carry a cell phone, didn't use the Internet, and talked longingly of "the good old days", whatever they were.

"Out, Dad. I have a few things I need to do."

Deliberately vague. She could be going to the grocery store or knocking over a bank. Ava crossed her fingers and took another step toward the door.

"Out where? When will you be back? Who will you be with?"

Just thought I'd hang with the Manson family.

Hissing out a breath, Ava juggled the folders she was carrying to her other arm. Setting boundaries with her parents was proving to be quite a chore. She was staying with them to attend Mary's wedding, and despite leaving home twelve years ago at the age of eighteen, her bedroom was still frozen in time.

It was kind of creepy.

The same posters, the same bedspread and curtains. It was as if some clone had been living in that room all this time while Ava went to college and started her career. She would have thought her parents would have turned it into a home gym or a craft room, but instead it stayed a shrine to her adolescence. That was a time of her life Ava could honestly say wasn't the greatest.

"I'm not sure, Dad. I have several things to do."

Her dad's footsteps on the carpet made her heart sink. He did this to everyone as if leaving the house was an insult to him and her mother. He walked into the foyer wearing a frown.

"There's a killer on the loose, Ava. Be home before dark. And call me when you get there. And when you leave."

She was thirty-frickin' years old and she was not going to do any of that.

"I doubt the killer has any interest in me," Ava said soothingly. "I'm not sure if I'll be home by dark. It will be okay. I'm a grown woman."

She might as well have said she was a Swahili voodoo healer for all the notice her father took.

"Promise me you'll be back before sundown. It's dangerous out there."

"Corville is not dangerous. Sheriff Wright runs a very orderly town."

At the mention of Logan, her father nodded. "He's the best sheriff we've ever had but wild as a mustang. I've never see him with the same woman twice."

Ava had heard the gossip about how hot Logan was between the sheets. Women actually sighed when they said his name. Sighed, for heaven's sake. Like he was some god or something. No man was that good in the sack.

"I don't think that will keep him from catching whoever murdered Mr. Bryson." Ava opened the door and tried to duck out. "See you tonight."

Her father's hand stayed the door. "Wait. You never said where you're going or when you'll be home."

Ava mentally counted to five as she didn't have the patience to count to ten. She needed to push back on this behavior if she was going to stay here in Corville for awhile and help Logan solve this murder. She looked her father in the eye.

"No, I didn't. That's because I'm thirty years old and no longer make a practice of checking in and out with my parents." Her father started to speak but she held her hand up. "I know you mean well, and I know you love me. But I'm all grown up, Dad. You and Mom did a great job. Rest on your laurels and relax. Your daughters will be fine."

"Mary will be fine because she has a good husband to take care of her."

Ava wanted to smack her head against the oak front door. "Are you saying Mary couldn't take care of herself? That I can't? If so, I've been doing a pretty decent impression of it these last few years."

Her dad's face was turning red. "While you're under my roof, young lady—"

"Bruce, leave Ava be. She's right. We need to trust her." Carol Hayworth appeared with a dishtowel in her hands and a smile on her face. "Honey, we'll leave a light on in the living room if we go to bed before you get home. Have fun and be safe."

"There's a killer out there!" Bruce Hayworth blustered. "You're sending your daughter to her death!"

Carol's eyebrows shot up and she gave her husband a quelling look. "If you are implying that I would be careless with my own daughter's life, you can fix your own dinner. I'll take my pot roast and eat at Doreen's."

The only person in the world who could handle Bruce Hayworth was his wife, Carol. He snapped his mouth shut and stomped back into the family room, turning up the television loudly.

Ava's mother rolled her eyes. "Your father is getting worse in his old age, I swear. You'd think this was Victorian times." Her eyes sparkled. "Are you going to see a young man, by any chance?"

Carol Hayworth had the wedding fever ever since Mary announced her engagement. Ava didn't have the heart to tell her she didn't really want to get married. She didn't see the need.

"Kind of." Ava was close to her mother, and they had very few secrets. "Actually, I was going to see Logan Wright. I want to help him find the murderer."

Everyone in town would have laughed at that statement, but Ava knew her mother wouldn't. Carol had been the only one who seemed to understand and support her daughter's fantasy life. She'd been the first person to buy one of Ava's books.

Carol tossed the dishtowel over her shoulder. "I suppose the safest place you could be is with Sheriff Wright." She turned to head back into the kitchen but suddenly stopped. "As long as that's all it is. Sheriff Wright is never going to settle down with one woman, sweetheart. If you're thinking along those lines, best put it out of your head. He's a good man, but a player of sorts."

"Everyone knows that. Besides, even if I was interested, I'm not his type."

"I'm not sure what Sheriff Wright's type is, but I just want you to be aware. He's a man that doesn't want to change."

"Do they ever?" retorted Ava.

"Only when they absolutely, positively have to." Her mother's eyes twinkled. "Have fun and drive carefully."

Ava would be a wealthy woman if she had a dime for every time one of her parents told her to be careful. It was as if they saw the world as this big, scary place with monsters around every corner.

She practiced her pitch to Logan in the car as she drove to his home. He hadn't exactly been excited about her offer to help the night before, but then they'd all been upset. Hopefully some sleep would have softened his mood.

She was still hopeful as she knocked on the front door of his house. This small ranch had belonged to the former sheriff but he had willed it to Logan. Despite the home being almost a hundred years old, it looked well-cared for. The clapboard siding was freshly painted in a cheery white with blue trim and the window boxes had bright red flowers that matched the flower bed in front of the large front porch. Everything about this place screamed a warm welcome to visitors.

She couldn't say the same for Logan when he finally opened the door.

"Ava? What are you doing here?" He looked over her shoulder as if to see if she had company. Either that or he was wondering how quickly he could hustle her back to her car.

"I brought you coffee." She held up a large to go cup from the local coffee shop who had assured her the dark roast was Logan's favorite. "I thought we could discuss the case."

He was less than thrilled. His jaw tightened and his lips pressed together, clearly holding onto his patience. She'd seen that same expression on her editor's face a time or three.

"We have nothing to discuss. You aren't working the case." He couldn't really pull off the pissed as hell routine considering he looked like a five year old pulled out of bed. He was wearing a gray pair of sweatpants that hung off his lean hipbones, a red T-shirt, and bare feet. His blond hair was tousled and even sticking up in a few places and there were creases on his cheek from the sheets. He must have slept hard when he finally went to bed. It was mid-afternoon now and she figured he probably hadn't even laid down until early this morning.

She waved the coffee under his nose. "It's your favorite."

His eyes followed the cup and for a moment she thought he was going to give in. Instead he shook his head and stepped more fully into the doorway.

"Ava, I know you're trying to help, but—"

"I know what you're going to say," she interrupted. "I only write fiction. I have my head in the clouds. Blah, blah. But I can help you. I brought the guest list. We have a lot of work to do and we need to get going."

She held up the thick folder filled with the guest list, vendor list, and even the reception seating chart.

Logan was suddenly wide awake. "How did you get that? We asked for it last night and was told by George they couldn't produce it. It had been thrown away."

"I printed them from my sister's laptop this morning." Ava shrugged. "It wasn't rocket science."

She could see the war going on inside Logan as different expressions flitted across his handsome features. Luckily for her, the last expression was one of acceptance.

"I suppose you won't give me those unless I let you in?"

Ava did a mental fist pump. Logan was going to let her past the threshold. Exultation made her want to do a victory dance, but this was only one of many battles to be fought. Logan wasn't going to give in easily.

"We're a package deal. Although I guess you could get a subpoena or something. That would take time."

Logan stepped back and waved her in. "Then by all means come on in. And give me that coffee. I desperately need it."

He didn't have his signature grin but a smile was playing on his lips. He was a good loser although she would bet he didn't have much practice at it. She handed him the paper cup.

"When did you get to bed?"

He drank the coffee, closing his eyes. "About ten in the morning. What a fucking night." He shut the front door and headed deeper into the house. "Well, you're here now. Are you coming?"

Scratching his stomach and yawning, he led her through the living room and into the large, bright kitchen. It had one of those old-fashioned double stoves she'd coveted in her grandmother's house and a large island in the middle stacked with file folders. A laptop was situated at one end and he pointed to one of two leather covered stools.

"Make yourself at home. I have coffee. Can I get you anything? I think I have juice and soda. Or water."

"A soda? You give in gracefully."

Logan pulled a can from the refrigerator and slid it in front of her as she settled at the island. She reached for one of the files but his large hand came down hard on top of it. She snatched her hand back and had to bite her lip to keep from laughing. He wasn't going to make this easy.

"First of all, I did not give in. I was blackmailed."

He wasn't happy, but he wasn't as irritated as last night.

"Second?" she asked sweetly, giving him her best innocent smile.

Logan growled and sat down in front of the laptop. She wasn't put off in the least. He was all bark and no bite. "Second, you are not a part of this investigation. I only let you in the house so I could get my hands on your evidence."

"That sounds kind of dirty." She giggled. "My evidence."

Logan finally smiled. "Did the deacon's daughter make an off-color joke? What would Daddy say?"

"Probably that I was heading straight to hell. Do not pass *Go*, do not collect two hundred dollars," she sighed. Her relationship with her father was complicated. In a nutshell, it went better when they were a thousand miles apart.

Logan gazed at her closely. "It doesn't appear to bother you."

It bothered her, but it was none of his business. "I'm not sure I believe in hell to begin with." Holding up the file, she gave him her biggest smile. She wouldn't be sidetracked. "We need to get started. I have a diagram of the reception area and the house. We need to put everyone in the places when the murder happened."

She hopped up and walked over to the large white board on the wall a few feet away. It was now clear Logan used this area as his office. She found a few magnets and clamped the large pictures to the board. She'd already filled in a few people in the reception area since that's where she'd been at the time of the murder.

Logan turned and eyed the chart. "You've been a busy bee while I slept." He pointed to some names on the dance floor. "How can you place them there when you don't even know the time of death?"

"I'm using the estimated time of death. We can fine tune the diagram later. It's going to take a long time to get everyone on here. There are over three hundred names on this guest list."

Logan winced and took another drink of his coffee. "I need a shower to help me wake up. I only got a few hours of sleep."

"I can work on this while you do that." Ava held her breath as Logan considered her offer.

Please. Please.

He reached and grabbed a folder, handing it to her. "I must be out of my fucking mind, but okay. Here are the statements of the guests that we gathered last night and early this morning. My deputies are out getting the ones we missed. Now raise your right hand."

"Um, what?" He looked completely serious.

"Raise your right hand. I'm going to swear you in as a temporary deputy of Corville."

She raised her right hand and dutifully repeated what basically amounted to a draconian vow of obedience and servitude. She was pretty sure this wasn't the same oath Deputy Drake had taken, but whatever. He was actually going to let her help.

"Now I'm going to take a shower and you are going to do only what I tell you to. You will not arrest anyone. You will not question suspects. Your job is one thing and one thing only. These files."

His finger tapped the stack and she sighed in capitulation. "You're mean. You take the fun out of everything."

Logan laughed and headed down the hall. "Ava Hayworth, you may be the first female to ever say that. I'll be right back."

She could hear his hearty laughter even when he closed a door between them and turned on the shower. Before she knew it, he was belting out a pretty darn good rendition of Bruce Springsteen's *I'm On Fire* at the top of his lungs.

Flipping open the folder, she started reading the first statement on top. It was going to be a long night.

Chapter Four

Logan rubbed his eyes and worked the kinks out of his back. He and Ava had been working through the stack of statements from the guests for the last four hours. He was tired, hungry, and his head hurt. They were, however, making progress. The reception diagram was starting to fill in nicely.

Ava was doing a good job. He hated to admit it but she did know her investigative techniques. She'd obviously done her homework and then some. She also appeared to have reserves of energy and enthusiasm he could only dream about. She was still bright eyed and bushy tailed, her eyes sparkling with excitement. She was a pretty girl with her dark curls and dimples in her cheeks when she smiled.

"I need a break. Are you hungry?" he asked, tossing a folder aside. "I think I have a frozen pizza in the freezer. They don't deliver way out here."

"I could eat," Ava shrugged and looked at her watch. "Wow, we've been at this a long time. I can't believe it's after six."

"I can. My stomach is screaming for food." He opened the freezer and pulled out two frozen circles, holding them up. "I've got a pepperoni and a sausage. Preference?"

"I like sausage but I'll do either. I'm easy."

Logan grinned. "That's not the word around town, Miss Goody Two-Shoes." Logan pushed a few buttons on the oven and slid the pizza directly onto the rack. He liked teasing her, seeing if she would take the bait. So far she'd been quite controlled.

"What is the word around town?" Ava asked, her expression bland.

Logan grabbed two fresh sodas from the fridge. "Word is you were a 'touch me not' in high school. Of course, that was several years ago. Things could have changed."

She tapped her fingernail on the counter and didn't look at him. "I didn't sleep around. Then or now. When I go to bed with someone it's because I like them. End of story."

"You think I sleep around though."

She finally looked up. "I didn't say that."

Logan laughed. "You didn't have to. Your prissy tone told the whole story. And I don't sleep around. I make sure the women I date understand who I am. I don't want a commitment, or marriage, or kids. If they're okay with that then we can have some fun. If not, I move along."

"My mother said you were a player and my father said you were wild as a mustang."

He liked her directness. It was refreshing in a world where most women were trying to get something from him. Sex, love, gifts, approval. Whatever it was, they were attracted to his looks or the way he filled out his jeans. They didn't know shit about him. Not really. They said they wanted to know him but what they really wanted was for him to know them. They wanted to be understood and admired. Ava didn't want anything from him at all.

Except to let her help.

He could give her that.

"A mustang. I like the comparison. Sounds like he doesn't think much of me."

Few fathers in this county did. Make that several counties.

"He said you were the best sheriff the town has ever had."

He turned and opened the oven pretending to check the pizza but really to hide his smile. He was glad the town recognized how hard he worked to keep them safe. He was truly proud of the legacy he was building in Corville. What he did had meaning and substance. It was real.

"That's nice of your father to say that. It's good to be appreciated." Logan popped open the can of soda. "Why are you trying to help me with a real murder instead of writing a new make-believe one?"

"This will make me a better writer." Ava was swinging her foot back and forth and avoiding his gaze. Logan played poker and had interrogated countless criminals. She wasn't telling the whole truth. He had found her tell.

"And?" He raised his eyebrows expectantly.

"And what?" Her small foot kicked faster. She'd pulled off her sandals earlier and he could see the flash of red toenail polish as her leg moved back and forth.

"You better check your pants, Ava. I think they're on fire. Now tell me why you're not working on a new book."

She sighed and her foot stopped swinging. "Melissa and Michael are falling in love."

"Is that a bad thing?" Logan didn't want to fall in love but he wasn't averse to reading about it.

"I didn't plan it that way. They were supposed to stay friends." She sounded annoyed.

"I'm not sure I follow you. They're your characters, right?"

"They really belong to themselves. They have minds of their own and they can be bossy."

He might just have a crazy woman in his kitchen.

"Do they talk to you all the time? Do they tell you to do bad things?"

She picked up the oven mitt and tossed it at him. "Stop smirking. I'm a writer. My characters talk to me."

He laughed at her outraged expression. "If you're okay with voices in your head, I am. You don't seem violent or anything."

"It's the life of a writer. Until now my characters were pretty well behaved. But lately they've wanted to do things that I'm not sure I can write about."

"Love?" Logan pulled the pizza from the oven and slid it on a cookie sheet.

"I've never been in love. I don't know how to write about it."

"Then don't. Ignore it."

"It doesn't work that way." Ava's stomach growled and she pressed a hand to her middle. "I didn't realize I was so hungry. That smells good."

Logan cut the pizza into slices and put two on her plate. "Eat. We still have a lot of work to do."

She blew on the steaming pizza. "So that's why I'm helping you. If I can hone my skills at solving a crime, maybe my readers won't notice that I don't know anything about love."

"You've never been in love? Ever?"

She was an attractive woman so it was hard to believe she'd never fallen. Love seemed to be all that females talked or thought about.

She shook her head. "Nope. I had a boyfriend who told me he loved me, but I couldn't say it back. He was nice but I just didn't feel it."

He decided to have some fun with her. "You could have just said it anyway. I don't think everyone expects it to be the truth."

Her eyes almost bugged out of their sockets. "Are you joking? Tell a man I love him but not really mean it? That's mean. Do you tell your women you love them?"

"No. Never." Love wasn't in his plans. "I told you I make that clear."

"Even if they tell you?" she insisted.

Logan winced at a recent memory. He didn't like hurting anyone's feelings but he wouldn't lie.

"Even if they tell me. But we're not talking about me. We're talking about you. You weren't in love with him."

"I should have been. He was perfect."

She bit into her pizza and hummed in appreciation.

"Perfect? How was he perfect?"

Logan was well aware he was interrogating her but he liked her clear, direct answers. She was too naive to even lie. It was like spending time with someone on truth serum. If she wasn't careful, she'd be crushed by the realities of life. It made him feel protective, wanting to shield her from the world.

"He was an artist of sorts. I've always dated that type. Actors, singers, writers. He understood my need to write at all hours of the day. He never pushed me when I was working on a book. He didn't drag me out of the house when I'd rather be home. We ate a lot of take out and watched television. He read me his poetry and showed me his art. He did graphic design for an advertising firm."

"He sounds like a deadly bore. No wonder you weren't in love with him. No excitement."

"I don't need excitement," she argued. "We were intellectual soul mates."

Logan almost snorted up his pizza. "I wouldn't know anything about that. I want passion and adrenaline. I want to feel something." He'd made her uncomfortable. She was picking at the sausage on her pizza. Good. It appeared she needed to be moved out of her comfort zone. "You need to get your heart rate up. That would help you write about love. And sex."

Her gaze lasered in on him, her eyes narrowing. He hid his chuckle as he realized he'd hit a nerve in the good girl. "I know all I need to know about sex, thank you very much."

He looked at her a long time, letting her get fidgety. "Somehow I don't believe that. Have you ever screamed so loud the windows shook? Have you made love so hard and fast the headboard put a dent in the wall?"

Her pretty cheeks were pink and she was eyeing him like he was slime. "That's not real. That's just in books and movies."

"Honey," he drawled. "That's my specialty."

From what she'd heard he was perfectly serious. He probably could get her screaming but she wasn't in the market for a man at the moment. She had too much on her mind, and besides she'd be leaving when they caught Bill Bryson's murderer. Being one of a crowd wasn't anything she aspired to.

"Yes, I've heard all about your reputation as the county stud." She reached for another slice of pizza. "Your name is on every bathroom wall between here and Billings. That must be quite an honor."

If she'd bothered him with her sarcastic tone, he didn't blink an eye. He just took a long drink of his soda and then grabbed another piece of pizza.

"There's nothing shameful about taking pleasure in life, good girl. I refuse to feel guilty for enjoying one of God's gifts to mankind."

She wasn't fond of him calling her a good girl. That's what the town thought of her and it was what she was, but she wasn't sure it was what she wanted to be.

"Sex is a gift from God?" Her voice sounded slightly choked. He was sitting there so smug and arrogant. Cool as you please.

He arched an eyebrow and smiled. "Isn't that what they mean when they talk about making a joyful noise unto the Lord?"

Heat suffused her skin. "I have no idea."

A knock at the door came just in the nick of time. Logan scowled but strode from the kitchen. She could hear a woman's voice, and something made her get up from her bar stool and peek around the corner. She knew better than to spy but Logan's silence made her wonder if the lady caller was welcome.

Logan was standing in the foyer with a tight expression on his face and his arms crossed over his chest. The woman, a drop-dead gorgeous blonde with a figure to die for, appeared completely unaware of his negative body language. The blonde had a bottle of wine and a cajoling tone in her voice.

"I know you've had a rough few days," she said. "I thought we could have a glass or two and listen to some music."

And Ava was Mary, Queen of Scots.

Ava doubted the only thing this woman wanted to do was drink wine and hang out. The blonde's eyes had a hungry quality that was clear even from six feet away. Ava turned to go back into the kitchen but she must have alerted Logan to her presence.

"Ava," he called. "Come out and meet Christina."

Why? Was he one of those guys who thought all females were friends simply because they all carried two X chromosomes?

She sighed and turned back, pasting on a smile. Holding out her hand, she tried not to stare. The woman was stunning to look at and obviously in love with Logan. Ava didn't know much about interpersonal relationships but a person could spot this a mile away. What was also obvious was that Logan didn't feel the same. To his credit, he was uncomfortable about it. Clearly he didn't want to be alone with her.

"Hi. I'm Ava. It's nice to meet you."

Christina's mouth drooped, but she shook Ava's hand.

"Nice to meet you. Are you a…friend of Logan's?"

Ava wasn't sure how to answer that question. She really wasn't. They were more acquaintances than anything else, but what she thought didn't matter. Logan answered for her.

"Ava and I have known each other for years. She's been living in Denver for awhile."

"Portland," Ava corrected. "I've been living in Portland, Oregon."

Logan's arm settled over her shoulders and she stiffened immediately. "I don't know why I keep getting Denver and Portland confused. Glad she's back though."

Logan had a big smile on his face, and Ava wanted to stomp on his toes. He was using her, dammit. She hadn't signed on for this.

"I came for my sister's wedding. I'll be leaving in a few weeks."

Christina was looking back and forth between them and for good reason. Who was going to believe sexy as sin, bad boy Logan Wright was interested in a barely attractive, goody two-shoes like her?

No one.

His arm hugged her close and she could feel the warmth from his body. "I'm hoping I can convince her to stay a little longer."

"Well, it's been very nice to meet you." Christina shoved the wine bottle at Logan, her smile shaky. "I guess I should be going."

The pretty blonde almost tripped over her own feet getting back out the door and down the porch steps. Ava felt her heart squeeze with sympathy as the car started up and shot down the long dirt lane to the main road. Ava twisted away from Logan and gave him a scathing look.

"That poor girl is in love with you. I thought you made sure they knew the rules at the beginning of the game?"

A muscle ticked in Logan's jaw. "I do."

Ava snorted. "This one didn't. I hope she doesn't drive off a bridge or something. Do you do this to all the women you date?"

"I do not." Logan leaned down and got nose to nose with her, causing her to take a step back. "Shit, Christina said she knew the score. She said she wanted casual and some fun. She changed the game on me. And no, I don't feel good about this. Hell, I wish she'd find someone else to fall for. I'm not worth what she's going through over me."

That took the wind out of her sails. "You were using me," she accused, not ready to admit defeat yet.

Logan straightened up. "I was, and I'm sorry. I just didn't expect her to show up here and I didn't know what to do. I've tried making things plain without being hurtful."

"I think you're going to have to hurt her a little," Ava admitted. "She's still hopeful obviously. Aren't you dating anyone?"

Logan's lips twisted. "I know everyone thinks I'm ass deep in women but I do go through an occasional dry spell. And I don't want to hurt her. She's a nice woman."

She had to give Logan credit. He seemed to be a genuinely nice guy.

"So you threw your arm around me?" she challenged.

A faint red stained his cheekbones. "I said I was sorry. I thought if she saw me with someone else, she'd give up and move on."

"And I was handy?"

"Yes." Logan sighed. "Are you going to take your foot off my nuts yet? I've apologized twice."

He had and she should. He'd only been trying not to hurt the woman.

"Do you think it worked? She ran out of here pretty fast."

"I hope so." Logan shrugged. "I'd hate to have pissed you off for nothing."

"I'm not mad. I just doubt she would be jealous of me. She's beautiful."

Logan stared at the doorway Christina had exited. "She is. But then all women are beautiful in their own way."

He sounded like he really meant it.

"All women? Even old lady Cartwright? She's about a hundred years old."

He turned and smiled. "Even her. She has a wisdom about her. She showed me pictures from her youth once. Man, she was hot back in the day. She must have had every man in Corville panting after her."

"Maybe you should have used her to make Christina jealous."

"I think she's already in a relationship with Malcolm Sweeney."

"My pizza's getting cold." Ava turned on her heel and went back into the kitchen, sitting down at the island. For some reason, she felt uncomfortable talking with Logan about relationships.

He followed her and settled back into his chair, watching her closely. "So will you help me?"

"Help you with what?" she asked evasively.

He chuckled. "I'm not letting you off the hook, good girl. Help me discourage Christina. Be seen with me. Come out with me and some friends on Tuesday night. It will help both of us."

She crossed her arms and shook her head. He was a smooth talker but she was wise to his game.

"How will this help both of us?"

"Christina will see me with another woman and you'll get out of your ivory tower. It might help your writing." He gave her a charming smile she was certain worked on women young and old. She felt her resolve starting to waver. It was tempting to give in. She was tired of her good girl image and being seen with Logan Wright was a sure way to destroy it. "I'm talking about going out on the town as friends. Have a few beers and some laughs. We'll go to the roadhouse and dance."

Oh hell no. Temptation withered and died there and then. He wanted her to be in a crowd of people. Those were situations she avoided like the plague. She had a small band of friends in Portland who enjoyed quiet evenings.

Boring evenings.

"I think I'll pass. That sounds like Dante's third circle of hell, honestly. I don't like crowds."

"I think you'll go." He grinned the patented Logan Wright smile.

"Why would I do that?" she asked, exasperated. Being around Logan was a little exhausting. He poked and prodded and asked way too many questions.

"Because you want to help me with this case so you can be a better writer."

"You're blackmailing me," she said flatly.

"You blackmailed me," he countered. "I let you help me with this case, and you let me help you learn how to wake the hell up, with the added bonus that Christina gets the gentle hint to move on. You're walking through life half asleep, Ava. I don't know why, but for some reason that bothers me."

There was a teeny tiny part of her that knew he was right. A big part of her, however, didn't like giving in too easily.

"I get to help you question people."

"No way." Logan shook his head. "No can do. You are an honorary deputy. Not a real one."

"No questioning, no dancing. No deal." She crossed her arms across her chest and tried to look tough.

"Your call." He shrugged. "Looks like you won't be helping me with this case at all."

She grabbed his hand. "I thought we were negotiating."

"What do you have that I need, good girl? I have all the resources I require to solve the case. What can you offer me to let you be part of the investigation?"

He looked like an immovable wall. An amused one. He had her over a barrel and he damn well knew it.

"You win. I'll go. But I won't have fun."

Laughing, he shook his head. "I bet you will. You just need to relax a little. Have some fun." He balled up his napkin and tossed it and the paper plate in the trash. "Are you done?"

She looked down at her plate and nodded. Just the thought of a loud night out with a bunch of people made her nauseous.

She'd rather be looking at crime scene photos of dead bodies.

"Yes. I'm full."

"Good. Let's get back to work then." He threw away her trash and they went back to combing through statements. Each one gave them a clearer picture of the whereabouts of all the guests, but there was still a long way to go.

And Logan wasn't going to take away her opportunity to help. She'd go dancing with him, discourage Christina, and he'd see what a stick in the mud she was. From then on, he'd give up on trying to get her to change.

Change sucked.

Chapter Five

Ava stood in the doorway of the Bryson house, hesitant to enter. The foyer and living room were packed with people and she didn't like crowds. It wasn't that she was shy. She could talk someone's ear off on the right occasion. She simply didn't like the closed in feeling of a room full of people. She was used to being alone most of the time and it suited her. She enjoyed the peace and quiet.

She looked right and left trying to find an alcove she could melt into and spied an unoccupied area behind a large wing back chair. She hurried toward it and tried to blend into the wallpaper, hoping to escape anyone's notice.

It was amazing how quickly a funeral could be arranged. Saturday, Bill Bryson was a proud father watching his son get married. Monday afternoon, they'd lowered his casket into the ground and he was being toasted by his earthly friends.

The entire town appeared to be here, with even more people than the wedding. Ava had attended the service in the local church, but had skipped the graveside ritual, much to her parents' chagrin. Her father especially had been disapproving, saying her absence would be noted.

How they would have been able to tell she wasn't there in this mass of people was a complete mystery. The crowd of bodies ruled out being able to catalog each and every attendee. She'd paid her respects to the family at the church already so her appearance here was simply to appease her parents who had to live in this town after she left.

She'd thought she'd found a good hiding place but clearly she was mistaken. Her sister, Mary, was heading right for her and there was no time to duck down behind the chair.

"I've been looking for you." Mary got right to the point.

"Why?" asked Ava. She couldn't think of a single reason Mary would want to talk to her. They'd barely spoken since Saturday.

"You gave Sheriff Wright the guest list from the wedding." Her sister looked less than happy, but that wasn't all that unusual. Mary could be moody at times and the ruination of her wedding hadn't helped her disposition. Her mother had been on the phone with Mary for two days trying to calm her down.

There was no point in pretending. "Yes. Was it a secret? I'm helping Logan find your father-in-law's killer. I thought you'd be happy about that. Don't you want to bring him to justice?"

Her sister had the decency to blush slightly. "Of course, but Uncle George told them it couldn't be retrieved. Then you produced it. It makes George look like a liar."

"Isn't he?" Ava challenged. "What made him say that to begin with?"

"I don't know," Mary admitted, looking uncomfortable. "I think he didn't like the way Sheriff Wright was questioning everyone like they were suspects or something."

"They are suspects," Ava argued. "We all are. Everyone at the wedding had opportunity. Now we have to find out who would have had motive as well."

"Are you really helping the sheriff? Mom said you were." Mary frowned. "That seems strange."

If her sister only knew.

"He's very open-minded." She couldn't think of much else to say. Confiding in her sister was not a habit Ava indulged in. She certainly wasn't going to tell her how she'd practically had to blackmail him into it. Or that he had blackmailed her as well.

Mary's eyebrows went up. "Really? Well, I hope you don't do anything stupid and get in his way."

"I'll try not to," Ava answered dryly. Her sister thought she was an air-headed nitwit. Some things never changed. "Excuse me, but I think I need something to drink."

Ava managed to dart away before Mary could reply or ask another question. Ending up in the dining room, Ava accepted a glass of wine from the bartender, sipping at the fruity liquid. She wasn't much of a drinker but needed the fortification for some reason today. Now the only question left was how long she needed to stay here to be polite.

"Drinking before five?"

Logan's deep, masculine voice in her ear jarred her out of her thoughts and she almost spilled her drink down the front of her staid black dress. She spun around and had to crane her neck to look up at him. He was easily over six feet tall and she was five-four in stocking feet. He was wearing another dark suit today but this one had a sedate navy tie instead of the bolo tie he'd worn on Saturday night. He looked every inch a Hollywood star instead of a small town sheriff. She could literally feel the gazes of several women on them at this very moment.

Pushing those disturbing thoughts away, she looked down at her wine glass. "I'm only sipping at it."

Logan held up a beer bottle for her inspection. "There's nothing wrong with having a drink on a day like today." He looked around the room. "I fucking hate funerals."

"I don't know anyone that likes them."

"When I die, just cremate me and spread my ashes up in the mountains somewhere. No services with people pretending to be sad. No emotional blackmail for my friends. Just peace."

She nodded to Wade, Aaron, Lyle, and George huddled together in a corner talking. "Do you think they're pretending to be sad? Isn't Wade your best friend?"

Logan's eyes narrowed at her question. "He is a good friend. As for pretending, the answer is no. The family seems genuinely distraught at Bill's death."

"So they're not suspects?"

"You know better than that. Everyone is a suspect until we can remove them." He leaned closer. "Even you, good girl."

He smelled really good, and she had to swallow hard to speak. "I had opportunity, but I think you'll find I lacked motive."

"That would make it the perfect crime. No motive." He smiled but kept looking around the room speculatively. "But I doubt you'd use a gun if you were going to kill someone. Nope. You'd want to kill them up close and personal. Maybe a knife or a blunt object."

"Professor Plum in the library with the candlestick," she said sarcastically. She didn't like the fact that Logan was so perceptive. It was what probably made him such a good lawmen but it was damn annoying too.

Logan chuckled. "I always liked that game when I was a kid." His smile fell. "Wade and I used to play it with his brothers."

She quickly changed the subject. "Mary's not happy with me. She found out I was the one who gave you the guest list."

"Then she guessed it. I didn't say where I received it, but it probably wasn't hard to figure out."

Ava peered around Logan to where her sister was talking to George Bryson. Their heads were bent close and the conversation appeared to be intense.

"She was upset because it made George look like a liar."

"He was a liar," Logan countered. "The question now is why did he lie? Why is he obstructing my investigation at every turn?"

"What else has he done?" George was looking back and forth between Logan and his nephews.

"He raised holy hell yesterday and this morning about releasing the crime scene. He also refused to turn over financial records for Bryson Development."

"Can he do that?" Ava watched George stride out of the living room and disappear into the back of the house.

"No, he can't. Wade agreed to open the records. Looks like you and I will be busy tonight and tomorrow."

She dragged her gaze away from the place George exited and back to Logan. "You mean it? You're going to let me continue to help?"

Logan's lips twisted. "Damned if I know why, but yes. I kind of like the way you think actually. You're logical and unbiased. You also don't shirk from boring, mind-numbing investigative work. You're detail-oriented and there is no way I would have plowed through those statements that fast without you. I'd be working on them for days."

His praise made her feel warm inside and it had nothing to do with the wine she was sipping.

"I do a lot of boring research for my books. I'm used to it."

"They're delivering boxes of paperwork for us to look through."

"So much for the digital age. Haven't they ever heard of computers?"

"For all I know they printed them from the computer. The good news is we'll be able to study them in the comfort and quiet of my home. Pick up a pizza on the way, will you?"

"Yes, my Lord. Anything you say, my Lord." Ava rolled her eyes. "That oath of office you had me take was cruel. You made me promise to obey you at all times."

"That was for your protection. If someone had a gun pointed at you, and I said duck, I need you to duck. I don't want you questioning me."

"Who on God's green earth is going to point a gun at me? All I do is look at files."

"That's also for your protection. Your parents probably wouldn't be too happy if I got you killed."

Ava chewed her lower lip, a shiver of something running up her spine. "Do you honestly think there's danger here?"

Logan looked at her straight on, a serious expression on his face. "Somebody got shot in the head, Ava. We don't know why, but we do know they aren't turning themselves into the police. So we know they don't want to go to prison. People will do desperate things to keep their deepest, darkest secrets hidden. I don't want you in the line of fire if they get a mind to do something rash."

"That doesn't explain the pizza."

"That's just because I'm going to be hungry. I'll meet you at my house at seven."

Logan turned and walked toward Wade, leaving Ava alone. She refused to let herself think about any sort of danger involved. She'd talked to policemen in her research and they'd told her the low rate of violence for most of them. Some went their entire careers and never discharged a weapon.

Nothing was going to happen to her. Or anyone for that matter. Whoever killed Bill Bryson had done it for a reason. A reason that probably didn't include killing anyone else. Corville didn't have a serial murderer running around it.

That would only happen in one of her books.

"You're making Uncle George nervous. Can't you lay off of him? He lost his brother for chrissake." Wade rubbed the back of his neck. "He didn't kill Dad."

Logan really wanted to believe that but George Bryson's behavior post-murder wasn't helping him in the least. He was putting up roadblocks at every turn, and Logan was already tired of the game.

"Then tell him to stop acting like an asshole and start cooperating. He's being evasive and difficult."

Wade winced at Logan's plain speech. "He's just upset. There's no way he would have hurt Dad."

"So far he's the last person to talk to your father. Do you know what they were talking about?"

Wade looked away. "No, but it was probably business. You know how Dad was."

Logan didn't like the shifty-eyed look his friend had just given him. What was it with the Bryson family? They'd circled the wagons and no outsider was going to be allowed to threaten them.

"I know how Bill was. Business first always." Logan tossed his beer into a nearby trash can. "Just tell George to start cooperating. No one wants to eliminate him as a suspect more than I do."

Logan spied Drake out of the corner of his eye and murmured some excuse to Wade, making a beeline for his best deputy.

"Any news on ballistics?"

Drake pulled his hat off and shook his head. "State lab said it's going to be Wednesday before they have anything to tell us. They're backed up but trying to make this a priority."

The state never made a small town's problem a priority. Drake was his best deputy but hadn't yet had to deal with the bureaucracy outside of Corville.

"First lesson in dealing with the state lab? Never take your foot off their neck." Logan grinned. "They'll feed you all sorts of bullshit and then put your stuff to the back of the line."

Drake's mouth turned up at the corners. "I'll make sure I call tomorrow at least twice."

Logan slapped Drake on the back. "Put Jillie on it. She's got contacts she can squeeze. Any good news?"

"I was able to get the last three statements from the guest list. All of them left the wedding early and weren't anywhere near the Bryson's when it went down."

"Corroborating witnesses?" Logan watched as Mary Bryson, Lyle's new wife, headed straight for Ava who was nursing what appeared to be the same glass of wine she'd had earlier. Mary had a determined look on her face. Ava's posture stiffened, her lips pressed together, clearly not happy to deal with her sister.

"They had a few drinks at Tommy's bar and there were several witnesses including Tommy himself," Drake replied, his gaze following Logan's. "Ava Hayworth is a nice girl. I went to school with her although she was a year behind me. She's smart too. She was president of the Drama Club."

Logan couldn't think of a woman less prone to drama than Ava. He liked her calm demeanor even when looking at a dead body. Mary was currently shaking her finger in Ava's face and a wave of protectiveness came over Logan unexpectedly. Ava rolled her eyes at her sister and looked to be handling things just fine, but he still didn't like it one bit. Nodding his head at Drake, he headed toward the two women in the corner of the room.

"We just want to know what Sheriff Wright is doing," Mary was saying. "Just keep us in the loop."

Ava's eyes went wide when she looked over Mary's shoulder and saw Logan. Mary must have seen the change in expression as well and whirled around, her expression going slack.

"Sheriff, how nice to see you. Thank you for paying your respects. The family appreciates it." Mary swallowed, her face flushed.

Logan took his time answering. "Bill Bryson was a good man. As for whether the family appreciates it, that's not a factor as to why I'm here."

"Of course," Mary nodded in agreement. "Well, I need to check in the kitchen."

She was gone in a flurry of movement, leaving Logan with Ava.

"I assume you heard that," Ava stated.

"Enough. She wants you to be sure to feed them information on the investigation?"

Ava sipped her wine. "Yes. Can you believe it?"

If she'd asked that question a few days ago Logan would have said no.

"She was talking to George earlier. I'm guessing he put her up to it." He crossed his arms over his chest. "Are you planning to do it?"

"No," she said, clearly offended. "Part of your draconian oath was that I keep my mouth shut about the investigation. But I wouldn't have said anything anyway."

Logan chuckled. "Always the good girl. Your sister isn't going to be too happy with you."

Ava sighed. "That's nothing new. She thinks I don't have any common sense."

"Do you?" he challenged.

Ava chewed on her bottom lip. "I admit I live in a fantasy world, but I do manage to pay my bills so the power isn't cut off. I miss a few meals when I'm working on a book. I know not to use the toaster in the bathtub and not to mess with a bull."

"All important things."

"Mary thinks I was crazy to become an author. After all, you don't get holidays, vacation, or health insurance."

Logan couldn't stop himself from teasing her. "You don't have health insurance? Hell, even I get insurance."

"I have health insurance," she protested. "I just have to buy it myself. It's good coverage."

"I bet it is." Logan held up a hand and smiled. "Listen, I need to get out of here. We'll start combing through the statements tonight. Don't forget the pizza, and don't be late. I get cranky when I'm hungry."

Ava groaned. "Yes, oh Great One. I wouldn't dare be late."

"And don't forget about tomorrow night. You're my cover, remember?"

Logan looked over his shoulder as he moved toward the front door. Ava was shaking her head and he had to laugh at her long-suffering expression. She didn't want to go out to the road house but he had her cornered. She'd go and help him with Christina. She'd also get out of her fantasy world a little bit which wouldn't be a bad thing.

He'd show her a good time tomorrow night. Make sure she had fun and meet some new people. She just needed to loosen up a little bit, and Logan had an idea of how to do it. Hopefully, the weather would hold.

No one could stay uptight on the back of a Harley.

Chapter Six

Ava straightened the frilly cuff on her red blouse with a sigh and picked her cell up from the bed, depositing it on the dresser.

"I feel ridiculous," she said. She was on the phone with her good friend Kaylee who was not only a friend but also a fellow author. Ava had needed the fashion advice prior to tonight's non-date with Logan. They'd settled on black jeans, a red blouse with wide sleeves, and a pair of cowboy boots from her college days that she'd found in the back of her closet. It was a far cry from her usual uniform of pajama pants and a T-shirt.

"Red always looks good on you. You'll wow this guy."

"I'm not trying to wow Logan," Ava corrected. "All I am tonight is a smokescreen so he can let this other girl down easy."

"That doesn't mean you need to look like a vagrant," argued Kaylee. "I love you to death but you could spend a little more time on your wardrobe. I've never met anyone who has as many pairs of pajamas as you do."

Ava liked to write in her pajamas but Kaylee liked to write in yoga pants, which wasn't much better.

"They're comfortable," Ava said defensively. "Besides I don't need to dress fancy for the UPS man. He doesn't care how I look." Ava laughed and applied some lip gloss.

"Isn't he married with three kids? He's probably seen a woman in jammies before." Kaylee was munching on potato chips in the background. "So what's this Logan guy like?"

"He's nice. Kind of a player though."

Ava dropped her keys, her lip gloss, and a wad of money into the small purse that already held a tiny wallet with her driver's license and one credit card.

"Good looking?"

"Way past good looking," Ava retorted. "Tousled blond hair, steely blue eyes, built like a Greek god. Better actually."

Kaylee whistled. "Why can't I find a man like that? He sounds yummy."

"It's not a date," Ava repeated.

"Why not? It could be. You're not ugly. He's a man. You're a woman. Go for it. Have some fun. For both of us."

"I wish I was staying home tonight and working on my book. That's what you'll be doing, isn't it?"

"It is. I'd rather be you. I don't remember the last time I went out on a date with a nice, handsome guy."

"Dale was pretty nice," Ava commented.

"He was okay." Kaylee sighed. "But he wasn't Greek god material. That would really be something. Do you think you could get a picture of him on your phone and send it to me?"

Ava laughed. "How would I do that? Sneak it while he's not looking?"

"Where there's a will, there's a way. If you get a chance, do it."

"I'll keep my phone at the ready. Seriously, what are you doing tonight?"

"You guessed it the first time. Writing. My hero is chatty today so I'm going to take advantage of it."

"Lucky you. Melissa and Michael aren't talking to me lately." Ava pressed the speaker button and lifted the phone to her ear. "I'm worried about them. They've never been this quiet."

"They'll talk when they're good and ready. Usually when it's most inconvenient. Listen, just relax tonight. Have some fun, maybe talk to a few men. You remember them, don't you? They're usually taller and rougher than we are, with deeper voices. They have penises."

"I remember," Ava answered sweetly. "The last one I dated was a faithless bastard who screwed every nude female model he hired."

Dustin had been an art teacher and he blamed his wandering eye and genitals on the fact that he was an artist. Ava had showed him the door and slammed it firmly behind him.

"When was the last time you got laid?" Kaylee paused for a second. "Time's up. If you have to think about it, it's been too long. Get yourself some tonight. You said the sheriff was eye candy."

"You didn't give me a chance to answer. It was six months ago, right before I started writing *Murder on Breaking Street*. As for Logan, he is hot, but not my type."

Nor was she his.

"Who cares? You're not planning to marry him, girl. Just use him for your own pleasure and walk away. Not every sexual encounter has to involve your heart, you know."

She'd never had casual sex in her life. She'd bet Kaylee hadn't either.

"Thank God I took you off speaker. If my parents heard that they'd have a stroke. I think they believe I'm still a virgin."

Kaylee snorted. "A thirty-year old virgin? Right. Get your freak on. Have some fun. Take a chance. For both of us. You've been brainwashed by that family of yours that your head is in the clouds. Personally I think it's up your ass. Stop living your life by how they see you and see yourself for what you truly are."

"And what is that?" Ava held her breath.

"A best-selling author who is financially stable. A good person, a good friend, and most of all a grown woman who is capable of making her own decisions."

Exhaling slowly, Ava fell back onto the bed. "They think I'm an airhead."

"So? Everyone has their blonde moments in life. Everyone. So you get involved with your work and forget to return their calls. Big fucking deal. It's not like you walk out into traffic and get hit by cars. Stop letting them lay this on you. This is their baggage. Not yours."

Ava's family did have their own issues. Plenty of them. "If I promise to try and have fun will you cut me a little slack?"

"Of course. Call me and tell everything tomorrow, okay? Maybe I'll put it in a book."

"Very funny. I'll call tomorrow. I doubt there will be much to tell. We'll have a few beers, dance, then come home."

"I still want to hear all about it. Just try to do one thing tonight you normally wouldn't do. One thing. Would that be so hard?"

Ava groaned. "Geez, you're a nag. Fine. I'll do one thing. One. Now I need to get going. I want to be waiting out front when Logan gets here. I'm not going to let my dad anywhere near him."

Kaylee's giggle came through the phone loud and clear. "Good luck. From what you said about your dad, he'll be lurking around dark corners to interrogate your date."

Crap.

Ava thought she'd taken precautions, turning on a ballgame and hoping her dad would start watching. It turned out her father hid in the garage. When Logan had come roaring up into the driveway on his huge motorcycle, she'd tried to hop on as quickly as possible.

It wasn't to be.

Logan had taken his time helping her into the helmet, seemingly in no hurry. The garage door opener had engaged and she'd heard the door lift slowly with a sense of foreboding. Her father would never in a million years let her ride out on a big, shiny Harley with Corville's original sex god.

And Logan did look like a sexual deity.

Dressed in old blue jeans paired with a black button-down shirt, heavy black boots, and a black leather jacket, Logan looked like every parent's worst nightmare and every girl's Saturday night dream. The only thing he lacked was an earring and a tattoo. She could visibly see he didn't have a pierced ear, but the tattoo was still a possibility.

A possibility that made her a little jumpy. Logan oozed sex without breaking a sweat. It must be deeply embedded in his DNA. She'd never dated a man this…well…masculine.

It's not a date.

He'd been polite to her father despite the near belligerent questions he was asked. It was only when her mother came outside and dragged Ava's dad into the house that they were able to break away. Now she was riding on the back of his big motorcycle.

It was awesome.

She'd never felt exhilaration like this before. The wind whipped around her and she leaned close to Logan's back, her hands wrapped around his middle. He'd pressed her palms to his washboard stomach and given her a thumbs-up as the engine had roared to life between her legs. Between the vibrations and the heat from Logan's body she was pretty much a mess by the time they pulled up to the roadhouse about fifty miles outside of town.

Logan swung his long leg over the bike and pulled off his helmet and black leather gloves before helping her. Her legs were shaky and she had to lock her knees to keep from collapsing. She'd had a quick tutorial as to why bikers were hot and sexy. He lifted the helmet from her head and gave her a grin.

"Are you okay?"

She nodded, still breathless from the ride. "Yes. That was great. I've never ridden on the back of a motorcycle before."

Logan laughed. "Good girls don't ride bikes, huh? I'm glad you liked it."

Ava knew she was grinning. "I loved it. Do you ride it all the time?"

"No," he shook his head regretfully. "Only when the weather cooperates, and not near as much as I'd like."

"It's like flying," she laughed.

Logan put his arm around her and led her into the loud honky tonk. "Uh oh. I think I've created a monster. Mommy and Daddy won't thank me when you buy a cycle and start wearing leather."

Ava would make sure Mommy and Daddy never found out.

She and Logan walked deeper into the crowded bar. His hand was at the small of her back and despite her dislike of crowds, he made her feel warm and protected.

No wonder he was such a good cop.

He leaned down so he was close to her ear. "Thanks for coming tonight and for helping with Christina. If I haven't said, I really am grateful."

"Grateful enough to let me help more with the investigation?" she asked, tongue in cheek.

Logan laughed. "No, good girl. You're strictly on paperwork duty. Your parents seemed pretty protective. I'd hate to get their darling daughter hurt or dead."

She stopped and twisted around so she was looking up at him. "I'm sorry about that. I tried to get us out of there before he saw you, but you moved too slow."

"Don't worry about it." Logan put his arm around her shoulders again, urging her forward. "He's not the first father I've met."

And he won't be the last.

The unspoken sentence hung between them. Unsaid, but clearly understood. This wasn't a date. She was here to help him out. It was a deal. Quid pro quo. They were both getting something they wanted.

"Who are these people we're meeting?" The roadhouse was loud and reeked of beer, sweat, and a cloying mix of feminine perfume. The crush of bodies made her press closer to Logan. Crowds really did make her uneasy.

"Just some friends. Christina will be there, of course. When I started dating her she became really good friends with the wife of one of my buddies. Karen and Bart have been married for less than a year. I went to high school with him."

"Bart Kensey? I knew his younger sister, Diane. She was in my class."

Logan nodded and pointed to a table in the corner where about eight to ten people sat. "Diane is here as well. She's dating a guy from Harper, Brandon Glass. Then there's Kiki and Bob, Jack, and Frank."

She was relieved she'd at least know one person. Diane hadn't been a close friend of Ava's but they'd always been friendly. Diane waved to them when they were about ten feet away before jumping up to give Ava a big hug.

"I'm so glad to see you! Come sit down and tell me what it's like to be a big-time author. I want to hear every detail."

Diane was a bubbly brunette with sparkling blue eyes, a feminine version of her brother Bart. He had his arm around his wife Karen, a pretty blonde who was sitting next to Christina. Ava shook hands with each person and took a seat next to Diane while Logan took the seat alongside. Christina was on his other side and damn if she didn't immediately move her chair closer to Logan's the minute he sat down.

Karen, who was sitting across the table, frowned when she saw Christina's move. Karen might be Christina's friend but the expression on her face was not one of happiness.

"It's nice to meet all of you." Ava tried to be friendly and gave them her best happy-to-be-here smile.

"It's nice to meet you, Ava." Kiki smiled. "It's not every day we get to meet a famous author. I've read all of your books. You're something of a local hero around here."

Ava inwardly cringed. She hated the celebrity stuff. She loved talking to her readers but she hated the autograph signing and the picture taking.

"I'm just a humble storyteller."

"I can't imagine how hard it would be to write a book! That's so cool." Diane practically bounced up and down in the chair. "Do you know Stephen King or James Patterson?"

She'd heard that question more than a few times. She hated disappointing people but she was about to do it.

"I'm sorry, but no." Ava shook her head. "I'm sure they're nice people though."

"Do you know anyone famous?" the man named Frank queried. He was frowning. "Anyone?"

"Um, I'm very good friends with Kaylee Blue." She looked at their blank expressions. "She writes erotic romance. She's very successful."

Karen smiled and picked up her drink. "I'll have to look her up. I love those kinds of books. So hot."

Ava opened her mouth to explain the solitary life of a writer but closed it again. It would be a futile endeavor. They had the usual idealized vision of a writer's life which included travel, glamour, money, and a tweed jacket with patches on the elbows. Ava looked terrible in tweed. How could she explain the reality which was flannel pajamas, massive amounts of coffee, and erratic sleep habits?

"You won't be disappointed," Ava replied. "Kaylee is a marvelous writer."

"Erotic romance, huh?" Bart waggled his eyebrows. "Why don't you write that?"

Karen elbowed him hard in the ribs and he coughed a few times. Logan's hand covered hers and she leaned into him. He felt solid and warm.

"I enjoy writing mysteries too much. I like the challenge of figuring out who the killer is."

Logan looked down at her, his brow knitted together. "Don't you know when you start the book?"

She shrugged. "Nope. I'm just as surprised as anyone else. The guilty party reveals themselves slowly as the story unwinds. It's exciting."

Logan laughed, his blue eyes warm. "I guess you and I have more in common than I thought. That's pretty much how police work is."

She gave him her best mean look. "I wouldn't know about any of the exciting parts of police work. All I do is look through paperwork."

Logan's lips twitched. "You just won't let it go, will you?"

Ava didn't get a chance to answer. Christina laid her hand on Logan's arm and leaned forward so he could get an eyeful of her cleavage. At least Ava got a good look. Since Logan was closer she assumed he did as well.

"How about a dance?" Christina purred, a seductive smile played on her glossed lips and her eyes glowed with promise. Ava couldn't have pulled off that move in a million years. She'd been doing something else when God had handed out the femme fatale power.

Logan patted Christina's hand but moved closer to Ava. "I think the first dance needs to go to my date. Ava, how about a dance?"

Ava liked to dance about as much as she liked to drink in bars. Not much. But she'd promised to help Logan and letting him go off with Christina would fall under the category of a fail. She nodded and he laced his fingers with hers tugging her toward the dance floor. Ava glanced over her shoulder at Christina. She looked decidedly unhappy. Karen was saying something in Christina's ear and nodding toward Jack and Frank as if urging her to dance with them. Jack stood up and he and Christina glided onto the dance floor several feet from Logan and Ava.

He pulled her into his arms, the palm of his hand burning a brand into her back. She looked up into his blue eyes and felt an unwelcome jolt of awareness. She didn't want to think of Logan

Wright as anything but a sheriff and a womanizer. She didn't want to be sexually aware of him at all. But here she was, slowly swaying to a mournful country tune with one of her hands entwined with his and her other on his muscular shoulder.

She could feel the heat emanating from his body, his scent clean and manly. She quickly averted her gaze but ended up looking at his wide chest instead which wasn't much better for her racing pulse. She dragged in a lungful of air to clear her head and tried to concentrate on the movements of her feet. If she stepped on his boots she'd be mortified.

His hand slid down her spine to just above her ass and he pulled her closer so their bodies were pressed against one another. It made it easier to follow him but it made it harder to breathe. He rested his chin on the top of her head and she could feel the heavy thud of his heart under her ear, slow and steady.

When the song ended, he stepped back and gave her an easy smile, totally unaffected by their nearness. She felt like a complete idiot. Logan had women throwing themselves at him all the time. One dance wouldn't send him over the edge. She, on the other hand, hadn't been close to a man in six months. That was a long time to go without touching, really touching, another human being.

"How about a beer?" Logan nodded toward the bar.

She shook her head. "I don't drink all that much, but I could use a soda or something."

He led her off the dance floor and leaned against the oak bar laughing with the bartender. She'd regained her balance luckily. This wasn't about Logan specifically. She'd been too long between dates and a woman was bound to be affected when close to one this good looking. It was simply a physical reaction. Logan was still not her type, and she wasn't going to get involved with him.

They'd danced. She'd liked it. Big deal.

"How am I doing so far?" she asked when he handed her a soda.

He frowned. "So far? What do you mean?"

"You know, helping you with Christina? How am I doing? She really seems to like you. I feel a little guilty."

His expression cleared. "You're helping. I've been avoiding hanging out with my friends because she's always here too. I don't want to hurt her feelings but I need to send her a message."

"That you're not available," Ava stated, sipping the cool liquid. The roadhouse was warm or maybe it had just been the dance floor.

"Exactly," Logan agreed. "Jack really likes her and I think if she gave him a chance she'd forget all about me."

Ava's gaze wandered to where Christina and Jack were still dancing. He was looking down at her with unabashed adoration. Christina was trying to look over his shoulder at Logan. It was a sad situation.

"I bet she's the type that likes emotionally unavailable bad boys. If you were more mainstream she'd probably lose interest."

Logan took a swig of his beer and grinned. "You mean if I sold my bike, bought a minivan, and spent Saturday nights with my coin collection she'd forget all about me?"

"You have a coin collection?" Ava snorted.

Logan laughed and he leaned his elbow on the bar. "I'm just your typical Renaissance man. I have many interests. Coin collecting is just one. I also brew my own beer and play the guitar in a treehouse I built myself."

"You built your own treehouse?" This wasn't what she'd expected from this man.

"I certainly did. It's a nice one too. I go there when I need quiet. I play my guitar and think. No cell phones allowed. What about you?"

"I write."

She sounded completely boring. Which she was. She liked to stay home and write.

"What do you do for fun?"

She shifted on her feet, uncomfortable with this line of questioning.

"I write. Writing is fun for me."

Instead of teasing her, he simply nodded. "It's good that you enjoy your work that much. I love what I do too, but it can be stressful. I have to find ways to unwind."

"I like to cook. And I like to read."

She sounded like somebody's grandmother.

"I like to eat so if you get a hankering to cook, let me know. I like to read too. Mostly thrillers and true crime."

They talked about books and authors while they finished their drinks. It turned out they had similar reading taste. He'd even offered to let her borrow the latest release from one of her favorites.

"I only read on my e-reader now." She shook her head. "But thank you for the offer."

"I need to get one of those but I haven't gotten around to it. I still buy regular books." Logan slapped his empty beer bottle down on the bar. "Are you done? How about another dance?"

Her mind wanted to refuse but her body was firmly in charge. She moved into his arms as the band started playing a slow song. This time she held herself rigid, not allowing their bodies to sink together.

Logan Wright was a player, and she wasn't the type to enjoy being played.

She really was what he called her. A good girl.

The best thing she could do is get through this evening and forget all about how good it felt to be held in his arms. And it did feel good. Too good. Mostly, it felt dangerous.

Well, shit. She so did not need this.

As the song ended they broke apart. Logan tucked a stray strand of hair behind her ear, leaving a streak of heat on her cheek.

"Are you okay? You seem tense all of a sudden." He'd leaned forward, his voice low. His expression was concerned.

She nodded, not sure what to say. "I'm fine. I just don't like that song," she lied.

"We'll go back to the table." He placed his large hand under her elbow and they went back to his friends who were laughing and smiling. Ava hesitated when Logan pulled out her chair.

"I think I'll visit the ladies' room if you don't mind. I'll be right back."

Diane hopped up from her seat. "I'll go with you. It's in the back of the bar."

Ava followed Diane to the restroom, the raucous crowd loud around them. By the time Ava was freshening her lipstick, Diane was eyeing her curiously.

"How long have you known Logan?" she asked.

"He and I were paired up at my sister's wedding on Saturday." Ava answered the question by not really answering it.

Diane pulled a gold tube from her purse. "I heard about what happened. So tragic. Is Mary doing okay?"

Ava tried to bring order to her shoulder length curls. "She and Lyle are doing fine. Heartbroken of course. Were you at the funeral? I didn't see you."

"I wanted to be there but I had some business out of town. A training class. I work as an auditor for the local bank now."

Diane drew the red lipstick around her mouth. "Listen, don't worry about Christina, okay? She and Logan used to date. She didn't take the ending very well. Karen gave her a stern talking to while you and Logan were dancing. She needs to move on. Logan's been patient with her, I'll say that. Any other guy would have told her off in a nasty way by now."

"Logan's not the type to do that." Even as the words came out of her mouth, Ava knew they were true.

Diane dropped her lipstick into her purse and smiled. "He's the type to make a woman happy is what he is. Very happy."

Shock ran through Ava. "You've dated Logan? I didn't realize."

Diane laughed. "I wish. Although in a small town like Corville, if we both stayed single long enough, I'd eventually get up to bat. Damn that man is fine. A friend of mine dated him and said she'd never had so many orgasms in her life. I should be so lucky. Is it true? Is he that good?"

Diane looked like she was holding her breath as she waited for an answer. Ava felt her cheeks get warm. "I have no idea," she drawled. "It's not like that with us."

Diane's eyebrows shot up. "I see. Well, if that's how you want it..."

"It is," Ava said firmly. "I'm not falling into bed with him. No way. No how."

But those orgasms did sound tempting.

Chapter Seven

Logan let his gaze rest on Ava as she sat at the table chatting with Diane. He hadn't really noticed it before but she was an attractive woman. Very attractive. Her golden brown hair fell in natural waves almost to her shoulders framing a heart-shaped face. Her skin was flawless and his fingers itched to stroke her cheek to feel if it was as soft as it looked. Her figure was curvy and generous, just the way he liked it. She had a body a man could hold in his hands. But what he liked the most was the dimples that appeared in her cheeks when she smiled.

And she smiled a lot.

Other than a strange moment on the dance floor, which she'd blamed on a crappy song, Ava had been great company all evening. She was polite and engaging with his friends, a good dancer, and a thoughtful person. She didn't ask him to fetch her drinks or complain about how her feet hurt or the dance floor was too hot.

In fact, she hadn't complained about anything at all. Even when other women had come up to him and asked him to dance, she hadn't said a word. He'd turned them all down and at one point she'd leaned in close and whispered in his ear that it was okay if he wanted to.

He hadn't wanted to. He had a bad reputation but he knew how to treat a lady. Ava Hayworth was a lady. Class all the way. It was probably a novelty for a good church-going girl like her to hang out with a guy like him.

And the evening wasn't over yet.

Normally, if he wasn't going to end up in bed with his date, which was rare, he took them home and then went for a ride. Tonight, he would take Ava with him on the bike. She'd loved it earlier but he knew she'd like it even better at night.

There was nothing like a nighttime cycle ride. The roads were deserted and there was nothing but the sound of the engine. He wasn't going to get involved with Ava, but he could share this with her. It would be a thank you for all she'd done for him.

"Is everything okay?" Ava asked. She must have felt his gaze on her profile.

"Are you ready to go? Have you had enough fun?" He smiled as her dimples appeared.

"I have, actually. I don't go out much at home. I'm always working. Thank you for bringing me."

"As I said earlier, you did me the favor. Thank you."

Ava's gaze strayed to where Christina danced with Jack. "She looks pretty happy with Jack tonight. Maybe she got the message."

Christina's behavior had improved as the evening had gone on. Jack had made sure she was very busy indeed leaving little time for her to spend with Logan. Things just might have turned the corner.

"I hope so. She really is a nice person and she deserves to be happy. She wouldn't have been happy with me."

Ava tilted her head. "Why not? Because you can't be faithful?"

For some reason her words stung. He lifted his hand. "Now hold on a minute. To be considered a candidate to be faithful, you have to be in a committed relationship. I don't do relationships, so I've never been unfaithful. I want to be clear on that."

Ava's respect was important to him and he wasn't sure why. Maybe it was because she was the first real female friend he'd ever had.

"I'm sorry." She shook her head. "I didn't mean to offend. When you say it that way, I guess you're right."

"You guess? You don't sound convinced." Logan had to lean close so he could talk over the loud music but still not be overheard by his friends at the table. This was none of their fucking business.

"When I think about dating I automatically think about one person at a time," Ava admitted. "Honestly, I couldn't picture myself dating several men at once."

Images of Ava with other guys flashed in front of Logan. His gut tightened and a scowl crossed his face. The thought of her with other men pissed him off. She was too good for anybody he'd ever met. She needed someone who would be as truthful with her as she was with them.

Most men would lie, cheat, and steal to get laid. Hell, he'd arrested a guy once who had pretended to work for Brad Pitt just to meet women. Of course he hadn't arrested him for his game of make believe, he'd arrested him because he ran out on his bill after running up a tab of food and drinks over a thousand bucks. Logan still couldn't believe females had actually believed someone working for Brad Pitt would be hanging out in Corville.

But women believed what they wanted to believe. Christina believed that Logan was a good man and that she was in love with him. Ava believed he was a hound and had to be blackmailed into going out on a date with him.

Logan stood and then helped up Ava with a hand under her elbow. They bid his friends goodbye and headed out of the loud roadhouse. Mounting the bike, they roared into the inky darkness. Ava's arms were wrapped around his waist and her thighs were pressed close to his.

They rode through the night on the back roads until finally she tapped him on the shoulder. He moved the bike to the shoulder and let the engine idle.

She lifted the shield on her helmet and looked up at him with a puzzled expression. "Where are we going?"

"Nowhere. Is that okay?" He held his breath as he waited for her response. If she wanted to go home, he'd take her straight there. He'd thought she would enjoy this, but if she didn't he wouldn't make her stay.

Her smile was slow in coming but no less dazzling. "Perfectly. I love this."

They hurtled into the darkness, nothing but the moon and stars to light the way. The hum of the engine soothed his soul in a way nothing else ever had. When he'd returned from the Army, one of the first things he'd done was buy a cycle. He'd had a few since then but they were worth their cost in psychiatric bills. Logan had never needed therapy after the war. He'd had this instead. It was a feeling he loved but never took for granted. This was freedom.

Logan hadn't consciously ridden to anywhere but he soon found them on the road that edged the lake outside of town. He pulled into an area canopied by several trees and just a few feet from the shore. He killed the engine and took off his own helmet before helping Ava with hers. She looked around and shook her head.

"I haven't been out to the lake since high school. It hasn't changed a bit. Do you come here a lot?"

He swung his leg over the bike and twisted around so he was able to see her clearly. The full moon hung in the sky illuminating the lake, making a silvery pattern on the surface and casting large shadows around the banks. He'd once heard that moonlight was a woman's best friend. He'd never given it much thought but tonight Ava looked luminous basked in its heavenly glow. His chest felt tight and it was hard to speak as he gazed down at her upturned face. She looked beautiful and innocent. Too innocent for a man like him who had seen and done so many things, most of them bad, but for once he wasn't in control of the situation.

Logan was used to calling the shots in his relationships with the fairer sex. At this moment, Ava was in the driver seat. Did she realize it? He felt like a kid on his first date.

And this wasn't a date.

A crinkle formed between her eyes as she studied him, waiting for his response. Damned if he knew what to say. All coherent thought was gone as instincts as old as time welled up inside of him.

Plunder. Explore. Conquer.

His hand snaked around the back of her head, plunging into her silky curls. His other arm wrapped around her, pulling her close until he could feel the heat of her body through his clothes. He lowered his head and paused, looking into those hazel eyes, waiting for her to push him away in disgust.

Ava's pupils were dilated and he could feel the thud of her heart close to his. Her lips parted and he didn't hesitate. Capturing her lips, he anchored his palm at her nape. She didn't even try to pull away. Instead, his good girl did naughty things with her tongue inside his mouth. Their lips fused together with a searing heat.

She didn't merely accept his kiss. She met him head on, giving as good as she got, an active participant. Her hands were around his neck and her fingers tangled in his hair. He slanted his mouth at another angle and deepened the kiss causing her breath to catch and her body to tremble. He could hear the beat of his own heart and the roar of blood rushing in his ears. His entire body was on alert and all from a kiss from Little Miss Goody Two-Shoes.

Holy fuck.

Sanity finally took hold and he dragged his mouth from hers, their breathing ragged. He avoided her gaze as he stood and stepped away, immediately missing her warmth.

This had to fucking stop.

Ava Hayworth didn't follow his relationship rules. She was the forever kind of woman, and he didn't have forever to give any female. He took several deep breaths and tried to slow his racing pulse. She was chewing on her lips, swollen from their passion, and watching him as if she was wondering what he might do next.

Next? He was fucking taking her home.

This was crazy. He'd started out taking her for a ride and now they'd swapped spit in a moment of madness. This was how men woke up married with two kids and a minivan. Panic rose up, shutting off his breath and sending him back a few more steps, almost tripping on a tree root.

"Are you okay?" she asked, her head tilted slightly. "You look a little green."

Logan felt it. His stomach was churning and his heart was pounding even faster now than when they had kissed. Ava was trouble with a capital T. Females like her looked all soft and innocent and then…

Bam!

They had a man roped, tied, and trussed up like a Thanksgiving turkey.

No thanks. Not him.

"You shouldn't have kissed me." He dragged his shirtsleeve over his mouth to remove her intoxicating taste.

Her eyebrows shot up and her lips firmed. "I shouldn't have kissed you? Don't you mean the other way around? You kissed me, Logan."

"You kissed me back. Well, I shouldn't have done it either. We both know it was a mistake. We're not for each other."

Her mouth twisted. "On that I agree." Her arms crossed over her chest, rising and falling quickly. "You just couldn't resist, could you? Man-whore Logan Wright just couldn't stop himself from making a pass. Do you even realize when you're doing it? Jesus, Logan. Way to ruin an evening."

No woman had ever accused him of ruining her night before and he didn't like it much. He'd been trying to be nice but somewhere things had gone wrong.

Ava hopped off his bike and walked to the edge of the lake, looking anywhere but at him. He'd acted like an idiot and she was right to be angry. He'd started it, blamed her, and now the fragile friendship they'd begun to build was ripped to shreds.

It was all for the best.

They couldn't be friends. Not really. They might have crime puzzles and motorcycles in common but that was it.

And sausage pizza. And music while they worked.

Shit. Shit. Shit.

"Listen, I'm sorry," he sighed. "I guess I got carried away by the moonlight. The full moon makes people do crazy shit."

Her back was to him but he could see her head nod in agreement. "That's true. I researched it once for a book about a serial killer who only killed on the harvest moon each year."

Irritation tapped at his brain. "Are you comparing our wimpy kiss to a fucking serial killer?"

Except it wasn't wimpy. It had almost brought him to his knees.

She twirled on her boot heels and looked him squarely in the eye. "Hardly. I was making small talk. Honestly, I'm not sure what to say at this point. We shouldn't have done that. Everything's changed."

"And I ruined it?" he challenged. "It's all my fault. I'll take the blame."

"I'm not blaming you," she argued. "I'm only stating a fact. Now we're going to be thinking about the kiss and not the case."

Logan picked up her helmet and handed it to her. "Honey, I lost count of the kisses I've participated in by the time I was fourteen. I doubt I'll lose any sleep over this one. I suggest we forget it ever happened."

Her little chin was lifted defiantly and he would have bet his Harley she would have loved to smack the smirk off his face. She wouldn't be the first or the last. Ava didn't do it however. She simply brushed past him, pulled on her helmet, and mounted the bike.

He did the same, taking his place in front of her. This time, her arms weren't wound around him. Instead her touch was tentative and she'd scooted as far back on the seat as possible. He grabbed an arm in each of his hands and pulled her forward.

"Hold on like you mean it," he growled. "I don't want you falling off the back."

He kicked the bike into gear and gravel shot out from the back tire as he took off. The entire evening had gone to hell in a hand basket and he only had himself to blame.

Bad boys didn't play games with good girls. He'd be crazy to get involved with a woman who probably thought happiness was a house with a white picket fence and a couple of kids. He'd be a lousy husband and a worse father.

Holy hell. Fuck that.

First thing tomorrow, he'd call up one of the many willing women who didn't ask for more than he could give. There would always be a bevy of females who only wanted some fun, and Logan knew how to have fun.

Chapter Eight

In his office the next morning, Logan was determined to put the night before with Ava out of his mind for good. He perched on the edge of his desk and punched in the number that had been written in his leather address book. Angie Vernon was a lively redhead he hadn't seen in over six months. She'd always been up for a few beers and some dancing. Then some naked fun afterward, of course. He vaguely recalled she liked to lick hot fudge off his abs after dinner. She was just the thing to get good girl Ava off of his mind. She picked up after a few rings.

"Hello."

"Hey babe. It's Logan. I've missed you, girl."

Angie laughed and Logan grinned at her delighted sound. She was happy to hear from him, dammit. "Logan Wright, as I live and breathe. I never thought to hear from you again. What brings you out of the woodwork after eight months?"

"Has it been that long? That's too long. Come dancing with me tonight. I'll pick you up at seven. Wear something that will make me work to take it off."

He was being outrageous but he remembered Angie liked him that way.

"Can my fiancé Joe come along?" He heard her laughter through the phone. "Logan, I've been engaged for two months. Hadn't you heard?"

Angie lived a few towns over and apparently no one had seen fit to pass on the news. Disappointment and something like relief twisted in his gut. He wasn't sure how he could be happy and sad at the same time. He put it down to a bad night's sleep.

"Well, congratulations." Logan tried to make it sound truly sincere when inside he was recoiling at the mere thought of marriage. "Joe's a lucky man."

"You'll have to excuse me if I don't pass on your message," Angie said dryly. "I don't like to remind him of my wild and woolly days. I'm a boring almost married woman now. We spend our time fixing up the house we bought and playing cards with other couples on Saturday night."

Dear God in heaven, that sounded like hell with window treatments and throw pillows.

"I wish you all the best, Angie. I hope you'll be very happy."

Logan hung up before she had a chance to answer, and then grabbed a pen and scratched her name from his address book.

Goodbye Angie.

He paged through and came to a name that made him smile with pleasant memories.

Hello Marie.

Twenty minutes and three more phone calls later, Logan wanted to toss the phone across the room. Marie had been married with her first child on the way. Lana had been dating someone "seriously", whatever the fuck that meant, and Terri's answering machine message said she was on her honeymoon.

Did everyone lose their mind at the same moment and suddenly couple up like animals before the storm? Had he missed some sort of memo? He was starting to feel like those naughty unicorns that had played in the rain while the ark sailed off into the sunset. Everyone knew those horned bastards had met their maker. Was having fun and some casual sex extinct too?

A tentative knock on the door brought him out of his brooding thoughts. Jillie, his secretary, was standing in the doorway with a peculiar look on her face. She was usually smiling and swigging fancy coffee from the place on the corner. Jillie took at least six coffee breaks a day.

"What is it?" Logan asked, trying to keep his irritation from showing.

She held up a piece of paper. "The state lab emailed me the ballistics report for Bill Bryson."

Logan held out his hand. He'd been waiting for this. "Thanks. I'll take it now."

She didn't give it to him, but simply stood there with an uncertain expression. He didn't really have time for Jillie to have a breakdown today. Tomorrow, after a decent night's sleep, he might be in a better mood and ready to hear her usual tale of woe about her latest boyfriend.

"Goddamit, Jillie. Tell me what they said."

Logan stalked over to the coffeemaker in the corner of his office, poured more into his mug, and fought the anger churning in his gut. Jillie had used her contacts at the state lab to move the ballistics test to the front of the line. The results were in this morning but she was standing in the doorway to his office gaping like a fish out of water. She wasn't normally reticent about passing along lab results. In fact, she normally tossed the email she'd printed up on his desk and waltzed down to the corner coffee shop for a latte and a muffin. Today she was pale and her grip on the paper was so tight it made her knuckles white.

"I need you to sit down, Logan," Jillie pointed to the chair.

Logan lost what little patience he had left. This case was a bitch, and he was fucking tired. He'd barely slept last night after what had gone down with Ava. He'd said he wouldn't lose sleep over a simple kiss but he'd turned out to be a fucking liar. He'd tossed and turned all night, at turns mentally berating himself and other times reliving those moments. As the sun had shone in his window, he'd woken grouchy and frustrated. Now women right and left were getting married and having babies. No amount of coffee was going to make this a good day.

"Just give me the report." Logan held out his hand and kept his voice under control. It wasn't Jillie's fault that he was in a piss-poor mood today, although her strange behavior wasn't helping. "Give it to me and go."

She looked undecided but finally handed the paper to him before slinking out the door and closing it behind her. It must be something bad as his door normally stayed wide open so he could hear the comings and goings in the office. Bill Bryson must have been shot by someone whose gun was in the system. Perhaps someone who was wanted for another murder.

Logan settled his big body into the comfortable old leather chair behind his desk and propped his feet on its surface. He scanned the report and felt his heart almost stop in his chest as he read. The black type seemed to blur on the page before coming back into focus. He blindly reached for the phone and punched in some numbers hoping like hell Tanner would answer.

"Tanner Marks."

Logan swung his legs down and sat up in the chair. "It's me, Logan. Listen, I need to talk to you. Shit, I still can't believe this."

"Believe what?" Tanner asked. "What's going on? You sound shaken."

Logan sure as shit wasn't feeling good. He kept reading the ballistics report over and over but it never changed.

"You know about the Bryson murder here in Corville, right? I told you about it."

"Sure. Bill Bryson, shot in his own home during the reception of his son's wedding. Have you found your killer?"

"Kind of." Logan leaned back in the chair, his mind whirling with questions. "According to the state lab, Bill Bryson was killed with the same firearm as a string of unsolved murders."

"Holy shit. We have a string of unsolved murders in Montana? Since when?"

"It's the vigilante, Tanner. The vigilante killed Bill Bryson."

There was a long silence on the other end of the phone. Finally Tanner responded, his voice low. "Are you sure? I thought you said this Bryson guy was pillar of the community stuff. Why would the vigilante go after him? His MO is taking out the scum of the earth, not rich businessmen."

"Apparently things have changed. Or not. Maybe Bill was into something we don't know about."

"Drugs? Did he beat his wife? Shit, the vigilante is usually quite particular about his victims. He likes to take out the ones few people mourn."

"Bill's wife did die under mysterious circumstances but that was twenty years ago. I doubt it has anything to do with what's going on now," Logan replied. He remembered the boxes of old records in the attic that had belonged to Sheriff Frank Jesse. He'd never paid them any attention before but now he knew he needed to bring them down to the main level of the house and look through them. Ava would be a great help in this task.

He mentally shook his head. He wouldn't be asking Ava for any help after last night. He turned his attention back to the phone call.

"Was Bryson ever a suspect?" Tanner asked. "About anything?"

"I don't know. Fuck, I was just a kid then. As far as I know, Bill Bryson hasn't done anything wrong. I don't think he's ever been arrested. Why would the vigilante break his pattern and murder Bill?"

Tanner cleared his throat. "Do you think it's personal? Maybe Bryson knew this guy and they had a disagreement? We've talked about how the vigilante must know someone in the area and was getting their information from them. Maybe Bryson was going to turn him in?"

Logan shook his head although Tanner couldn't see him. "Bryson was a businessman through and through. How would he get mixed up with the vigilante? It doesn't make sense." He took a deep breath to steady himself. The last few minutes had tilted his world on its axis. "I'm going to need your help. Everyone's help."

"I'll call the other guys. Sounds like we need an emergency meeting," Tanner replied.

The meeting would be a gathering of Logan and five other sheriffs he knew in the area. They were all small town lawmen who had banded together to share information and help one another. It had made them exponentially more effective at their jobs.

"The sooner the better," Logan agreed. "Name the date and the time. I'll be there."

"I'll call you as soon as I get it set up. I know you don't want to hear this, Logan, but this could be the break we've been waiting for. If there is some connection between the vigilante and Bryson we might be able to catch this guy. Finally."

"I wish a good man didn't have to be dead if that's what you're implying. I hope you're not saying that I don't want to see this guy behind bars. I do."

"That wasn't what I was saying at all. I know you respect law and order. You're just not fond of rules, that's all." He heard Tanner chuckle.

"Rules were meant to be broken, my friend. Call me or Jillie and let her know the meeting time, okay? In the meantime, I'll keep you in the loop if anything else comes up."

They hung up and Logan stared at the phone. His gut didn't like what was going on at all. Usually murderers killed for one of a few reasons. Money, love, or revenge.

Which one was this?

Later that day, Logan slammed the door shut on his old pickup truck and paused in the driveway of the Bryson estate. Yesterday he'd been surprised to get a call from Deke Kennedy, the Bryson family lawyer. Logan's presence was requested today for the reading of the will. He couldn't imagine why he was needed there but Deke had insisted. Perhaps Bill had left everything to the county animal shelter, and Deke was expecting a family rumble to break out. Logan inwardly chuckled at the image of Wade, Lyle, Aaron, and George beating on each other with sofa cushions.

Pressing the doorbell, Logan looked around the grounds. It was a sunny day but there was no activity outside the home. Whatever was going on, the action was inside. The door opened and Deke was standing there with an apologetic smile. Deke was on the wrong side of sixty with thinning hair and sagging jowls. His brown suit always looked rumpled whether you saw him at eight in the morning or late at night.

"Logan, I'm glad you could be here. Come on in." Deke stood back and let Logan enter.

Logan pulled off his hat and followed Deke back to an oak lined office dominated by a large desk. Logan knew it had been Bill Bryson's office from the million and a half times Logan had been in this house. At one time, it had almost been a second home.

"You said one o'clock so here I am. Where is everyone?"

Deke pulled at his tie and sighed. "They went to lunch in town. I sent them. The reading of the will is actually at two. I wanted you here early."

Logan had had enough with the mystery and games. He leaned forward, placing his palms on the desk, and looked Deke right in the eye. "Why the hell am I here, Deke? Are you expecting trouble at the reading? Is it going to get ugly? Did Bill leave everything to some young floozy?"

Deke flushed and waved a hand toward the leather chair. "Have a seat. Please?"

Logan reined in his impatience and sank into the chair. "Okay, I'm sitting."

Deke sat on the other side of the desk and shuffled some papers, pulling out a white, legal sized envelope, before clearing his throat. "I do expect some trouble today but not for the reasons you think." Deke rubbed his chin as if looking for the right words to say. "Bill Bryson was a complicated man. Few people knew him well. I certainly can't say I knew everything about him, but I did know him and called him a friend for almost thirty years."

"Congratulations," Logan drawled, his fingers tapping a beat on his blue jeans. "Can we get to the trouble part?"

Deke rubbed the envelope between his fingers. "Bill thought a great deal of you, Logan. He spoke of you often and how you had grown into a fine man. He was proud of how you handled the early blows you'd been dealt in your life. He was impressed with your military record and then how you took over for Sheriff Jesse."

Logan sat straighter in the chair, his eyes narrowing. He didn't talk about his past. Period. "So? Are you saying he left me something? Whatever it is, I don't want it. Give it to Wade and his brothers."

Deke shook his head. "It's more than that, Logan." He tugged at his tie again nervously. "I don't know if you knew this but Bill knew your mother."

Logan didn't like the way this conversation was progressing and felt a bar of tension start to grow in his abdomen. He shrugged as if it didn't matter. "It's a small town. Lots of people knew my mother."

"They were very good friends," Deke insisted. "They were…close."

Logan leaned forward in the chair, his gaze locking with the obviously uncomfortable attorney. "Are you trying to tell me something? Best spit it out now."

He kept his voice low but his heart pounded in his chest.

Deke pushed the envelope across the desk toward Logan. "I wanted you to have a chance to read this before everyone gets back. In private. When the will gets read in an hour, well, all hell is going to break loose. I knew you'd need a chance to read this and digest it."

Gritting his teeth, Logan placed his hand on the envelope. "Get out while I read this."

"Logan, I can help you with this—" began Deke, his voice almost desperate.

"Get out." Logan's voice was barely above a whisper but the words seem to register. Deke stood and headed for the door, only pausing for a moment before he exited the room.

"I'll be right outside the door when you're done reading the letter," he said, shutting it softly.

Logan stared at his own name written in bold print on the stark white paper. He finally ripped through the seal and tossed the envelope aside, holding the paper with shaking hands.

Logan,

I write this letter today as you leave for the military. You are in the dining room with my sons having a small party as a sendoff. I thank God we are not at war and you will be safe. I am sure by now you are wondering why you are receiving this letter from me after my death.

This is so hard to write but I know I must tell the truth at last. I met your mother many years ago when your father brought her to this town after they were married. We were all young couples and we all socialized with one another. Jackie was beautiful, a golden girl, with her blonde hair and blue eyes. She was always happy, always humming a tune even when doing simple things like cooking or shopping.

There's no excuse for what we did. We were both desperately unhappy and we turned to each other. We hurt others and for that I'm sorry. Very sorry. By the time we ended it, our marriages were shattered and any feelings we may have had for one another were torn to pieces.

My biggest regret was that we could never tell you the truth. Please know that I was just as proud of you as my other three children. I watched you grow into a man that anyone would love to have for a son.

But I'm not a courageous man. You must have gotten your bravery from your beautiful mother. I'm weak and when things ended with Jackie she felt it was best to let you go on thinking that John Wright was your father. It seemed the right thing to do at the time. After all, I'd done so many things wrong by then I was desperate to do something good.

My punishment was never being able to tell you the truth. I hope you can find it in your heart to forgive me. You'll never know the joy I felt as you became best friends with Wade. It was how things should have been. All four of my sons together as a family. I'm sorry again I couldn't make that happen for you. When your father left, you were all Jackie had left. I couldn't come between the two of you. She was a good woman and she loved you so much.

But you are just as much my son as Wade, Aaron, or Lyle and because of that you will inherit your share of my estate. At this point, it is the very least I can do to make up for what you lost out on. My hope is this will bring you even closer to my sons, pulling you together as a family.

Protect each other, for in the end, family is all you have. You, Aaron, Wade, and Lyle are my legacy. I know it's in good hands.

Your father,
William Remington Bryson
June 3rd, 1997

Logan read and re-read the letter until he could have recited every word from memory. Hurt, anger, and other emotions he couldn't begin to name churned inside of him creating a physical pain that almost brought him to his knees. He was glad he was sitting down as his shaking legs wouldn't have been able to support his weight. He dragged air into his aching lungs and tried to calm his hammering pulse.

Crumpling up the letter in his tight fist, he cursed as he slumped forward in the chair. His elbows on his knees, he buried his face in his hands. He never wanted to leave this room and face Deke or anyone else, but staying here was simply not an option. He shoved the balled up letter into his pocket and stood on legs that felt like jelly.

He jammed his hat back on his head and straightened his shoulders. He'd learned early on not to show emotion or weakness. It was better to act like you didn't give a shit one way or the other. He opened the door and found Deke waiting on the other side, his forehead covered in sweat.

"Does anyone else know?" Logan was surprised the words came out evenly despite the lump in his throat. "Anyone?"

Deke's throat bobbed. "George. No one else." He reached out but Logan dodged the comforting hand on his arm. That wasn't going to make anything better. His world had been ripped apart in a matter of minutes. Everything he'd thought was true was now in question. "The family will be here soon for the reading. We're all going to meet in the dining room."

Are you fucking kidding me?

"I think I'll pass on the familial scene, Deke. I'm out of here."

Logan started for the front door with the attorney on his heels. "What do I tell the family? They're going to hear that you inherit a fourth."

"I don't give a fuck what you tell them," Logan growled, pulling on the door knob. "Tell them the bastard son had to get back to work."

He was out the door and down the steps before Deke could reply. Logan jumped into his truck and gunned the engine before reversing out of the driveway. He needed to get out of here right now. He needed to find a way to stop this agonizing pain.

Chapter Nine

Logan twisted open the bottle of whiskey, breaking the seal. He reached for the cabinet door to pull down a glass but quickly tossed the idea. This wasn't a sipping occasion. Current events called for gulping the Wild Turkey straight from the bottle. Hopefully the alcohol would bring him the blessed numbness and oblivion he sought. Booze was the answer and Logan didn't even know the fucking question.

He felt raw. Exposed for all to see.

He tipped the bottle and let the fiery liquid slide down his throat and into his belly. He'd barely noticed his surroundings as he'd driven home from the Bryson estate, stopping only briefly at the liquor store. Stubborn disbelief and denial still warred with the dawning realization that nothing would ever be the same after today.

Fuck it all. Get drunk.

That was his plan. It wasn't much of one but it was all he had. In the Army, they'd dealt with adversity as a team. He'd learned to trust others then but now there was no one but himself. He'd just acquired a family and yet he'd never felt more alone. Even when his mother had left.

An image of her flashed before his eyes and he took another long drink. Bryson had been right when he said that Jacquelyn Wright was a sunny golden girl. She'd taught Logan to sing and play the guitar. She'd taught him to hold doors open for females and to help them with their coat. In the end, she'd taught him that love couldn't be trusted. She'd vowed to love him forever but she'd lied. He wouldn't give anyone a chance to fool him that way ever again.

He took another drink from the bottle and settled back on the couch. The dull ache that always permeated his chest whenever he thought about his mother was back. He hated the feeling, hated the weakness. Most days he went about life and didn't think about the past. He'd vowed to never become its bitch, disgusted by people who allowed victimhood to take over their life. Now he had no choice but to let long forgotten memories come crowding back one after the other until he thought his head might explode.

Searching every corner of his mind, he looked for some clue or hint of the truth that had been revealed to him today. What had he missed? Should he have known?

He ran through every conversation in fast forward. His mother had never shown that she was anything else but delighted when he'd made friends with Wade, Lyle, and Aaron. Or maybe she was glad he was close with his brothers. Since she wasn't fucking here to ask, he'd never know.

As for Bill Bryson, Logan hadn't spent that much time with the man but he'd always been given a warm welcome in their home. Nothing had seemed amiss or strange. Logan had never been favored over anyone else.

There was always the possibility that Bill's letter was a huge lie. But then why would he leave Logan a quarter of his estate? It seemed an elaborate ruse to simply play some sort of sick practical joke.

No, Bill had to be telling the truth.

The thought that had been niggling in the back of Logan's mind finally came front and center. This was the reason Logan's supposed father had left. There couldn't be any other reason. At some point, his father – John – must have found out and the marriage had broken up. He'd left without a backward glance because Logan really wasn't his son.

The insistent ringing of the telephone brought Logan out of his reverie. He scowled at the machine as if his mind could vaporize its mere existence. He sure as fuck didn't want to talk to anyone. His anger was simmering too high and his feelings were too confused. The machine beeped and a halting-voiced Wade left a message that Logan should call him.

He wasn't even tempted to pick up the phone. He didn't want to talk to Wade. Or Lyle. Or Aaron. Or any other Bryson right now. Logan wasn't even sure how they'd taken the news. They had every right to be pissed that the bastard son had inherited. This had the potential to ruin his long-standing friendship with the family. He didn't want anything from Bill Bryson. Logan should simply sign everything over to them and be done with it.

Then what?

Corville, for better or worse, was his home. He'd been born and raised here, only leaving when he was in the Army. Even then, whenever he'd had leave, he'd come home to visit, staying in this very house with Frank.

Which brought up the question – had Frank Jesse known about Logan's parentage? Is that why he'd received special treatment? Admittedly, five years in the Army wasn't exactly a gravy train. As a matter of fact, it had been damn hard work and he was lucky to have come out alive. Many of his fellow soldiers hadn't.

But Frank had looked at him differently. Even leaving Logan this ranch when he'd died. Some had been puzzled when that happened, but Logan knew he'd earned it. The last few years of Frank's life he'd been so eaten up with alcoholism that Logan had run not only the sheriff's office but the ranch as well.

Suddenly he couldn't stand to be inside the house. Logan grabbed the bottle and headed out the back door, tossing his cell phone on the kitchen counter as he went. He walked across the green grass until he was standing in front of his tree. Grabbing a branch with one hand, he tucked the bottle under his arm to keep it safe.

He'd spend the night in the treehouse he'd built with his own hands several years ago. There was no telephone to bother him. Only the silence surrounded him and his thoughts.

Or not think at all. Just drink until he couldn't feel anything. Until there was peace.

The only problem was he wasn't sure he'd recognize it when he found it. He'd known little in his life and it didn't look like he'd be getting even a glimpse anytime soon. He swung up into the treehouse and settled on the bed watching the sun start to fade in the distance.

He took another drink of whiskey and settled in for a long night.

Ava pulled a soda from the refrigerator as her mother bustled into the kitchen to start dinner.

"It's about time you came out of your room. You've been locked in there all day," her mother observed.

For good reason. Ava hadn't wanted to face any questions from her mother and father about her date with Logan last night. She still didn't know how she felt about it herself. It was one measly kiss and it certainly wasn't her first. It shouldn't be a big deal but somehow things had grown all out of proportion. She wanted to hate Logan but she didn't. There was something about him that she couldn't identify.

"I was writing, Mom. It's what I do." Ava plopped down at the kitchen island to watch her mother make the meatloaf. Despite the entree not having a good culinary reputation in general, Carol Hayworth made an excellent meatloaf. Her secret was saltine crackers instead of bread crumbs.

"I know but it's a lovely day. You should go out for a walk or something. It's not healthy to stay cooped up in one room for hours."

If her mother only knew. Ava had been known to not leave her home for days on end.

"I'm out of there now. What else are we having?"

Her mother smiled as she dumped the ground beef into a large bowl before adding two eggs. "Mashed potatoes and corn bread."

Carb heaven. Ava's mother had never met a starch she didn't like. From the rounded curve of her own hips, Ava was pretty fond of them as well.

"With honey butter?" she asked hopefully.

"If you make it." Her mother laughed and poured the broken up crackers into the bowl. Ava grumbled but stood and headed back to the refrigerator, but the slamming of the front door and frantic footsteps interrupted her. Mary burst into the kitchen looking quite unlike her usual unruffled appearance.

"Heavens, child. You're slamming doors. You know how your father feels about that. Thank goodness he's at work."

Mary grabbed Ava's soda can and she watched in awe as her normally cool sister slugged half of it back in one shot. She raised her eyebrows as Mary set the can back on the island.

"Help yourself," said Ava a trifle sarcastically. "What the heck is wrong with you? You look like you've seen a ghost."

Mary took a deep breath. "I kind of have. I wanted to get home to tell you before you heard it from anyone else."

"Heard what?" her mother asked, digging her fingers into the bowl to combine the ingredients.

"The reading of the will today." Mary looked annoyed that no one seemed to be getting the urgency of the situation.

"Did Mr. Bryson leave everything to a long lost relative or something? Or the cat?" Ava joked.

"Kind of. He left a quarter of his estate to Sheriff Logan Wright." Mary looked back and forth between her sister and her mother as if waiting for a reaction.

"Logan?" That didn't make any sense. "Why? Did he help out the family in some way? Is he distantly related?"

Mary's lips curved in a Cheshire cat smile, triumph in every line of her expression. She loved it when she knew something no one else did.

"Logan Wright is Bill Bryson's son."

Shock and then denial ripped through Ava's body. "No way. You're kidding."

"I'm not. It was revealed today at the reading of the will. You should have seen everyone's faces. I thought George was going to have a stroke."

Ava's mother wiped her hands down with a paper towel. "Why aren't you with your husband right now?" she asked with a sharp tone. "I would think he would want his wife at his side at a time like this."

Mary had the decency to blush. "I wanted to be the first to tell you."

Her mother's lips twisted. "Well, you are. Was it as glamorous as you imagined?" she asked wryly. "I'm surprised at you, Mary Ellen Hayworth Bryson. You usually have better sense than this. The Bryson family, your own husband, is probably in great pain from this news and you come tearing into this house to spread gossip."

Pressing her lips together, Mary dropped her gaze. "I'm sorry, Mom. I guess I forgot what was important."

"Yes, you did. I hope you remember it now."

Ava watched her mother turn Mary into a stammering schoolgirl. The only person that could keep Mary in line was Carol Hayworth. Lyle didn't have a prayer of wrangling his headstrong wife.

"How's Logan taking this? Did he already know?" The question was wrenched from Ava but she couldn't help herself. He must be completely devastated.

Mary looked up and shrugged, shifting uncomfortably on her feet. "From what Deke Kennedy said only Bill and George Bryson knew. I didn't see Logan. He was gone by the time we got to the house. Wade, Lyle, and Aaron have been looking for him but no one can find him."

Ava chewed on her lower lip as emotions she'd tried to suppress last night squeezed her heart. Logan could be a royal jerk at times, but mostly he was a really nice man. She liked and respected him, and this had to have hurt him deeply. To find out he'd been lied to his entire life would be a betrayal he might never get over.

She slid off the barstool and moved towards the stairs to get her purse. "Mom, I may not be back in time for dinner. Don't wait on me."

Her mother put her hand on her hips. "Just where are you going?"

"To talk to Logan." She waited for her mother's disapproval but instead Carol Hayworth's expression softened.

"Honey, do you think it's a good idea? He must be in a powerful lot of pain right now. Maybe you should wait a day or two."

"No, I need to see him. Tonight." Ava couldn't explain the inexplicable urge to be with him. Right now. She only knew she couldn't deny it.

Mary shook her head. "No one knows where he is. You'll never find him."

Ava had a pretty good idea where Logan was hiding. She remembered the conversation they'd shared last night only too well. It was worth a try.

"I'm going anyway," Ava replied. "I have to."

Mary snorted and tossed back the rest of the soda in the can. "And another one bites the dust for the amazing Logan Wright. I should have known that's what you were doing hanging around him so much. You know he's only going to break your heart, don't you?"

"It's not like that. We're friends," Ava denied.

"Friends?" Mary laughed bitterly. "Logan Wright doesn't have any female—"

"Hush, Mary," Ava's mother intervened. "If Ava says they're friends, that's good enough for me."

"Thanks, Mom." Ava headed toward the door, slinging her handbag over her shoulder on the way. She felt a touch on her arm and turned to see her mother's worried expression.

"Honey, I don't want you to get hurt. Are you sure about this? Logan Wright is a good man, but…is he your man?"

Her voice was gentle and it tore at Ava's heart. She was only beginning to comprehend her feelings for Logan. This wasn't going to have a happy ending, of that she was sure.

"No, Mom. He's not my man but that's alright."

Her mother looked at her for a long moment and then nodded. "Drive carefully."

Ava climbed into her car and headed toward Logan's ranch. It was the dumbest, stupidest thing in the world to go after him. But she couldn't stop herself. He needed someone and she needed to be that someone.

No matter what it cost her.

Chapter Ten

Ava found Logan's treehouse tucked into a back corner of the lawn about two hundred feet from the house and barn. Peering up into the tree, she realized with dismay there was no ladder to access the house.

She was going to have to climb the damn tree.

She hitched her purse higher on her shoulder and reached up for the lowest branch, digging her sneakered toe into a knothole in the thick bark. She muttered a few impolite words as her foot slid down and she had to do it all over again. This time it held and she swung herself up on the branch, swinging her leg over it so she was in a straddle position.

One deep breath and she reached for the higher branch as she stood on the other, hiking her leg up as high as she could reach. By pushing with both her hands and feet she found herself kneeling on the upper branch. A peek down to the ground made her dizzy and she closed her eyes for a moment so the world would stop spinning.

If Logan wasn't up here she was going to kick his ass when she did finally find him. That was if she lived through this. She still needed to inch across the branch about a foot and a half to get to the opening of the treehouse.

And it was an impressive structure. It had been partially obscured from the ground by branches and thick leaves, but this close she could see it was about twelve by twelve in size and tall enough for a grown man to stand in. It looked professionally made with windows and a peaked roof with real shingles. If she wasn't about to plummet to a horrible death she would have taken the time to admire his craftsmanship.

Right now all she wanted to do was to live through this. Hopefully Logan would know an easier way back down to the ground because she didn't have a clue how she was going to manage that now she was up here.

She carefully dragged her left leg forward and then her right, balancing on the branch until she was finally at the entrance. She slowly reached up for the doorknob and twisted it, praying it wasn't locked. The door fell open and she collapsed in a heap on the treehouse floor grateful for something solid underneath her.

She looked up to see Logan about four feet away, reclining on a bed and holding a liquor bottle. He held up the bottle with a grin.

"Ava, come have a drink with me."

His voice didn't sound slurred so she couldn't be sure if he was drunk. A second look at the bottle showed about a third of it was gone. If it had been unopened when he'd started he probably wasn't sober.

She crawled the few feet and climbed up onto the bed, really just a mattress on the floor. To make it more inviting, Logan has fashioned a cushioned headboard and the bed was covered with clean linens, blankets, and oversized pillows.

She slid her purse off her shoulder and settled back, giving him a sour look. She wasn't in the best of moods after risking her life. "Everyone is looking for you. I wanted to make sure you were okay."

He scowled and took another drink straight from the bottle. "I came up here because I didn't want to talk to anyone. You weren't supposed to find me."

"Well I did," she retorted. "Not that you make it easy. I almost killed myself climbing the tree."

He took a swig, his forehead crinkled in confusion. "Why didn't you use the ladder?"

Ava wanted to smack Logan hard despite the fact that she was here to comfort him. He was obviously delirious, drunk, or both. "There is no ladder," she snapped. "Or I would have, of course. Did you climb the tree?"

"No," he shook his head. "I used the ladder." Logan started to smile and then to laugh, his entire body shaking. He pointed to the far side of the treehouse. "There's another door there. That side of the tree has pieces of wood nailed to the trunk so you can come up. Did you really climb the tree?"

Ava had to grit her teeth to keep from kicking him in the balls. "I did. It's not funny, you know. I could have killed myself."

Logan was still chuckling, his patented grin spread across his too handsome face. "More likely you would have spent the next six months in a plaster pantsuit but that's not the point. You did climb the tree and you did find me." His smiled disappeared. "What did you want?"

She didn't want to tell him people were gossiping about him but he'd lived in this town long enough to know that secrets were hard to come by. "I heard what happened today. I thought you might need some company."

"Company, huh? I can't imagine why you would think that. I came up here to be alone. That's what I am, Ava, alone." He held out the bottle to her. "Since you're here, you might as well have a drink."

She wrinkled her nose and shook her head. "Uh uh, I don't drink Wild Turkey."

He held it closer. "If you stay, you drink. If you don't drink, you leave." He jerked his head toward the entrance. "The same way you came in."

"You'd make me climb down the tree?" she gasped. "That's mean."

"I can be sweet. If you want, we can burrow down under these covers, just the two of us. I'll show you just how nice I can be. I'll have you screaming so loud we'll scare the birds from the trees."

She took the bottle from his outstretched fingers and grimaced. "I think I'll pass on the sex, if you don't mind. I can only imagine how many women you've brought up here and seduced."

"Seduced?" Logan laughed. "Honey, women come to me, not the other way around. I haven't had to lift a finger to get a woman in my bed since I was in my teens. Just so we're clear, I've never brought a woman here. This is my space."

And she'd invaded it, clearly. He didn't look angry but he didn't necessarily look thrilled either. He obviously found her funny, but for all the wrong reasons. She hated being this attracted to a man this boastful about his prowess with women but what could she do? Attraction wasn't something you could control. It was there whether she liked it or not. The only thing she had control of was how she reacted to it.

Maybe. She hadn't had much control about coming here to be with him. It had been a compulsion she couldn't deny.

He was watching her closely, his eyes a trifle glazed, probably due to the alcohol he'd already imbibed. She lifted the bottle to her lips and took a drink, the fiery liquid scalding her throat as it slid down.

She made a face and her eyes started to water. "Ugh! That's terrible. How can you drink that and not puke?"

"It's an acquired taste, good girl," Logan mocked. "Have another. Who knows? You might start to like it."

Her belly was already starting to heat up but she shut her eyes and took another drink, smaller this time. She'd heard about enjoying the mellow smoothness of a fine whiskey but at the moment she'd give anything for a caramel latte.

"That's just nasty." She pushed the bottle back to him, and he lifted it to his lips. He took a long swallow before setting the bottle between them. He reached to his left and placed a Western guitar on his lap, strumming the strings idly.

Leaning back against the cushions, Ava didn't say anything. She let him have his quiet while he played a few tunes, one after the other. Finally, he took another drink and handed the bottle to her. After she had made another face and shuddered as the whiskey heated her insides, he looked up at the ceiling.

"My mom left when I was a senior in high school," he said abruptly. She shoved away the urge to respond and waited for him to continue. He drank deeply from the bottle. "I went to school one day and when I came back she was gone. No note. Didn't take anything with her. Just gone. She never came back. I waited for her but she never did."

He played the guitar again and she recognized the tune of *Puff the Magic Dragon*. It had been one of the first songs she'd learned to play on the piano as a child. His mother abandoning him must have been a horrible moment in his young life. Ava couldn't imagine her mother leaving her like that. No wonder he didn't get serious with women.

"I like that song," she said. Not sure how to reply to his revelation. She'd known his mother was gone but not the circumstances.

Logan studiously avoided looking at her. "She taught it to me. It was just me and her for a long time. My dad up and left when I was ten. Only when he left, he packed all his things and said goodbye. He said he'd write to me." He plucked at a string. "He never did. I never heard or saw him again."

Her heart squeezing in her chest, Ava wanted to reach out and comfort him. Somehow she knew he wouldn't welcome it at this moment.

"She started drinking after he left. Not so much she couldn't work, but enough I knew she wasn't happy. I wasn't enough to make her happy."

Pressing her lips together, Ava batted at a stray tear, hoping Logan didn't notice. He wouldn't appreciate the pain she felt on his behalf.

"I think she really loved my dad." A bitter expression crossed his face and Logan shook his head. "Wait, not my dad. John Wright. I think she really loved him. I don't know if she loved my real dad."

Logan drank from the bottle before handing it back to her. She winced but took another drink, already getting used to the fire it created.

"Wade, Lyle, and Aaron are my brothers. Half-brothers anyway. I don't know how I feel about that." He turned to face her, his eyes almost black from emotion. "How am I supposed to feel about this?"

"I don't know," Ava admitted softly. "I don't think you're supposed to know this soon. You need to give yourself time."

Logan laughed but it wasn't a happy sound. "Time? Yeah, that's what I need. Time. Do you know that I waited for months for Mom to come back? Every day I'd come from school and I'd hope and pray she'd be back. I never gave up hope until the day I left for the Army."

"I bet she would have been proud of your military record. I heard you're some kind of hero." This time she did reach out to him and place her hand on his. His gaze dropped to where their fingers were joined but he didn't pull away.

"In combat, a hero is somebody who does something stupid and lives to tell about it. In my case, I saved some of my fellow soldiers by risking my own life. I had a death wish back then." Logan set the guitar beside him. "It wasn't even my idea to go into the Army. It was Sheriff Frank Jesse's idea."

Logan sat up restlessly. "After my mom disappeared I started doing stupid shit. Hanging out with troublemakers. Looking back, it was obviously a cry for attention. Anyway, me and a couple of kids broke into the drug store and stole some candy and soda. Kids' stuff really but the sheriff caught us. I guess he saw something in me because he made a deal. If I kept my nose clean and graduated from high school, then joined the military, he wouldn't arrest me."

"Did he arrest the other kids?"

"He did. Said they were 'punks', I believe. He was right. I've arrested every one of them while I've been sheriff. The ones that aren't dead or in prison already."

"So you joined the Army?" Ava wanted to keep Logan talking. It seemed the only way for him to work through what had happened to him today. She also had to admit she selfishly wanted to know more about this fascinating, complex man.

"Yep. Sheriff Jesse said if I did five years he'd make me a deputy when I came home. It seemed like a good deal. I didn't have any other ideas as to what I wanted to be. Of course I ended up doing ten years because of 9/11. Frank taught me everything he knew about being a lawman. He kept his promise."

That would be important to Logan after everything he'd been through. He'd only surround himself with those who kept their word. She understood now why being up front with women was so important to him. She also understood his frustration with Christina. She'd gone back on her word about no strings or commitments. Logan would never trust her again.

It also sounded like Sheriff Jesse was the closest thing to a father figure Logan had had at the time. It was amazing that he'd turned out as normal as he had.

"Logan," Ava began, still unsure as to what to say or do when faced with the truth about this man's life. He'd borne more than she could have imagined but come out the other side, obviously stronger and better for it. "I don't know why your parents left but I'm sure it didn't have anything to do with you. Things happen and life gets difficult. Whatever it was, it wasn't about you."

"Both of them?" he asked drily. "They both left me but it didn't have anything to do with me? Then Daddy Dearest could have told me when I didn't have anyone, but did he? Fuck no. Shit does happen, good girl. Bad shit. But what the fuck would you know about it? What bad thing has ever happened to you?"

His jaw was tight and he didn't look at her. She was shaking inside, recognizing his tightly controlled anger but knowing he wasn't mad at her. He was furious at the world and she just happened to represent it at the moment.

"Nothing," she conceded. "Nothing like you. My father is a pain, my sister is a piece of work but it's not even in the same league as what you've had to deal with. You win."

He quirked an eyebrow. "Funny, this is one I gladly would have let someone else win. I'm sorry I got mad. It's not your fault. It's nobody's fault."

Ava nodded her head. "It's somebody's fault, Logan, but not yours or mine. It's their fault. This has to do with them. Their shortcomings as human beings. No one else. You don't blame your issues on others, do you? No." She answered her own question.

"Why are you here again?" Logan queried, lifting the bottle to his lips.

"I came to make you feel better," she admitted. "I think I may have done the opposite."

"I felt shitty when I got here and I feel slightly less shitty now. Could be you or could be the booze." Logan held up the bottle. Most of the amber liquid had been drained. "Doesn't matter which."

He held out the bottle to her and she drank from it only semi-reluctantly. The whiskey had warmed her inside and made her feel slightly drowsy and mellow.

"I really was worried about you." Ava settled back against the pillows as the room seemed to be undulating before her eyes.

Logan rolled over on his side, a smile playing on his lips. "If you really want to make me feel better, you could get naked. Naked women always make me happier."

She started to sit up sharply but the room spun and she had to lie back down. "Don't be a jerk. I'm not taking my clothes off."

"Too bad. I bet you look pretty hot naked." Logan had lay down also and was staring at the ceiling.

"That's where you're wrong," she answered tartly. "I look like every other woman."

"Naw, I bet you look like you."

It was kind of a nice thing to say but she was too tired to think any more about it. Logan tipped the bottle up and drained it before tossing it away. It clattered and rolled across the floor but luckily didn't break.

"The room is spinning." Ava placed her arm over her eyes but the bed continued moving in relentless circles. Her stomach lurched and she swallowed hard to keep her stomach contents from reappearing.

"Hold onto me," Logan replied, pulling her into his arms. She thought about fighting him but the room did indeed stop spinning. Her stomach settled and she put her head on his chest, listening to the thump of his heart.

"I'm so tired. Does drinking whiskey make you tired?" she asked. Logan didn't answer and she lifted up to look at him. His eyes were closed and his expression peaceful. A snore erupted from his mouth and she couldn't hold back her giggle. He'd drunk so much he'd fallen asleep. She'd just lie here and keep him company. Maybe just close her eyes for a few minutes. When she knew he was okay, she'd climb down the tree ladder and head home.

Logan's snoring settled into a deep but disturbingly loud pattern. It was a wonder women were trying to get into his bed. Luckily they weren't there for the sleep. She'd never be able to get any rest with that racket.

Chapter Eleven

Ava started to open her eyes but winced as a sharp pain pierced her skull. She cautiously lifted one lid but quickly shut it again when the shooting pain turned into a hammer on her forehead. Licking her dry lips, her stomach lurched threateningly. The inside of her mouth tasted like dirty socks and felt as dry and grainy as a desert.

What happened last night?

With one eye now open, she took in her surroundings. She was still in the treehouse but instead of dark outside the windows, sun was streaming in making her squint. She levered up from her prone position and her head and stomach protested vigorously. One look at the rumpled bed next to her showed Logan was nowhere to be found. He'd left her up here to die obviously.

Death sounded pretty good at the moment. Her head hurt, her body ached, her stomach felt like it wanted to leave her abdomen, and she could feel every individual strand of hair on the top of her head.

So this was a hangover. She'd never drink again.

"You're finally awake." Logan's cheery face appeared in the doorway. He looked disgustingly healthy and had clearly showered and changed. She, on the other hand, never looked good in the morning under the best of circumstances. These were the worst. She bet she looked like a zombie. A wrinkled, hungover, pissed off zombie.

"Apparently. What happened last night?"

She reached up to try and smooth her hair down as he climbed into the treehouse. Despite feeling like death, she couldn't help but notice he was only wearing a pair of jeans. His broad chest with just a sprinkling of blond hair was bare and she had to look away from all that potent masculinity on display. It made her want to run to her laptop and write a character in his honor. At the moment she wasn't in any shape to run anywhere.

"We got drunk. We fell asleep. Pretty straightforward. I brought you some coffee."

Logan held up a styrofoam cup with a smile. Later she would probably thank him for climbing up a tree ladder with only one hand free to bring her a beverage. At the moment, the wafting aroma of coffee made her stomach contents rise in her throat. She slapped her hand over her mouth and groaned, her eyes wide with panic. Throwing up in front of Logan was simply a non-starter. She'd never be able to face him again if she did.

His expression turned from happiness to confusion then to understanding. He quickly tossed the cup out of the open door and wrapped his arm around her shoulders.

"Let's get you into the house. We'll splash some cold water on your face and get you some saltines."

She didn't know how Logan managed it, but somehow he got her down to the ground, practically carrying her into the house. The smell of coffee and eggs hit her the minute she stepped in and she whimpered as her stomach twisted and rolled. She flew through the living room and down the hall to the bathroom where she became wretchedly sick.

A gentle hand was at her back holding her hair and running up and down her spine. When she was done, Logan gave her a cool washcloth and a glass of water. Tears leaked from her eyes and she cursed her weakness in front of this man. She didn't want him to be this nice to her. She wanted to think of him as a selfish womanizer.

"I think the lining of my stomach is gone," she sniffled. "Possibly some of my intestines too."

Ava heard him chuckle as he flipped the lid of the toilet down and helped her up from the floor to sit on it. "I think it's all still there. You'll be okay. I promise. You must be really pissed off at me, good girl."

Ava looked up at him in surprise. She'd thought he would make fun of her illness. She'd hoped it. "Why would I be mad at you?"

"Because I told you to drink. It's my fault. It never occurred to me you'd be this sick. I'm sorry, honey. Are you ready to lie down for awhile?"

She nodded and pondered his apology. It really was his fault. She never would have drank that whiskey if he hadn't said to.

No, wait.

She knew he wouldn't have made her leave if she hadn't. He would have let her stay. She'd drank it because she wanted to belong. Peer pressure at its finest. She'd thought she'd outgrown it.

Nope.

She let him help her, his arm supporting her weight, as he led her back into the living room and settled her on the couch. She leaned back against the cushions and sighed. It felt good to lie down. Now that her stomach was empty, it didn't feel too bad either.

"I'll be right back," Logan said and he disappeared into the kitchen. He returned with a sleeve of crackers which he handed to her. "Can I make you some tea or something?"

He seemed to know how to take care of a hangover. This whole situation was going from bad to worse. He was sexy and nurturing. Was he trying to ruin her for any other man?

"Okay. Thank you," she replied belatedly. She opened the crackers and bit into one, the saltiness actually tasting good on her tongue. She nibbled on them as she listened to him moving around in the kitchen. It was kind of nice being waited on by a handsome man but she knew better than to get used to it.

He brought out the steaming cup and set it on the end table. "Drink up. It will help settle your stomach."

She blew on the liquid and took a sip, making a face. "Sweet."

"The sugar will help revive you. You look a little washed out."

"Is that a nice way of saying I look like death warmed over?" She took another sip. "I don't look good in the morning. Some people do, some don't. I'm part of the latter, I'm afraid. I bet you do though. Jerk."

She was trying to build up her crumbling defenses but he was knocking them down so easily, brick by brick.

"I doubt it. You look fine, good girl," he assured her. "Just pale from being sick. Do you want to take a punch at me for getting you drunk?"

Ava looked at Logan over the edge of her cup. He was smiling but managed to look contrite at the same time. Hitting him was tempting, but she wasn't going to do it. "I don't want to hurt my hand. Maybe I can kick you in the balls when I'm feeling better."

Logan laughed and the sound hurt her head a little. "Sorry, I'm only offering a punch in the jaw. My balls are off limits." He waggled his eyebrows. "Unless you had something pleasurable in mind, that is. Then I might be persuaded."

She might be persuaded too, but letting him know that would be stupid. Groaning, she closed her eyes to block out the sight of him looking too good for this time of day. "Logan Wright, the last thing on my mind is sex. How can you be so cheerful this early in the morning anyway?"

She mentally apologized for lying but she was in sheer self-preservation mode here.

"Because it's not early for one thing. It's almost ten o'clock." He sat down on the coffee table next to the couch.

She sat up so fast she almost spilled her tea. "Ten! Oh my stars, my parents will have called out the National Guard."

Logan's hand stayed her movements pressing her back against the cushions. "Stay put," he ordered sternly. "You can call your parents and let them know you're okay. You need to lie down and rest. Give your stomach a chance to settle. Running off now isn't going to do you any good."

Ava sat back, albeit reluctantly. Her overprotective father had probably already had a litter of kittens by now. She'd never hear the end of this from him. Even her mother who was more open-minded would be worried to a frazzle. They would think she'd had wild sex with Logan last night. Anyone who knew him would of course.

And anyone who knew her?

Don't go there.

Logan grabbed the landline from the kitchen and handed the receiver to her. "Go ahead and let them know where you are."

Staring at the phone, Ava was flummoxed as to what to say to her parents. She couldn't tell them she'd gotten drunk and spent the night with Logan. She didn't want to lie either. They would already have their suspicions about what might or might not have happened last night.

Ava was a grown woman and here she was arguing with herself about how to break it to her parents that she'd done something most grownups do once or twice in their life.

Logan's eyebrows were pulled down. "Aren't you going to call them?"

She looked up at him and something in her expression must have told the story. He smiled gently and plucked the phone from her hands. "Why don't you let me do the talking?"

She wasn't the type to let a man take control of things but she was tired and sick. Logan was confident and assured. If anyone could talk her parents off a ledge, surely it was him? After all, he had her contemplating doing wild naked things with him. He could handle two hysterical parents.

He punched in their number and waited for an answer. "Mrs. Hayworth? Good morning, ma'am. This is Logan Wright."

Thank God it had been her mother answering. Of course it could be because her father had already stroked out some time in the night when Ava hadn't come home.

Logan was smiling and nodding as he listened patiently to whatever her mother was saying.

"Ava's fine," he assured her. "I think something she ate didn't agree with her and she got sick to her stomach. She's feeling better now and lying on my couch."

More talking from her mother. Ava liked how he didn't really lie but he didn't tell the whole story either. The whiskey had certainly not agreed with her.

"It's all my fault. After she finally fell asleep, I was tired too. I should have called you last night and for that I can't apologize enough. Please blame me. She was safe here, I promise."

Logan was using every ounce of charm and it appeared to be working. The voice coming from the phone sounded much less agitated than before.

"She's going to rest a little more and then I'll bring her home. She should probably take it easy today."

Logan exchanged more pleasantries with her mother before hanging up. He tossed the receiver on an armchair. "You're in the clear. Somehow your mother kept your father from figuring out you didn't come home by telling him you were still asleep this morning. She was very worried. I'll take you home on my way out of town."

"I have my car here," she said stiffly, faintly put out by how easily he handled her parents. She'd been dealing with them for years and it rarely went that smoothly. Did he have to be good at everything? It was pissing her off.

"Then I'll follow you," he replied easily. "I'm going to a meeting in about an hour."

"How did you do that?" She hated herself for asking the question but she couldn't hold it in. "What's your secret for dealing with my parents?"

He sat down next to her on the couch, his expression gentle. He lifted the cup of tea to her lips. "Drink some more, okay? As for what I did? A couple of things. First, I deal with people every day in my job so I've learned a lot about what makes people calm and what gets them angry. But the real secret is that I'm not invested, good girl."

"Invested? What do you mean?" The tea and crackers had settled her stomach and she was starting to feel human again. Instead of worrying about her nausea she was thinking about how it felt to be this close to him. She could feel the warmth from his body and smell the clean scent of his body wash. He was sexuality and tenderness all wrapped up in this delicious package. She was only human for heaven's sake. If he'd been a jerk this morning she would have been okay. But he wasn't in the least. He was a good person and she was a sucker for caring, sensitive men.

"I'm not their daughter. I don't have a need to make them happy or proud of me. It frees me up to be firm and set boundaries with people unemotionally. Simple as that."

"So you're saying my need for their approval is what's keeping me from breaking free completely?"

His words had hit home. Hard.

"Did I say all that?" Logan grinned. "All I said was I'm not their kid. You thought up the rest on your own."

She picked up one of the throw pillows from the couch and smacked his arm with it, trying to put some emotional distance between the two of them. She felt way too vulnerable with him. "Sometimes I hate you."

She really didn't. She liked him way too much. He'd taken good care of her this morning.

"Sometimes I hate myself." Logan laughed and leaned forward to press a brief kiss on her forehead. It made her feel about five years old but the alternative was much scarier. She'd be lost if he treated her like a desirable woman. "Drink your tea and then you can freshen up in the bathroom before we go."

"The whiskey didn't affect you at all, did it?" She sighed and drank more of her tea. "I guess you're used to it."

"Could be," he agreed. "Or it could be I'd already puked up my stomach contents long before you woke up."

Grinning, he headed into the kitchen, whistling a lilting tune. She couldn't tell if he was serious or kidding, which was probably the point.

The sooner she returned home to Portland and got her head on straight the better. The more time she spent in Logan's company the more she liked him. He was more than just sex on a stick. He was the kind of man she'd been looking for in her life. Caring, tender, smart, and fun. For her peace of mind, the sooner they solved this case the better.

"Christ on a cracker, can't you keep it down?" Logan asked the other five men as they sat at a long table in the roadhouse. Tanner had managed to get the entire group together this morning to talk about the latest with the vigilante. Normally Logan loved joking and spending time with his closest friends but this morning he felt decidedly ragged. He hadn't puked as he had suggested to Ava, but his head wasn't feeling all that great. He'd taken several aspirin and they had yet to kick in.

Griffin Sawyer's brows shot up. "Are we feeling poorly this morning? Did someone have a little too much fun last night?"

The last thing he'd call last night was fun. Learning about his heritage the way he had could more readily be labeled as torture. The part with Ava had been okay though. It had been really sweet of her to come find him to make him feel better.

No one else had.

People might have been looking for him but they hadn't looked very hard. Anyone who knew him would know where he was. Ava had found him after only hearing about the treehouse once in passing.

Waking up next to her this morning hadn't been unpleasant in the least. He'd liked feeling her curves flush against his body. She'd been warm and womanly, her hand resting on his chest as if she was trying to feel his heartbeat.

He'd watched her sleep for quite awhile noticing how thick and dark her lashes were and how her full lips trembled as she dreamed. Her fist had been tucked under her cheek and a few dark curls had fallen over the satiny skin. He'd carefully reached out so as not to wake her and caressed it, then let her silky hair fall through his fingers. For the first time in his life he hadn't been in a hurry to evict a woman from his bed.

He'd had to climb out of bed and get his shit together before she woke up. She'd knocked down all his defenses the night before leaving him raw and exposed. He'd told her more about his life than he'd ever told any woman.

Stop thinking about Ava.

It was getting him nowhere fast. Good girls like her didn't date or have sex with bad boys like him. Just as well. He couldn't promise her a future. Women like her would want that.

"There was no fun involved, I assure you," Logan answered, popping open a can of soda. "How many days, Seth? What's the latest countdown?"

Seth Reilly's wife Presley was pregnant and due any day. Groaning, Seth grinned. "Ten days and counting. We both can't wait. Poor Presley can hardly sleep or eat. She's so uncomfortable. Luckily the doctor says it could be any time now."

"Don't wish these days away," Tanner cautioned. "It's much easier to take care of a baby that's inside the mother than outside. You think you can't sleep now? You don't know what sleep deprivation truly is."

Reed Mitchell shook his head with a grimace. "Shit, all this talk about babies gives me the creeps. When did we stop talking about hockey and football and start talking about diapers for fuck's sake?"

Jared Monroe strummed his fingers on the table, an amused look on his face. "Relax, Reed. No one's going to make you get married and have a baby. You can be single and alone the rest of your life."

Apparently Reed thought that sounded like heaven. "Promise?" His face split into a grin. Reed was the most mysterious of the five lawmen that met on a regular basis to share information. "Alone sounds just right."

Griffin slid a soda can down Reed's way and snorted. "Who'd have you? I went camping with you that one time and didn't get a wink of sleep. You snore like a buffalo. Holy shit, you should see someone about that. It can't be a healthy thing."

"If they come a half a dozen times, they're too tired to complain." Reed winked, a mischievous grin on his face. "I guess you wouldn't know anything about that."

Griffin's lips twisted into a half smile. "I haven't heard any complaints. In fact, they're usually calling me 'Oh God'."

Tanner pounded the table with his fist to bring the meeting to order. "We get it. You're all studs. Some of us don't have to brag. We're secure enough in our manhood to keep it to ourselves."

His lips were twitching so Logan knew Tanner was just busting their balls. Any other day he would have laughed but his head hurt too damn much.

"I'm as secure as they come. Can we get started now? I have work to do," Logan declared. He wasn't kidding. He'd taken a vacation day yesterday, then this whole thing with the reading of the will, the whiskey, and Ava being sick this morning had played hell with his schedule. Logan liked to keep to a routine and today he was supposed to be doing surprise checks on a few guys on parole.

Seth chuckled and looked around the room at the other guys. "I'm with you there. Why don't you start?"

Logan filled them in on the ballistics report and then told them about the reading of the will the day before, telling them only enough of the pertinent details. He hated revealing anything about himself. He'd told Ava everything but these men would get the digest version. They didn't need to know Logan's old man had left him when he was young or that his mother had disappeared one day.

The room was silent and his friends didn't seem to know what to say. Finally Tanner spoke. "I'm sure this has come as a great shock to you. We appreciate you being this open about why you want to put this killer behind bars once and for all."

They didn't have a fucking clue. Not really.

Logan lifted the soda can to his lips, draining the last of the liquid before responding. "I hope I don't have to talk about this again. Let's find out all we can about my…father and his business. I need to know why the vigilante would go after him. He doesn't fit the pattern."

Reed stroked his chin. "I have a few contacts I can talk to. Maybe there's something in his real estate dealings."

Griffin nodded. "I have a few contacts in government. There might be something there. I assume they applied for permits and variances, things like that."

"That's what I was hoping for. I have my hands full sifting through financial paperwork at the moment. I'm also planning to pull some old files of Sheriff Jesse's down from the attic."

"He kept police files in his attic?" Jared asked, clearly surprised. "Isn't that against regulations?"

"Let's just say when I took over Corville's sheriff department, there were several things that were against regulations. I had bigger issues." Logan chuckled. "I've never needed the files and the station storage room is packed to the rafters with boxes already. They're as safe at the house as they are at the office."

"You should think about digitizing all those files like Presley in Harper. It's fantastic."

"Jillie's great but she hates computers. It's all I can do to get her to read the email that comes in. She has to print off every one she wants me to read. She won't just forward it to me. You could simply lend me Presley," Logan said in a hopeful tone.

Seth laughed and tossed his empty can in the trash behind him. "Sorry. She's going to be pretty busy here real soon. She could show Jillie but she can't do it herself."

"I may take you up on that offer after the baby's born. I could always bring in a temp to get it done." Logan was already mentally calculating where he could find the funds in his tight budget.

"Any other business?" Tanner asked from the head of the table. Logan couldn't believe how happy and relaxed his friend looked these past months. Since meeting and falling in love with Madison he was a new man. A much more content man.

The men shook their heads and the meeting broke up. Logan headed to his truck but Griffin was right on his heels.

"Are you okay, man?" he asked. "A lot of shit has come down on you these past few days. Can I do anything for you?"

Logan opened the door to his truck. "Just what you're going to do. I appreciate your help. I want this guy in the worst way."

Griffin slapped Logan on the back. "We'll get him. It's only a matter of time before he fucks up. This murder could be the turning point. If he broke pattern and killed this Bryson guy, I mean your father, it could lead to information that will reveal his identity."

"You don't have to call him my dad. He didn't act like it. I sure as fuck don't feel like he's my father."

Logan felt a tightening in his chest whenever he talked about Bill Bryson. He wasn't sure how he was supposed to feel. Right now he was pissed as hell that the man had never told him while he was alive.

Griffin shrugged. "You probably don't. Honestly I wasn't sure how you wanted us to refer to him."

"Right now I'd gladly call him that son of a bitch."

Laughing, Griffin headed towards his own truck. "That sounds more like the Logan we all know and love. I'll call you if I learn anything. See you."

Griffin swung into his truck and gunned the engine. Logan did the same and backed out of the parking lot, turning towards Corville. He needed to get some work done today. Tonight he needed to finish going through the financial papers. It was a shit load of work.

He could use some help.

An image of Ava as she'd looked this morning, all sleepy and soft, rumpled from the night drifted through his brain. It wouldn't hurt to ask her if she had some time. After all she wanted to help. She'd begged him to let her work on solving the case.

He pulled his cell phone from his pocket and punched a few buttons.

Chapter Twelve

"I'm worried about you, that's all." Ava's mother sipped her coffee as they sat in the diner. "I know you're a grown woman but you're also my child. A mother never stops worrying about their child."

"You don't worry when I'm in Portland. I could be staying out all night, every night, there and you'd never know," Ava pointed out. She understood her mother's feelings but she needed to set some boundaries with her parents. She was thirty years old after all.

"True. I just want you to be happy, sweetheart. I get the feeling you're not. Not really." Red tinged her mother's cheeks. "When you have children you want them to have everything."

"What would you do if I wasn't happy?" Ava challenged. "You can't make me be happy. I have to find that on my own. Do you worry about Mary like this?"

Ava's mother shook her head. "Not in the same way. You and Mary are very different people. Her idea of happiness is not the same as yours. You'll only be happy when you find love."

"Love?" Ava echoed. "Mom, I'm not a woman who needs a man in her life. I do fine on my own."

"I didn't say you needed a man. I'm sure you can kill your own spiders by now. I'm talking about a man that adores you, who wants to love and protect you. A man that thinks you hung the moon."

Ava couldn't think of one man she'd ever dated that fit that description.

"I don't see that happening. Modern men don't do that."

"Then find an old-fashioned one. I'm sure they're out there. But you have to leave the house to look." Ava's mother teased.

"I leave the house. You know I've been helping Logan with the Bryson murder."

Although after this morning Ava wasn't sure she would ever see Logan again. He'd been kind but a man like him would feel vulnerable after what he'd revealed to her.

"That's true. It would be nice if you stayed here for awhile. I'm selfish enough to want both my daughters close."

"I'm not leaving right away," Ava assured her. "Now can I have a bite of your cheesecake?"

Carol laughed and pushed the plate across the table. "As long as I can have a bite of your tiramisu."

Ava slid her own plate into the middle of the table. They were happily munching away on their fattening desserts when they heard voices from the next table.

"She's been spending a lot of time with the sheriff," one voice said. "A lot of time, if you know what I mean."

"I heard she went dancing with him at the roadhouse the other night. Shocking," the second voice said, her tone prissy and uptight. "A nice girl like her with a playboy like him. Next thing you know he'll get her in trouble and leave her for a prettier face."

"Hmmm, he usually dates the more glamorous ones," the first voice responded. Ava could feel her anger rising and heat suffused her entire body. These busy-bodies were obviously talking about her. She didn't like it one bit and it was all she could do not to turn around in her chair and let them know how rude they were being.

Ava gritted her teeth and set her fork on the table, her appetite vanished. Her mother was looking at her very calmly and finally said, "Is Logan Wright a playboy? I know he appears that way on the surface but one never knows what's underneath."

Chewing her bottom lip, Ava thought about the question and shook her head. "No. He's a nice man. He took care of me when I was sick. There's more to him than meets the eye."

Ava's mother smiled. "Being that handsome is certainly enough. Doesn't seem fair to womankind that he's not a jerk."

"I wish he was." Ava sighed and tried to eat more of her tiramisu. "It would be better for me."

"You're falling for him, aren't you?" her mother asked gently.

There was no censure or judgment in her mother's tone. It was simply a question.

"I don't know," Ava admitted. "If you'd ask me yesterday, I would have said no. I wish I didn't like him."

"If wishes were horses," her mother began.

Ava tried to smile. "I know, beggars would ride." She'd heard her mother use that saying many times over the years. "I think it's just a crush."

"Probably," her mother nodded in agreement. "Although I would be happy if you fell in love, married the sheriff, and stayed in town."

Laughter Ava couldn't contain bubbled up. "Whoa. Just because I have feelings for Logan doesn't mean he has them for me. I don't see us setting up housekeeping, Mom. Far from it."

The two women at the table behind them got up to leave and Ava caught sight of them. Harriet Weatherby and Louise Farmer were two of the biggest gossips in Corville. Louise had the grace to turn pink when she saw that Ava was sitting right next to them. They must not have seen her and her mother sit down.

"Harriet. Louise. How are you today?" Ava's mother asked politely, looking them right in the eye. "I think we'll have good weather for the church picnic on Sunday."

"Indeed we will," agreed Harriet, sneaking glances at Ava out of the corner of her eye. "This weather we've been having the last few weeks has been excellent. I don't remember a stretch this long since oh, ninety-eight, I think."

Louise shook her head. "It was ninety-six. That's the year that Jackson boy ran off with—"

Louise broke off abruptly as if talking about someone else's exploits would reveal she'd been talking about Ava's.

Harriet rushed in to cover the gaffe. "I hope you're going to make your famous pistachio salad, Carol. I look forward to it every year."

"I am. I think Ava's going to make a chocolate cake as well."

Both women nodded enthusiastically as if they hadn't tasted cake in years. Louise waved toward the door. "Well, we must be off. See you Sunday!"

The two women exited the diner and headed quickly down the street, probably already talking about Ava and her mother. Some people just never learned to keep things to themselves.

"I hope you marry Logan Wright and have ten kids and thirty grandchildren, dying in each other's arms when you're a hundred years old." Her mother was staring out the window of the diner at the retreating figures of Louise and Harriet.

Ava laughed at her mother's outraged expression. "I really don't see that happening. Logan and I are just friends."

Even saying it made her depressed. She wasn't sure it was enough anymore.

Carol Hayworth snorted in disgust. "I'd love to tell those two busy-bodies that my daughter had tamed the biggest man-whore in town."

"Mother!" Ava exclaimed, appalled and amused at the same time. "Such language."

Carol Hayworth laughed and picked up her handbag and car keys. "There was a time, Ava, before I met your father that I was young. I knew how to have fun. I also liked the bad boys."

Her eyes had a faraway look to them as if she was remembering past glories. Ava clapped her hand to her forehead. "Don't tell me. I don't want to know."

Her mother stood and Ava followed suit, hoping this bizarre exchange was at an end. She didn't need to picture her mother on the back of a Harley. It was disturbing. And creepy.

"Just know you get this from me, dear." Her mother led the way out of the diner. "You're not doing anything that hasn't been done before. You kids didn't invent sex, you know."

"For the love of God, please stop," Ava groaned. "I don't want to hear this."

They walked toward the car and Ava's mother simply laughed at her daughter's mortified expression. "I never knew you were such a prude. I think Logan Wright has come along just in time."

Logan opened a box and pulled out a stack of manila folders, handing half to Ava. "We need to get through these financial records so we can start on the files in the attic. This is the last of it."

She'd been surprised to get Logan's call earlier asking for more help on the case. His impassive features gave no clue as to whatever emotions he might be hiding. He appeared calm and in control at the moment, nothing like the man he'd been the night before. She knew better. He was suppressing his emotions, skating along the surface like he always did.

The only time he'd shown any emotion was when he'd told her about the ballistics report. George Bryson had been shot by an as yet unidentified serial killer performing vigilante style murders. Apparently the murderer had shot more than a dozen victims in the last ten months.

"We haven't found anything yet," she countered, flipping the file open and starting to peruse the contents. "I'm beginning to think there's nothing here."

Logan opened the fridge, pulled out two cans of soda and popped them open before sliding one to her side of the kitchen island. "I'm starting to think that myself. So far I haven't seen anything I wouldn't expect. It's frustrating as shit."

Logan started on his own file and the silence stretched on as they worked. It was hell being so close to him but not being able to help him with the pain he surely felt. The words were dancing on the paper in front of her and she finally couldn't keep the question from bursting from her lips.

"Are you okay?"

He looked up, his eyes narrowing. "Why wouldn't I be okay?"

"You know." She wasn't sure how to say it, how to break through the wall he'd built between them. She'd felt it the moment she'd arrived, a polite facade she wanted to shatter.

"With everything that's gone on in the last few days, well, I was wondering how you were doing."

He looked back down at the file, dismissing her concerns. "Leave it alone, Ava." His tone had a hard edge but she was in too deep to stop now.

"Ignoring it won't make anything better."

A muscle jerked in his jaw. "Typical. Get back to work."

"What do you mean *typical*? How am I typical?" She completely abandoned the pretense of working. Denying his emotions wasn't going to help him in the long run. He was being stubborn and she hated stubborn men. At this moment he reminded her of her father.

Logan looked up again, his blue eyes almost black. "A typical woman. Women are always asking what I'm thinking or what I'm feeling. But they don't really want to know."

"I do want to know," Ava insisted, grabbing his hand with her own. "I'm worried about you."

Logan snatched his hand back and got up from the barstool to prowl the kitchen. "Right. When a woman says she wants to know what I'm thinking, what she's really saying is she wants me to know what *she's* thinking. She wants me to know what *she's* feeling. Feigning interest in me is just a game to get me entangled in her life. It's a test, Ava, and I don't like being tested." He stopped and whirled toward her, his teeth gritted together. "Women are always trying to get me to be more involved than I am. Basically honey, I'm not that deep. I like to drink. I like to fuck. And I like riding my bike and being alone. That's it. I'm not any more complicated than that."

Ava didn't know whether to hit him or hug him. She was pissed that he still lumped her in with every other woman he knew. But another part of her, a big part of her, wanted to pull him into her arms and tell him that every woman didn't want something from him.

"I'm not trying to do that," she said evenly. "I truly am concerned. I don't want to tell you about my feelings." Boy, was that the truth. "I just can't imagine going through what you have in the last two days and being hunky-dory. I swear on a stack of all my novels that I'm not trying to test you."

"So you like me just the way I am?" he taunted. "I find that hard to believe."

"I don't like you much at the moment," she retorted. "You're being a big horse's ass right now. You're spoiled, Logan Wright. You're a spoiled brat."

He took a step back, astonishment written on his face. "Spoiled? How in the fuck am I spoiled? You're the little princess who's too good for the bad boy."

Righteous anger that had been building inside her burst open. She shook her finger under his nose. "You're spoiled. Females have been catering to your whims since you were a teenager. Preening and primping to get your attention, you've never had to work for it. Never had to lift a finger to get them to like you. They've allowed you to be the shallow playboy you've become. It's fine for now but think of yourself in ten years. You'll be a pathetic figure, Logan. A middle aged man hitting on young girls in bars. You'll be a joke."

Her words were scornful and she hoped they hit home with him painfully. She wanted him to see himself through her eyes. The road he was on was a sad one.

"I never met a woman that was worth changing for." Logan straightened, his features carved in granite. He knew what to say to inflict the maximum damage. She felt like she'd been punched in the solar plexus, gasping for oxygen.

"I'm sorry," Ava whispered. "I think that's a little sad. I also think you have to accept some of the blame for that. You only let women in that will play by your strict set of rules."

"Have you ever let anyone in?" he jeered. "Ever? I think you're waiting for a knight in shining armor to sweep you off your feet. You want a man to be perfect, Ava. You've set standards so high no man could ever live up to them."

His words pierced her heart sending pain straight to her soul. She'd let him in, albeit reluctantly, briefly. She hadn't wanted him to be perfect. Far from it. She'd only wanted him to be what he could be, not this shadow.

"I've never wanted a perfect man." Ava thought of her mother's words earlier that day. It was funny how a parent knew a child so well. Ava hadn't even known it herself until this moment. "I've only ever wanted a man who had the capacity to love deeply."

Her shoulders slumped and tears pricked the back of her eyes. Nothing would ever change Logan. He'd been hurt too deeply and too often. The shell around his emotions was thick and she'd be a fool to think she could breach it. This was a battle she wouldn't win. Logan didn't want to face what life had thrown at him. She should leave him to live however he wished.

She walked slowly into the living room, slinging her purse over her shoulder, and then toward the front door, not looking back. Each step took her farther from Logan and closer to never seeing him again. Despite what she'd told her mother, there was really nothing to keep her in Corville. She could pack her things tonight and be on the road in the morning.

She was halfway down the porch steps when she felt his hand on her shoulder, the heat scorching her skin through the fabric. She couldn't look at him and let him see the tears she knew were glistening in her eyes. She couldn't let him know that he'd gotten to her like this. He wouldn't welcome it.

"You can't leave." Logan's voice was hoarse, almost choked.

"I have to." She didn't elaborate but his fingers tightened, almost bruising the flesh in his urgency.

"Don't leave me, Ava. I can't have one more person I care about walk out on me."

Tears spilled down her cheeks, the pain in her heart almost more than she could bear. She wanted desperately to believe his tortured words but her cautious nature wouldn't let her turn around and throw herself into his arms. She'd never been this vulnerable before with a man and she didn't like the feeling one bit. She tried to shore up some sort of defenses but they were in short supply. She'd have to make do with what she had.

She placed her hand on his. "I know you feel alone and confused right now. I know you feel betrayed by the people that were supposed to protect you. But you don't really mean what you're saying. If I turn around and come back nothing will change. Tomorrow you'll go back to being the same person you were twenty minutes ago. I couldn't take that, Logan."

Her voice shook and her body trembled. She prayed that he would leave her and go back in the house. She wanted to crawl away somewhere and lick her wounds. She needed to find the resources to build up the same shell he wore so easily and carelessly.

"Ava Hayworth, nothing has been the same since the moment we danced together at the wedding. I don't know what I feel, but I know if you walk away from me I may not be able to survive it this time."

Her heart. God, her heart.

She couldn't walk away from this man no matter what damage he might do later. The plea in his tone called to her and she found herself turning around to face him. She caught sight of his pale features before he pulled her into his arms. His lips came down on hers, almost brutal in their intensity, and then more gentle when he realized she wasn't going to pull away.

Her purse slid down her arm and landed with a thump on the porch steps. Her heart accelerated in her chest and heat swept her body as his hands roamed up and down her curves as if he wanted to learn every line. Emotions she'd tried hard to tuck away broke free.

Her arms went around his neck, holding on for dear life as her legs gave way. He must have felt her surrender because he leaned down and swept her into his arms, carrying her up the steps and through the front door. Kicking it shut with his boot, he strode with purpose towards the back of the house where she knew his bedroom was located.

She was going to make love with Logan. Right here. Right now. She only hoped she wouldn't regret it in the morning. She only hoped she could survive the broken heart she would surely have when he was done with her.

Chapter Thirteen

Something inside of Logan had snapped when he'd watched Ava walk out of his house. At that moment he'd known he couldn't let her go. She'd breached the walls he kept firmly around his emotions, guarding him from feeling too much. He didn't know what would happen tomorrow but tonight he'd spend worshipping her, showing her how it could be between them.

He laid her on the bed and came down on top of her, pressing butterfly light kisses all over her face and throat. Her fingers were holding tightly to his shoulders and her head was thrown back to give him better access to the sensitive curve where her shoulder met her neck. He nipped and then licked at that spot, feeling a heady triumph when she shuddered and a small moan escaped from between her kiss-swollen lips.

His cock pressed insistently against his fly but he didn't want this to be a bump and run. He wanted to take his time and explore the lush curves and valleys of Ava's gorgeous body. She wasn't a bag of bones like so many women these days who existed on lettuce leaves and rice cakes. She had the figure of a woman, full and ripe, waiting to be plucked into his greedy hands.

The problem was she was wearing too many clothes. He reached down and popped open the button of her jeans and pulled the zipper down, the metal teeth loud in the silence.

If he'd thought she might hesitate as the reality of what was happening hit her, he was quite mistaken. He slid to the floor as her jeans glided down her legs. She pulled her pink T-shirt over her head and tossed it aside hurriedly. The jeans joined it along with her white anklet socks with pink thread along the toes.

Reclining on her elbows, Ava's eyes turned to molten gold as he trailed kisses from her instep, up her calves, to the silky skin behind her knees. She giggled as he hit a ticklish spot so he kissed it again and again until she was laughing and twisting on the bed. He repeated the pattern with her other leg and sat back to survey his handiwork.

She looked delightfully mussed with her flushed skin, sparkling eyes, and tousled curls. How she managed to look so sexy in her sensible white cotton high-cut briefs and matching bra he didn't know. There was something earthy and sensual about her. She didn't need fancy lingerie, perfume, or a face full of makeup to get his motor running. He was as attracted to her mind as he was her body, and the thought should have scared the shit out of him.

Ava was the first woman in his life that hadn't asked anything of him. She didn't want him to conform to her idea of what a man should be. She'd quietly snuck in under the radar and taken down his emotional walls brick by brick. Calling him on his bad behavior had only been the beginning. She challenged him at every turn to be more, to be better. She believed he could be even when he wasn't sure himself.

"Logan." Her soft voice caught his attention and his gaze wandered from her legs to her smiling face. She was holding out her arms and he went into them gratefully. He wanted to blot out everything that had happened before this moment, even just for a few minutes. There would be a long list of things he had to deal with in the morning but for now he'd find some sort of peace with her.

The weight of his body pressed her into the mattress. He reached a hand behind her and squeezed the fastening on her bra until it snapped open. Sliding it down her arms and tossing it over his shoulder he feasted his eyes on the bounty before him. For a small girl she was generously proportioned on top and he wanted to enjoy every exposed inch of flesh. His palm cupped her jaw and he could see her cheeks had turned a pretty shade of pink that just matched her nipples.

"Are you going to just look?" she asked huskily. "It's kind of embarrassing."

"You've got nothing to be ashamed of, good girl. Nothing at all."

Even as he spoke her rose tipped breasts tightened and crinkled in response. He loved that just his voice could get her going. He leaned down and lapped at the nipple, hearing her breath suck in at the touch of his tongue. Scraping his teeth lightly on the sides of the hard point, he sucked it into his mouth and her hands went to the back of his head, tangling in his hair.

He chuckled to himself and moved his attention to the other side, plucking the nipple with his fingers while he attended to its twin. He didn't stop until she was writhing underneath him, rubbing herself against his aching cock. He dragged her panties down her legs so she was completely bare to his gaze. He suddenly couldn't stand the feel of fabric on his overheated skin and he stood to strip off his clothes.

Ava sat up, her gaze raking him head to toe. "I want to see."

His dick jumped in his pants at her purely carnal expression. His sweet little good girl had a naughty streak in her and damn if he didn't love it. He wanted to be the one to help her set it free.

Logan's fingers went to the top button of his shirt. "Take it all in, baby. I'm all yours tonight."

Even as he said the words, he knew they were true. She owned a part of him that he might never get back. His mind ruthlessly pushed the truth away. He wasn't ready to deal with it. Not now.

Tomorrow was soon enough.

Ava couldn't drag her eyes away from Logan as he stripped off his shirt revealing his muscular chest and arms. She reached up with her fingers and traced the ridges and bumps of his flat abdomen, brushing the silky trail of blond hair that disappeared into the waistband of his jeans.

"Easy, baby. We've got all night." Logan's breathing was as shallow as her own and he took a small step back, freeing the buttons on his fly and shoving the blue material down his thighs. His socks followed and he stood in front of her in nothing but a pair of black boxer briefs. Most men would have looked ridiculous in them but Logan had the physique to pull it off.

She licked her lips at the impressive tent his cock made with the material, and his gaze zeroed in on her movements. Her insides turned to molten liquid and her arousal hitched even higher as he hooked his thumbs inside the elastic of his underwear and quickly shucked them off, tossing them on the ever growing pile of discarded clothing.

His cock sprang free, hard and long, making her fingers itch to explore it as well. He must have read her mind because he stepped closer, inching his manhood closer to her mouth. She leaned forward and traced his six-pack with her tongue leaving a wet trail down his flesh. His hand went to the back of her head and she knew what he wanted.

Surprisingly she wanted it too. She'd always found oral sex to be more than a bit embarrassing. There were smells and bodily fluids, not to mention the evaluation of one's technique. Avoiding it had become something of a habit.

She was surprised the urge to taste as well as touch was this strong. She wrapped her fingers around the base of his cock, so thick her fingers didn't touch. A shiver of apprehension and anticipation ran through her as she thought about how it was going to feel inside. He was bigger than any man she'd known before. Women were always saying bigger was better and it looked like she was going to find out for herself very shortly.

She ran her hand up and down the velvety shaft drawing a tortured groan from Logan. She looked up at his tense expression before leaning forward and kissing the tip of his cock.

"Honestly I'm a little concerned," she said, letting her hand slide down and explore further. She cupped his heavy balls already pulled close to his body.

His lips curved in a smile, his eyes heavy-lidded. "About what, good girl? Doing something naughty?"

"About this," she dipped her head and sucked on the head for a moment. "I'm not sure it's going to fit. You're…thick."

His fingers tilted her chin up, his hands warm and gentle. "It'll fit just fine. We'll take things slow and work up to it. I can't wait to be inside you. Are you wet for me, good girl?"

She nodded but apparently that wasn't enough. He shook his head and pulled on a curl until it was straight and then let go, watching it spring back. "Show me how wet you are for me. I need to know you want me, Ava."

His voice was deep and dark, and she couldn't resist him. She spread her legs wide so he could see her honey glistening in the pale moonlight that shone through the open curtains. His hand slid slowly up the inside of one thigh leaving a trail of heat behind it. A finger traced her slit and he held it up in front of her face, shiny with her own juices.

"This is so hot, baby. I want you that much too. Tell me what you want, Ava. You can have anything tonight."

His voice sounded like ground glass and her entire body tightened in response. "I want it all. Everything."

If she only had tonight with him, she needed to make it count. Without waiting for an answer, she sucked his cock as deeply into her mouth as she could take him. Her hands grasped his thighs, the hair rough under her palms. She bobbed her head, taking him until he bumped the back of her throat, then pulled back until she only had the mushroom-shaped head. She flitted her tongue on the other side and his fingers reflexively tightened in her hair.

She would have continued her sensual foreplay but he pulled back, his face flushed and his chest rising and falling rapidly.

"That's enough." He grinned and leaned down to kiss her lips until she was breathless and wanting. "You have the lips and tongue of a very bad girl. Not that I'm complaining."

Her hands rubbed his thighs and he pushed her back onto the bed. "What do you do to bad girls?" she asked, trying to keep the atmosphere light.

He positioned himself between her parted thighs, pressing them further apart. "Bad girls? Lots of things. Usually I spank them. Or tie them up and keep them on the edge of coming for hours. But tonight I think I'll do this instead."

A jolt of electricity had run through her at his words. She was so distracted she missed his movement and before she knew it his tongue was between her legs making mischief. His hands held her firmly down and she couldn't wriggle away from his insistent tongue that teased and tormented her swollen clit.

Her orgasm surprised her, taking her breath away. The waves of pleasure turned her world upside down and she closed her eyes to savor this unexpected development. He paused at this triumph for only a moment and went right back to work, more gently now on the over-sensitized flesh. This time the build was slower and she clutched the sheets in her hands as the arousal grew in her abdomen, drawing her as tight as a bowstring.

When she finally exploded for a second time, the room spun and her world tilted on its axis. He was every bit as good as he'd boasted and she realized belatedly she'd screamed his name as her climax had taken her over the edge, curling her toes and sending her into orbit.

She heard him rummaging in the bedside table and then the crinkle of a condom wrapper. The head of his cock nudged her entrance and she slid her feet wider apart. He pressed forward then paused, letting her get used to his girth. Her unused muscles stretched to accommodate him and she started to feel pleasure fizz in her veins like bubbles in a fine champagne.

His weight on his palms, he entered her at his own leisurely pace, their gazes locked. She watched his jaw tighten as he gave her every delicious inch. Gasping at the sensation, he filled every nook and cranny of her pussy with his cock. Her world rocked and she grasped his wide shoulders desperate for something solid to hold onto.

He fucked her slowly at first, never looking away or breaking the tenuous connection that tethered them together. Never in her life had she felt this close to another human being, this wide open and exposed. It was as if he could see all her secrets and thoughts written boldly across her features.

She could certainly see his. His expression was stamped with passion but something else as well. He looked surprised, as if he hadn't expected to feel this deeply or this much. There was also a look of edgy control as if he wanted to hide everything from her.

She wouldn't let him.

Wrapping her legs around his waist and her arms around his neck she abandoned herself to the onslaught of pleasure their synchronized movements evoked. His jaw tightened and then went slack as he too gave himself over, giving up the control he'd hidden behind for so long. He rode her hard and fast, their bodies shimmering with a fine sheen of sweat.

Amazed, she felt her orgasm building inside her again. Ragged breaths and murmured encouragement gave way to unintelligible groans. His cock swelled inside of her and he reached between them, his thumb caressing her clit and sending her flying off the edge of the cliff.

He buried his face in her neck and whispered hot, filthy words into her ear. She could feel her pussy tighten around his cock and the ripples of pleasure crested into waves so overwhelming all she could do was hold on for dear life.

When it was finally over, they slumped together on the bed, sated and sweaty. Ava deliberately kept her mind from straying anywhere but this moment. There would be time later to think; now she only wanted to revel in this feeling she may never know again.

Her hand stroked his spine and she heard him drag air into his lungs before levering himself up from the bed. She immediately felt cold without his body heat and she pulled a blanket over her to cover her nakedness.

"I'll be right back." He padded into the bathroom on bare feet, and she caught a glimpse of his muscular backside as he went. She took the opportunity to let her heart rate return to something like normal and curled up deeper into the covers. Unsure of what was expected of her now, she waited for the ax to fall. Would he expect her to get dressed and leave? She didn't want to put any pressure on him or ask for more than he could give. She'd known doing this was a gamble. The odds weren't in her favor but she'd been powerless to resist his plea to stay.

Face it, she'd wanted to be here with him. She'd wanted this.

He quietly returned to bed and she moved over to make room for him. He pulled her into his arms, pillowing her head on his shoulder. It felt like she belonged there but she knew better.

"Sleep. I'm going to want to make love with you again in a few hours. I want to make love with you all night, good girl. You're going to need your rest."

She lay there quietly until his even breathing signaled he was deeply asleep. She extricated herself from his arms and headed into the bathroom, taking care of a few things and splashing cold water on her face. She leaned over the sink patting her face with a towel ineffectually.

Tears were running down her cheeks, the liquid salty on her tongue. She didn't bother to swipe at them. Instead she stood braced against the vanity and let the silent sobs rack her body until she was worn out, her eyes red and swollen.

When she was done, she pulled herself together, blew her stuffy nose, and slipped back into the bedroom. Clumsily, she found her clothes in the dark and dressed as quietly as she could. She looked around for her purse before realizing that it still sat on the porch steps. She walked out of the house, locking the door behind her so she wouldn't be tempted to go back in.

Picking up her purse, she fished for her keys and headed for her car. She needed space and she needed it now. She simply couldn't face Logan in the bright light of day and watch him back away from her. The pain would be too great.

She would never ask Logan for something he wouldn't give of his own free will. If she stayed tonight, she just might beg.

Chapter Fourteen

Logan stomped up the steps of Ava's parents' house, banged on the front door, and tried to calm the fuck down. He'd been breathing fire since about five in the morning. It had been hard to cool his heels until the sun was up but he didn't want to wake up Ava's parents in the middle of the night.

When he'd woken up around midnight and found nothing but cold sheets he'd been shocked at first but it had quickly morphed into anger. Three cups of coffee and several hours later, his rarely seen temper had ratcheted up from simmering to fucking livid.

It didn't help that he had a good idea why she'd left. In a way, he couldn't blame her. He didn't have the best of reputations with women. But fuck it all, after everything that had gone on between them, she should have given him a chance. He'd told her things he'd never told another human being. Didn't she see that he'd made himself vulnerable?

Then she'd gone and kicked him in the nuts. Figuratively, but it still fucking hurt.

Carol Hayworth opened the door with a surprised smile. "Logan! Good morning. Are you here to see Ava? She's in the kitchen having some breakfast. Are you hungry?"

Carol stepped back so he could enter. He took off his hat and his stomach growled at the delicious smell of eggs and bacon. He hadn't eaten this morning. He'd been too pissed off, which was saying something. He rarely missed a meal over anything.

Carol leading the way, he followed her through a comfortable living area with a powder room off to the side. The kitchen and family room combination was at the back of the house overlooking the oversized lawn with several shade trees. Ava was sitting at the island in a white terry cloth robe with little blue stars and gold moons on the back and sleeve. Her curls were wild around her head, and her face was innocent of any makeup. She shouldn't look so damn adorable in the morning. He wanted to be mad at her but already his temper was dropping a degree or two.

At the moment, she didn't appear to be the judgmental pain in the ass he'd been calling her a few hours ago under his breath. In fact, she looked pretty pathetic. He moved further into the room so he could get a good look at the woman who had triggered this much emotion. Ava was hunched over, her shoulders slumped, holding a coffee cup with both hands and wearing a miserable expression on her pretty face. If he wasn't functioning on about three hours of sleep he might have forgiven her completely.

"Ava dear, Logan is here to see you."

Carol Hayworth's gaze went back and forth between her daughter and himself, obviously assessing the situation. Ava's eyes went wide and he saw her swallow hard before placing her cup on the counter.

"Logan. What are you doing here?" Trying to avoid looking directly at him, she was studying her untouched plate of breakfast.

"I need to make a trip to the market," Carol announced, clearly deciding they needed to be alone. "It was nice to see you, Logan. Ava, why don't you make up a plate for your guest? I bet he's hungry."

Before Ava could reply, her mother bustled away with her purse and keys. Carol Hayworth was a smart and sensitive woman. Ava certainly took after her mother. Mary, on the other hand, must take after the father.

Logan just stood there in the middle of the kitchen, his temper still engaged, until he heard the slam of the car door and the engine fire up. He sat down on a stool across from Ava and pulled her plate towards him, filching a piece of bacon. He idly munched it while he waited for her to speak. Anger churned in his gut but he needed to be in control for this discussion.

"What are you doing here?" she finally asked, lifting her eyes so her gaze met his.

He swallowed the bacon and tried to rein in the impulse to pull her into his arms and kiss her until none of this shit mattered. He'd do just that but then they'd be right back in the same boat tomorrow morning.

"I'm here because I'm angry," he said, snatching another piece of bacon. "Very angry."

"You don't sound angry. And stop eating my bacon." Ava tried to pull the plate back but he tapped at her fingers.

"After what you pulled last night I think the very least you could do is let me eat your bacon." He was trying very hard not to yell. He didn't get angry very often but when he did he usually shouted. Females had a tendency to cry, and he couldn't handle any fucking tears from this woman.

She straightened her shoulders, a mutinous expression on her face. Good. He wanted her to have some fucking emotion. So far she'd been almost bland, a pale imitation of the passion he knew was inside of her.

"I'm not sure what you're talking about."

So she wanted to play it like that? Little Miss Avoider. He wouldn't let her. "You know exactly what I'm talking about. I'm not one of those dreamy artists you usually date. I won't let you get away with distractions or obfuscating. Now answer my question." He hardened his voice. "Why did you leave?"

Shifting uncomfortably in her chair, she started swinging her leg, the fluffy pink slippers she was wearing looking like two pink cats on her feet. The swinging was her tell. His good girl was about to lie. "I didn't want my parents to be upset again. So I left. You were asleep and I didn't want to wake you up."

"You're lying, Ava. Try again." He picked up her fork and dug into the scrambled eggs. They weren't hot but they were still fairly warm. Carol Hayworth had added some sort of cheese and black pepper. They were as good as any he'd tasted. He wondered if Ava could cook as well. He wouldn't mind having her cook him breakfast in the mornings.

"I'm not lying," she denied.

"You are." He quickly finished the eggs and started in on her toast. "I really don't have time for this. I have to get into the office, but we need to settle this first."

She opened her mouth to deny it again but one look at his angry expression must have made her decide against it. She shook her head and got up from the stool. She paced back and forth a few times before leaning against the refrigerator and playing with the belt on her robe.

"There's nothing to talk about, Logan. Last night was a bad idea. It shouldn't have happened." She couldn't even look at him when she said it.

"You are such a liar, Ava Hayworth. You're lucky lightning really doesn't strike people who don't tell the truth." He dropped the toast on the plate and stood, walking right up to her so she had to look up at him. "Last night was inevitable. It was also amazing. You know it and I know it. Admit it. You got scared and ran."

He expected her to argue with him but instead her composure crumbled on the spot. Her lower lip trembled and her eyes grew bright with unshed tears. "Do you blame me?" she accused, her voice almost a hiss. "I know what would have happened if I'd stayed. You would have gotten cold feet this morning. Given me some bullshit about how we can be friends with benefits or something equally insulting. I would have got the 'baby don't get hooked on me' speech. That's the last thing I wanted to hear in the cold light of day."

She turned to walk away but his hands caught her shoulders making her face him. "So you did it first? You decided to hurt me before I could hurt you?"

He could see she was surprised. He stepped back and scraped a hand down his face. "Yes, Ava, you hurt me by leaving. Wow, you really don't have a very high opinion of me, do you?" He leaned down and got nose to nose with her. "It was a shitty thing to do."

He let her go and walked to the other side of the island. He couldn't trust himself to touch her right now. He was halfway between kissing her senseless and turning her over his knee.

Ava crossed her arms protectively over her chest, looking scared and unsure. "I'm sorry. I do have a high opinion of you. Really." She must have seen his disbelieving look. "But I know you don't do relationships. Right? Tell me you weren't going to say that this morning."

Logan spread his arms out wide, feeling helpless. "You know what? I have no fucking idea what I was going to say this morning. And you know why? You didn't give me a chance. You ran before we could talk. But I know what I want to say now. So here it is." He paused to make sure she was listening. Really fucking listening. This shit was important. "Last night meant something to me. You mean something to me. You're right. I don't do relationships. At least I haven't in the past. But something changed last night. And I can't believe you didn't feel it too."

His tone was angry and his stomach tight with frustration. If she couldn't see that he was different then this wasn't going to work at all.

Shit, he didn't even know what "this" was but he knew it was something he couldn't pretend wasn't there.

She was wringing her hands together. His words had hit their mark. She was shaken and finally showing her emotions. "I'm not your type," she insisted, her voice thick.

Holy fuck.

"Apparently you are!" This time he did yell. He'd managed to stay patient and calm up until now, but that statement blew it all to hell. "I feel more for you—way more—than I've ever felt before. So you must be my type. Shit!"

"You never said anything!" Ava shouted back and shook her finger at him. "How was I supposed to know?"

Logan threw up his hands. "Hell if I know! I just figured it out myself. You're the woman. Aren't women supposed to know shit like this? As for telling you, I did."

She grabbed a dishtowel from the counter and threw it at him, hitting him in the chest before falling uselessly to the floor. "You never said anything!"

"I didn't say it with words. I said it in bed," Logan seethed. He'd never understand women if he lived to be a hundred. Actions meant more than words to Logan. He'd shown her last night. Words hadn't been necessary. People lied with words all the time.

Her eyes went wide and her mouth formed a perfect "O". "You mean with sex?"

He shrugged and shook his head. "We didn't have sex and you know it. We made love. I showed you with my body."

"I didn't know. I don't know the difference." Her voice was a whisper. "How was I to know?"

Logan's anger seeped out of him like air inside of a balloon. Ava was truly puzzled and distressed. Of course she wouldn't know how it was different for him. But she should have known it was different for her.

"Are you like that with every man you go to bed with?" he challenged, trying to make her see that what he did was more important than what he said.

"No." She shook her head. "I haven't been with that many men. But no. That's why I was so upset. You have to understand. It had never been like that for me before. I felt so—"

"Exposed." Logan finished the sentence for her. She nodded in agreement. "I felt the same way, honey. But I didn't run out the door the minute it was over."

Tears started to slide down her cheeks and Logan's heart felt like it was being ripped out of his chest. He never wanted to see her cry. "Aw, honey. No tears. I'm not worth crying over."

In two strides he was across the room wiping her cheeks with the hankie his mother had taught him to carry in his pocket. She sniffled and batted at his hands.

"Wait. Logan, what are we going to do about this? What does this mean?"

"Hell if I know," Logan answered, handing her the white square of linen. "You're the smart one. But we need to figure this out together, not apart. That much I know."

She swiped at her eyes and her little chin lifted as if ready for battle. "I won't share you with other women. If you're with me, well, then I'm the only one. I won't let you hurt me."

"I sure as fuck don't want you with another guy," Logan snarled. The thought of Ava doing the things they'd done together with anyone else made his head hurt. To his utter surprise a smile bloomed on her face.

"Really? Would you be jealous?" she asked, hope written in her expression.

"Yes," he answered with finality. He didn't want to discuss it, for fuck's sake.

"So…we're a couple?" The innocent question set off a cacophony of warning bells in his head but he ignored every one of them. He couldn't do his usual disappearing trick with this woman. If he tried he knew he'd be back eventually apologizing and asking for another chance.

"A couple of fucking idiots," he groused. "We need to talk more about this but I have to get to work." He grabbed his hat and jammed it on his head. "I'll take you to dinner tonight and then we'll continue working on the case."

"We still have to talk more." Ava sighed and tugged at the belt on her robe.

"We do," Logan agreed. "But we can do that tonight. Just know that last night wasn't a one night stand."

"I've never had one of those in my life."

"You still haven't." He nodded and pulled open the front door. They did have more talking to do but the important point had been made this morning. She wasn't like everyone else. "I'll pick you up at seven, good girl."

Swinging up into his truck he headed for the station. He was halfway there when the reality of everything he had on his plate hit him. He had a murder investigation, a new-found family, and now a relationship. A real one.

What the fuck was he supposed to do with that? He'd screw it up for sure.

Logan was finally sitting down for lunch after a morning of chaos. As soon as he'd walked in the office this morning he'd received a call from a local rancher about possible cattle rustling. He'd spent the last four hours getting statements and collecting evidence. From what Logan could see it appeared to be more of a prank than anything. Sometimes the young people drank too much beer and played hide and seek with cows, trucks, and even lawn ornaments.

He sat heavily down in his chair and opened up the styrofoam container that contained his lunch. He'd ordered whatever the special was today at the diner and it looked like he was in luck. The smell of pot roast, potatoes, and carrots in a rich gravy wafted up from the tray. There was a side of their sour cream mashed potatoes and one of their homemade dinner rolls.

Score.

He wolfed down the meal in record time washing it down with a soda from the small refrigerator in his office. Jillie stuck her head in the door, back from her own lunch.

"You had a couple of calls while you were out. Wade Bryson and Griffin Sawyer."

"Thanks. I'll call them back."

Logan would call Griffin right away but Wade would have to wait. He'd already dodged several calls from Wade, Lyle, and Aaron. Logan knew he would have to talk to them eventually but that didn't mean he had to do it today. Tomorrow or the next day would be soon enough.

Jillie closed the door as he knew she would when he told her he was returning a phone call. She might not be the greatest secretary in the world but she understood him. Or at least she understood the way he worked. She didn't try and tell him what to do and she wasn't nosy about ongoing investigations.

He punched in Griffin's number and pressed the speaker button. The phone rang a few times before his friend picked up.

"Sawyer."

"Hey, heard you called this morning." Logan stuffed his lunch into the trash can and snagged another soda.

"I did. I have some information for you. Hold on. Let me get into my office where we can talk."

Logan heard some voices and then the click of a door closing. "Are you at the sheriff station?"

"I am and it's a madhouse here. Shit, now I know why I only do deputy training once a year."

Logan laughed as he pictured the usually calm and quiet Griffin tearing his hair out over a couple of rookies. "How many do you have?"

"One, and it's more than enough. He's a nice enough guy but he can't remember anything from one day to the next. Of course that might have something to do with the fact that he's staring at his phone ten hours a fucking day. He appears incapable of speaking with his voice. Yesterday he texted me a question. He was sitting next to me in the truck. I don't think he's going to make it."

"Has he been through the academy?" Logan asked.

"Are you kidding me? He wouldn't have lasted a day there."

Logan shook his head and grinned. "How many days has he lasted with you?"

"Ten. Ten long fucking days. Shit, I'm tense just thinking about him. Let's change the subject."

Everyone knew Griffin liked his town quiet and uneventful. His preference was to go fishing when things were boring.

"So tell me what you found out."

"Interesting stuff. When I asked my government friend about Bill Bryson he knew exactly who I was talking about. It appears that Bryson wasn't above using dirty tricks and bribery to get what he wanted. My friend said that Bryson was known for getting zoning changed on a whim and putting competitors out of business. Apparently they'd have a run of extremely bad luck."

Griffin's words went straight to the pit of Logan's stomach. How had this gone on for so many years and not a whiff of trouble in Corville? He really needed to look at those old files in the attic.

"What about George Bryson? Did your guy say anything about him?"

"Funny you should mention that. I asked about him and my friend knew nothing. It was like George Bryson didn't exist within Bryson Development. So I looked up the articles of incorporation. George Bryson isn't on them. Anywhere. He doesn't have any piece of the family business."

Now they were getting somewhere. Logan had assumed George hadn't inherited because he had a fortune of his own. It now looked like he'd been kept out of the business, maybe deliberately.

"I don't suppose you did any research on George?" Logan asked.

Griffin chuckled. "Actually I farmed that out to Reed but he called me this morning. Good old Uncle George doesn't have a pot to piss in. He has his own business which was set up with an injection of cash from brother Bill. According to Reed's sources George loves women, booze, and the ponies. Not necessarily in that order. He spends it as fast as he makes it."

"Expensive hobbies," Logan replied. "If he thought he would inherit, it might be a motive for murder."

"If he thought he would inherit," Griffin agreed. "Did he have any reason to believe that?"

Logan didn't know but he intended to find out.

"I'll bring him in for questioning. This is the first lead I've had. Thanks for helping me out. I've been combing through financial statements for days. Sometimes police work is boring as hell."

"Glad I could help. It's nice to work on something other than cattle rustling and petty vandalism. I'll email you all the details so you can read through it. Let me know if there's anything else I can do."

Logan tapped the desk, indecision warring inside of him. He sighed and gave in, knowing he was going to regret this. "Actually there is one more thing."

"Name it, man."

Son of a fucking bitch, he hated this shit. "I need some advice. About a woman."

Laughter erupted on the other end of the phone and Logan had to take it off speaker, picking up the receiver.

"Women? I thought you had every woman for five hundred miles panting after you. Since when do you need advice?"

"Stop fucking laughing, asshole. I'm serious about this. I don't need advice about women. I need advice about *a woman*. And about relationships. Shit, I've never been in one. I like this woman and I don't want to fuck it up."

Griffin choked and coughed a few times. "A relationship, huh? That's some serious shit. I'm not sure I can help you. I've never been in love. I have dated a few women seriously."

"I didn't say I was in love." Annoyed, Logan almost slammed down the phone. "I said I liked her."

"Oh. Maybe you should call Tanner. Or Seth. They might know what to do. But it can't be all that difficult. Millions of men are in them and they seem to do okay. From what I've experienced women don't expect very much. Just don't stick your dick where it doesn't belong and buy her flowers. You'll be fine. Don't over think it."

"You have a point. If Seth and Tanner can do it then it can't be all that tough." Logan was sure both of his friends had screwed up a time or two.

"Be sure to tell her she looks nice. Women like that. Even if she looks like she's been dragged through a hedge, be sure to say it," Griffin offered.

"I can do that. You're right. I just need to relax."

"If things start to go south, just fall back on what you know. That's what I'd do."

What Logan knew? He knew how to make her scream when she came. It would certainly stop any talk about feelings and the future, that was for sure. Griffin was onto something here.

"Thanks. I'll let you go. I need to set up an interview with George Bryson."

"Keep us in the loop, man. See you." Griffin rung off and Logan set the receiver back in the cradle.

He should have known better than to ask his friend for advice but a desperate man did desperate things. He needed to show Ava he could be faithful without making her think about forever. Logan was in no way ready for that kind of commitment.

He would make sure Ava understood. He wanted her, wanted to be with her. He simply couldn't make any promises about the future.

Logan wasn't the husband and kids type.

Chapter Fifteen

"He came after me," Ava told Kaylee. They were talking on the phone while Ava waited for Logan to pick her up for dinner.

"That's so romantic," breathed Kaylee. "Like at the end of *An Officer and a Gentleman*."

"He didn't sweep me off my feet or anything. But I was shocked when he showed up. I thought he'd be happy I gave him a way out."

Ava had been an emotional wreck when she'd walked out of Logan's house. Their lovemaking had been a revelation and she'd been overwhelmed as she thought about him being like that with another woman. To hear him say it had been different for him too had come as a relief. The fact that he'd said he had feelings for her was overwhelming.

"Tell me again what he said," Kaylee begged. "Do you think he wanted to tell you he loves you?"

"Ah no," Ava laughed. "Besides, it wasn't what he said that was important. It was the way he said it. He was…sincere. His body language wasn't deceptive. I mean, he came after me."

She was still in awe that he had. After she'd gotten over the shock of seeing him standing in her kitchen, she'd been filled with opposing thoughts. Anger that he expected any different behavior, and joy that he had cared enough to make the effort to come to her.

"I still think it's romantic. Was it good?" Kaylee giggled on the other end of the phone. For a writer of erotic romance she could be surprisingly girlish when discussing the more intimate details of their lives.

Ava rolled her eyes. "It was beyond good. They haven't invented adjectives that would correctly describe last night. Writers would be crying in their cappuccinos with the frustration of trying to capture just how hot Logan is in the sack."

"Why can't I find a man like that?" Kaylee wailed. "Are there more men like that in Montana? I can be there in less than twelve hours."

"I think I can safely say Logan Wright is one of a kind. I'm not sure this is even going to work between us."

"You just need to set some ground rules. Don't let him start any of that bad boy behavior. Nip it in the bud before it takes root," Kaylee declared.

Ava chewed on her lower lip. Kaylee had a point. It might be easier to set expectations at the beginning than later. Heaven knew Ava was going to have to lay down the law more than once with a man like Logan.

"You may be right," Ava conceded. "I just don't know what rules. What would you do?"

"If he's as hot as you say he is then I'd set a rule he has to give me two orgasms to his one." Kaylee was laughing so hard Ava had to pull the phone away from her ear.

"That doesn't sound very fair." Although it was tempting.

"Fair, shmair. Just set the rules so he has to treat you with respect. That's what you really want."

Logan's truck pulled up in the driveway. "I think I can do that. It might help us both. I don't know much more about being in a relationship than he does. He's here so I gotta go. I'll call you tomorrow."

"You better! I want all the dirty details. Remember you're having sex for both of us." Kaylee exclaimed before hanging up.

Ava grabbed her sweater and purse and hurried out the front door. Her father was in the back yard and she wanted to be gone before he realized someone was here. She rushed to the passenger side of the truck but not before Logan got out on his side and came around to open the door for her. It was a sweet, old fashioned gesture that made her blush and she murmured her thanks as she slid inside. He'd turned on the radio and a Jason Aldean song was playing softly in the background. A single pink rose was on the seat between them.

"Is this for me?" She picked it up and breathed in its heady fragrance as he backed out of the driveway.

Glancing over briefly, he nodded his head but kept his concentration on the road. "It is. I didn't know if you liked flowers or not. I got pink because red seemed too ordinary."

Did that mean he didn't think she was ordinary or that he didn't think he was a man who did ordinary things?

The latter was certainly true and she could only hope about the former. "I like pink. It was thoughtful of you. Thank you."

His profile was outlined in the dim light of the truck cab. "You're welcome. It was a friend's idea."

"You asked a friend?" It was kind of endearing to think he had. She already liked him but this made him seem as vulnerable as she was about all this.

"I was talking to him about the case anyway."

"Oh." So he hadn't called a friend just for help. That was kind of disappointing. Logan turned into the parking lot of one of the better restaurants in town. Parking the truck, he finally turned toward her.

"I hope you like steak."

"I do." Ava nodded, feeling suddenly nervous and shy now that she had his full attention. "I haven't been here in years."

Logan's rich and throaty laugh made her warm all over. "It hasn't changed, good girl. Not much around here does."

By the time they'd been shown to a table and ordered their drinks and meal, Ava was starting to break out into a cold sweat. She didn't know what to expect and Logan's expression was frustratingly inscrutable. He was like one of those faces on Mount Rushmore. No emotion whatsoever. She wanted to kick him in the shin just to see him wince.

"So I talked to my buddy Griffin about the case today." Logan sat back in his chair and lifted the beer glass to his lips. "He told me some very interesting things about Bill Bryson."

Her discomfort was forgotten the minute he brought up the case. Talking about this wouldn't be awkward in the least. "Are you going to share?"

His mouth quirked up. "It seems Bill Bryson was known to bribe a government official or two to get zoning changed for his benefit. He was also known to play dirty tricks on his competition driving them out of business."

Ava tapped her chin. "Motives for murder."

"Possibly. Seems extreme though. Griffin wasn't able to get specifics so it's hard to tell just how evil Bill was. He may simply have been about as bad as everyone else in business."

"True. But with the wrong person even a seemingly mild provocation can become deadly. You hear about people being shot and killed over stupid things every day. Someone cut them off in traffic or they talked too loud on their cell phone. Bang. They're dead."

"The reason you hear about that is because it's so rare. Most people are killed for the usual reasons."

"Love, money, and revenge." Murder required passion and those things inspired it.

Logan nodded in agreement. "That's right. So which one was Bill Bryson?" Logan leaned forward. "I also found out a few things about his brother George."

"George? What did you find out about him?" Ava had always been under the impression the Bryson family was very close. They'd certainly circled the wagons recently.

"George isn't a part of Bryson Development. At all. Did you know that?"

Ava frowned, trying to remember anything that would have indicated that, but if anything what she'd seen pointed to the opposite. "Doesn't George own and manage apartment buildings in this and neighboring counties? I always thought Bryson Development did that."

"I did too. I'm guessing that's what they wanted us to think. In actuality, George had his own company—"

"GTB Management," Ava and Logan said simultaneously. Logan's eyebrows shot up.

"Have you been reading my email?"

"I've been reading those files." Ava shook her head, excitement coursing through her veins. She loved the feeling when she found a clue. "There were regular payments from Bryson Development to GTB Management. Twice a year – one hundred thousand. I thought it was strange because no reason was given for it. It was categorized as a miscellaneous expense."

Logan whistled. "A big miscellaneous expense. Even pencils are categorized as office supplies. I wonder what it was for?"

"I don't know but the payments stopped last year," she revealed with a sense of triumph. This was the first real lead they'd found.

"Nothing this year?" Logan stroked his chin. "That is interesting. I think I need to bring George in for questioning tomorrow."

"What should we ask him?" Ava asked eagerly, already formulating questions in her head.

"Not we, me," Logan replied with a shake of his head. "You're not a cop, remember? You're an honorary deputy. I can't have you interrogating a person of interest."

He was right. She'd gotten ahead of herself with the excitement of a lead. "That sucks. Will you tell me what he said?"

Logan gave her one of his patented grins. "I can do you one better. How would you like to be there?"

"I can be there?" He was probably yanking her chain. Kicking him in the shin was sounding better and better.

"You can. You can watch on a monitor in my office. I can't have you in the room with me."

"You mean it?" She hardly dare believe it but he looked sincere.

"I mean it." The waitress placed their plates in front of them. "You've taken a vow of silence so I'm not worried about you talking."

"I wouldn't say a thing." Ava made an X with her finger across her chest. "Cross my heart."

"That's as good as a pinkie swear I guess." Logan dug into his steak with relish. "I trust you."

Ava felt warm with that small bit of praise. She had a feeling Logan trusted few people in his life. From what he'd told her, he had scant reason to.

They finished their dinner and Logan insisted they order a decadent chocolate cake to share for dessert. She licked at the fudge icing on her fork and sighed in sublime happiness. Somehow chocolate made a good evening even better.

"Like it?" Logan asked, his eyes twinkling. He obviously knew her answer. "They're known for their good steaks and desserts here."

Ava helped herself to another forkful. "I'll second that. This is delicious."

"Next time we'll try the white chocolate cheesecake."

He'd obviously been to this place before. An image of him sitting in this very restaurant eating dessert with another woman made her feel like a giant boulder was pressing on her chest. She didn't like feeling vulnerable with him. He was a serial womanizer and she needed to make her expectations clear. Kaylee was right. It was best to head things off at the pass. If he was going to be a jerk, she needed to get out now.

Ava toyed with her fork. "I was thinking we should talk about some ground rules. You know, for this relationship we're trying."

"Rules?" Logan's fork paused in midair. "What kind of rules?"

"Just a few to help us understand what the expectations are. You've never been in a relationship before. I've been in a few but I wouldn't say they were all that great. I'm sure you have ideas of what we should do. What I should do. I'd like to hear them. I think we both should come to some agreement as to how this is going to work."

Logan smiled and stroked his chin. "I'm not fond of rules. You'll find I go out of my way to break them. Just because I can."

She should have known he would say that. He wasn't one to conform to societal norms. "If we agree to a rule then I expect you to follow it."

"Do I get to make some too?" From the amused look on his face he wasn't taking this too seriously.

"Of course. We both have to agree," she said firmly.

"Fine. I'll agree to three rules if you will too." Logan tossed out the challenge casually as if he made rules with women every day of his life. He didn't appear worried in the least. And that worried her. What kind of rules would he want?

"Fine." Ava licked her lips nervously. "My rules first." Hopefully if she set reasonable rules he would follow suit. "Rule number one. No dating or sleeping with other women."

Logan shrugged. "We talked about not seeing anyone else. I'm okay with that. What's rule number two?"

Ava nodded, searching her memory for things her friends might have mentioned when complaining about their boyfriends. "What about frequency of dates and phone calls?"

His eyebrows drew down. "What's the usual?"

"Maybe…a couple of times a week?" Ava thought about some of her past relationships but they hardly seemed like a blueprint for success. "But you're supposed to call the morning after."

"After we have sex?" He laughed when her blush deepened. She had to fight the urge to press her hands to her hot cheeks. "There won't be any need. We'll be waking up in the same bed. No more running out afterward, good girl."

The thought of waking up with Logan next to her sent a rush of heat and excitement through her body. He must have noticed as his blue eyes were a shade deeper and he reached out to capture her free hand with his own.

"It's going to be hard. My parents aren't the most open-minded people in the world."

"You're a grown woman, Ava. I'm sure you can handle them."

She wasn't as sure as he was, but he had a point. She was a grown woman and they needed to back off. Her mother wouldn't be an issue. Her father was a different story. He'd lock her in a chastity belt if he had his way.

"Rule number three," she began, trying to get her mind out of the gutter. Logan was so blatantly sexy she had a hard time concentrating on everyday matters. She actually didn't have another rule but since he'd set the limit she felt like she needed a third one. As long as he treated her with respect, just as Kaylee had said, things would be fine.

Logan's lips twitched as if he was aware of her predicament. "Go ahead. I can't wait to hear this last one. Don't waste it."

"Rule number three," she began again. "You'll always treat me with respect even around your friends."

Scowling, he leaned forward in his chair. "Have I ever not treated you with respect?"

"This doesn't really have anything to do with you," she admitted.

His expression cleared. "Some asshole acted like a jerk whenever he was around his friends?"

She nodded, remembering how Lucas had belittled her writing when they were around his literary friends. After all, she only wrote *commercial fiction* that made money. They sold *literature*.

"I just don't want a repeat of that. It was very uncomfortable for me." So uncomfortable she'd broken up with him shortly after. His condescending attitude had been almost insufferable.

"Agreed." Logan grinned and waggled his eyebrows. "Now it's my turn."

Ava felt a moment's trepidation at she studied his delighted expression. She'd opened up a can of proverbial worms.

Ava wanted rules. Logan wasn't a big fan of them but if they made her feel more secure he could handle it. Logan knew cheating and being a dick wouldn't be an issue but she still needed more reassurance. She wasn't asking for all that much. Basically she was asking he not be a total jerk.

He could handle it.

She was now sitting across from him, impatiently waiting for his own rules. He'd set few of them in his life. Mostly Logan lived by the golden rule. Treat others how you want to be treated and don't be an asshole. He was a firm believer in karma. He'd seen it in the Middle East and it was a heartless bitch.

Logan decided to have some fun with her. "Rule number one. If I have a hard day at the office you have to rub my shoulders."

He watched her expression closely as she digested his outrageous request. The only reason he'd ever received a back rub was because a woman was trying to seduce him into bed. The state of his day had never been a question.

She nodded, her body relaxing slightly as if she had been braced for the worst. She hadn't heard the next two yet though.

"Rule number two. You have to make me those eggs your mother had for breakfast today every morning after."

Her eyes went wide and her mouth fell open. "You want me to cook for you? That's a rule?"

He stretched out his long legs and enjoyed her discomfiture. "They were excellent. I don't remember the last time someone fixed me breakfast. I liked it."

Her expression clearly told him she thought he was crazy. He was having a great time with this. Finally she nodded. "I guess that's no big deal. Although I think it's a weird rule."

"You didn't have a rule against weird rules," he said cheerfully.

"That's what you really want?" she asked, confusion clearly written in her delicate features. "Breakfast and shoulder massages?"

He shrugged. "Everything else is negotiable. Rule number three."

Her shoulders straightened and her chin went up as if he was going to give her a right hook. "What's next? Housework?"

Logan chuckled and shook his head. "I've got that covered. Rule number three. You'll be open to trying new things in the bedroom. Things you haven't done before or wouldn't normally be comfortable with."

She gaped at him, her face turning a flaming crimson. She opened her mouth, closed it, then opened it again. "You want to do something kinky?" Her voice had dropped to a whisper which really wasn't necessary. Their table was off in the corner and the piped in music muffled most conversation.

"I most definitely want to do something kinky. I think you do too. So let's make it a rule."

Indecision was written all over her face. He knew how to sweeten the pot having already figured out her weak spot.

"I thought it would help you shake out of that good girl mode you've been in." He watched her reaction closely knowing this was something she desperately wanted.

Her teeth sunk deeply into her bottom lip. "I do want to do that."

"Then let me help you." Erotic images ran through Logan's mind and all of them starred this beautiful woman.

"Help me?" Her eyebrows went up. "I think you'd be helping yourself."

"Let's just call it mutually beneficial. Agreed?" He could see the indecision in her eyes. "I only said open to it, good girl. You have the final say."

"Okay." She pulled a face at him. "You have strange rules."

"You have boring rules," he retorted. "You're the only woman I've given the opportunity to do this and look what you do with them. Just a lot of talk about respect and calling the next day. I would have done those things anyway."

She clearly wasn't convinced of that, ergo her rules. Maybe he should give her three more and see if she came up with something more interesting. Appearing to have something else on her mind, she frowned and dropped the fork on her plate.

"What about when I leave? What happens then? I can't stay here forever."

Why not?

Logan ignored the little voice inside of him. Luckily he hadn't asked the question out loud. She had a life in Portland, a home and friends she wanted to get back to. He felt a twinge of unfamiliar jealousy and pushed it away, not liking the feeling in the least. He'd never been the jealous type and he wasn't about to start now.

"How long do you think you'll be here?" Logan's fingers drummed on the tablecloth. "Are you planning to leave right away?"

"Not right away," she denied. "Just until you find Bill Bryson's murderer."

"Ava, it could take months to find Bill's killer. Or I might never find him," Logan said gently, squeezing her hand. "Are you prepared to hang around that long? Is there something you need to be back in Portland to do?"

"I need to start my new book but I can do that anywhere really. I have a friend watering my plants. I guess I just figured you'd solve the case in the next couple of weeks."

It was just as well she wasn't looking too far in the future. He'd never been the forever kind. Although if he ever did settle down, Ava would be the type of woman he would want.

Logan nodded. "Then we won't look further than the next two weeks. When those two weeks are up, we'll reassess the situation and decide if we want to carry this forward."

"And if we do? We might have to do the long-distance thing."

"If in two weeks we still feel the same, that will be the least of our worries." Logan gave her a lopsided smile. "I'm not sure how to say this but I'm not looking for a wife and a couple of kids, Ava. If you want the fantasy, I'm not your guy."

"I've never wanted to get married." Frankly, her simple statement, spoken sincerely shocked him. He'd assumed that she was looking for a husband, a commitment. She'd make a wonderful wife and mother. Just not for him. "I like being independent. I don't need to marry a man to take care of me or anything. As for kids, well, I'm still young. I can decide that later."

"As long as we're on the same page," Logan said, waiting for the rush of relief but it never came. "I'll try to be a good boyfriend while you're here."

"I'll try too. I'll even follow your stupid rules."

He leaned forward and her perfume teased his nostrils. Now that they had the mundane matters taken care of he was ready for more pleasurable pursuits. He'd been thinking about it all damn day.

"Would a good girlfriend go home with her man and do unspeakable acts of debauchery with him? Rule number three, good girl."

He watched with amusement as her hands fluttered to her throat and then nervously pushed her curls off her forehead.

"I think she would."

Logan admired her bravery. He'd be sure to reward it handsomely. Just as soon as they got home.

Chapter Sixteen

They scampered into Logan's bedroom, tripping on the stairs. Breathless and panting, Ava paused in the middle of the bedroom, suddenly unsure as to what she was supposed to do. Logan had snapped on the bedside lamp and she wasn't sure she wanted to strip to her birthday suit while he stood there and watched.

Logan tossed his hat on the dresser and started to pull off his boots. "Take off those clothes, Ava, unless you want them torn off."

No man had wanted her enough to tear her clothes off in a fit of passion. It sounded kind of fun. At least it would be until tomorrow morning when she had to go home in a towel. After making him eggs, of course.

"You're bossy." She gave him a teasing smile but he chuckled and grinned in response. Arousal curled in her belly as he kicked his boots to the side and stepped closer. She could feel the heat from his body and couldn't resist the urge to run her hands down his muscular chest before wrapping them around his lean middle.

He bent his head and kissed her so thoroughly it made her head spin and her knees weak. It really wasn't fair that he was this potently male. But he was all hers for the next two weeks. When he lifted his head he continued to nibble on her lower lip.

"You don't know the half of it. I like getting my way so start shucking those clothes, woman."

Ava tilted her head, a smile playing on her lips. "Are you going to do that all the time?"

"Do what?"

"Issue orders like that. You could try asking me."

He looked every inch the arrogant male at that moment. He pulled her close and locked her lips with his, letting her know in vivid detail who the man was in this relationship. It was a dominating kiss, but at the same time gentle. He simply kissed her as if she belonged to him body and soul. She had a feeling when the two weeks were up that would be true. By the time he let her go, her cheeks were hot and she wanted more, much more. From the amused look on Logan's face, he was well aware of her predicament.

"Asking takes too much time, good girl. I'd rather just tell you how things are going to be. If you have an issue we can talk about it. Then we'll do it my way."

He certainly knew how to poke and prod at her normally placid temperament. "You're not the boss of me, Logan Wright."

"That's what you think." He was obviously enjoying this battle of wills, supremely confident he would win any skirmish. She had to admit the back and forth had lit a fire inside of her that made this entire interaction seem bold and sexy. She'd never realized competition could heighten her arousal. "By the way, you have a punishment coming for leaving last night. I think you're going to spend some quality time over my knee."

Shock and arousal flew through her veins like wildfire. If this was Rule Number Three she had to at least consider it. It took mere seconds to realize her body had already responded in the affirmative while her mind was taking its sweet time catching up.

He ran his finger over her hot cheeks and down to trace her lips. "From that expression it looks like you like the idea. I give spankings to naughty naked girls so off with those clothes. If I have to tell you again it will only make your punishment worse."

She froze, searching his features. He appeared to be completely serious. She tugged at her clothes trying not to think about the other women he might have done this with. There was no place for jealousy at a moment like this. She'd been with other men too.

Just not this kinky.

She pushed her panties down her legs and tossed them away but Logan caught them easily in midair. To her surprise he'd picked up her discarded clothing and carefully folded them before setting them on top of the dresser. He laid her panties and bra with her slacks and shirt.

"You don't want your clothes to be wrinkled in the morning. Mommy and Daddy, remember? We don't have to make it obvious."

She would have made a smart ass comment about his domestic skills but he started plucking open the buttons to his shirt and her mouth went dry. His tan, muscular chest was revealed inch by inch until he was finally out of it. She followed his movements as if in a trance as he popped open the buttons on his fly and shoved the denim down and off along with his boxer shorts. Wanting to admire him she took a step back but he was already moving forward.

He pulled her into his arms, their bare bodies pressed close together. She could feel the rough hair on his thighs as their limbs brushed together. Her hard nipples were smashed against him and his cock rubbed her belly.

She let her hands roam up over his biceps and shoulders and down his back. His skin felt smooth and warm under her palms. His lips blazed a wet trail of kisses from her ear down to her neck until he found the sensitive spot where her pulse beat wildly. He nipped at it and then soothed the hurt with his tongue until her knees gave out. Lifting her into his arms, he laid her down on the bed and let his mouth tease her already sensitive nipples.

He drew circles with his tongue around and around until her back arched and her fingers dug into his scalp. Sucking the nub into his mouth, he let it go with a pop before moving to the other side. She was writhing underneath him, breathless and begging within minutes.

He lifted his head giving her a brief respite from his skillful hands and mouth. "Does that feel good? Do you want me to stop?"

He had that grin splashed across his face again, well aware he'd shattered her control.

She shook her head – her ability to speak had deserted her. He chuckled and planted open-mouthed kisses down her abdomen. Ava closed her eyes and savored the sensations but he paused at the top of her mound.

"First we need to get your punishment out of the way," he announced.

Her lids snapped open and she lifted her head to give him a look of disbelief. He'd been mere inches away from her clit. His brow was lifted as if daring her to question him. She had tacitly agreed only moments ago to let him spank her. The idea tantalized and aroused her. She'd read some of the books Kaylee had written and knew many women enjoyed submitting to a man in an erotic setting. She trusted Logan wouldn't truly hurt her, but there was still that good girl part of her that was holding back.

"I said I was sorry. Do I have to be punished?"

She couldn't decide if she wanted him to say yes or no. The idea of being spanked by him had taken root in her brain and blossomed.

"You do. I don't like people walking out on me. You knew that but did it anyway. This will ensure you think twice next time."

From what he'd told her in the treehouse he had good reasons for not liking people to walk away. Too many had in his life.

Nodding, she sat up on the bed, not sure what to do next. His strong arm came around her waist and lifted her so she was draped across his knees. Her palms came to rest on the soft woven area rug beside the bed, her legs too short for her toes to touch the ground.

Logan's callused hand rubbed circles on the exposed flesh of her bottom in almost a soothing motion. Unfortunately for Ava, it had the opposite effect. Tingles from her pussy shot through her body and she squirmed on his bare thighs until he lightly smacked an ass cheek.

"Stay still," he commanded, his voice dark and deep. It sent arrows of pleasure straight to her clit and pussy. "I'm going to spank you now for walking out on me. Don't ever do that again."

Bracing her hands on the floor she waited. Logan took his time, rubbing her bottom more firmly until he'd brought the blood to the surface. His ministrations stopped and she squeezed her eyes shut as time seemed to stand still. It could have been a minute or an hour she stayed frozen in position.

When his palm finally did come down on her defenseless rear end she jumped as the sting and heat hurtled through her. Her mind barely had time to register the pain before he smacked her again and again. She was just about to call a halt to it when the fire in her bottom turned to something else. The heat had traveled directly to her pussy and clit, her honey dripping on Logan's thighs.

Rubbing herself against him, the spanking continued, raising the temperature on her ass cheeks. Mewling with frustration, he had her positioned so she couldn't get enough friction to send herself over. When she heard him chuckle, she knew it was by design.

The spanking stopped as abruptly as it had started. She moaned with need and tried to twist away, angry with him for denying her. Her entire body was on fire and she needed desperately to come.

"Easy, good girl. I know what you need." His voice was soft and gentle and she stopped struggling as he easily held her down. His hand crept between her legs and his fingers stroked her swollen clit. She screamed his name as she tumbled into the abyss, her climax stronger than she'd ever known. Her body shook as wave after wave rolled through her. Slumped over his lap, she was sated and wrung out.

When she opened her eyes again, she was lying on the bed. Logan was rummaging in the bedside drawer and pulling out a condom.

"I think you enjoyed that," he said as he tore open the package and rolled it on. "I know I did."

She wasn't quite ready to admit how much she'd liked it. Besides he was entirely too full of himself. "It was fine." She held out her arms to him and smiled. "I know I'll like this next part."

He'd started to move toward her but he paused and quirked an eyebrow. "Fine? You were rubbing yourself against me like a cat and gushing honey from that pretty pink pussy. I think you'll be wanting to do that again."

Scowling, she dropped her arms. "I did not."

"Did too," he argued right back, but then his expression softened. "There's nothing to be ashamed of, good girl. It's okay to enjoy it. Want it. Even need it."

"I know that." She turned away, not wanting him to see the conflict she was feeling inside. Already she was remembering the pleasure. He was right. She'd be begging for it.

His fingers under her chin were gentle as he made her look into his eyes. "No judgment here. I don't think any less of you for liking it. Do you think any less of me for enjoying giving it to you?"

She shook her head at the challenge. "No. It's just not what an independent feminist type should want."

"Isn't feminism about living your life by your own rules, not a man's?" he asked.

"I guess." She shrugged. Women's liberation hadn't been discussed in her household when she was growing up.

"I can guarantee you it was a man who came up with the rule that women shouldn't enjoy sex, or spankings, or toys, or whatever brings them pleasure."

She smiled at his logic. "And you don't like rules."

"I don't. Let's break them all tonight."

It sounded like a hell of an idea.

Positioning himself between her legs, Logan didn't hesitate. He filled her with one thrust, taking her breath away. Lifting her legs so they were slung over his shoulders, his cock drove deep inside her, rubbing sensitive spots she'd never known existed. Higher and higher he drove them until her head thrashed on the pillow and her body trembled on the brink.

It was wild, abandoned, and more than she'd ever imagined. With Logan she felt free. She could never do this with another man but there was something so accepting about him. He lived his life by his own rules and didn't judge others who did the same.

She felt his lips exploring the flesh of her neck and heard the sound of their ragged breathing.

"Now, good girl," he whispered into her ear just before he bit gently into her shoulder. A bolt of electricity seemed to fly from that spot straight to her clit. She froze for a moment then dug her nails into Logan's back as her soul flew into the stratosphere. Her pussy tightened on his cock, and with a groan he tumbled after her. Their frenzied movements slowed and then finally stilled. He rolled to his back and pulled her close so they were curled together on the bed.

Logan stroked his hand up and down the curve of her spine and placed tiny kisses on her forehead. She didn't have the words to describe how close she felt to him when they made love. It would have to be enough that he'd expressed he felt the same.

Reluctantly she pulled from his arms; he tried to drag her back down to the bed. "I need to freshen up. I'm also thirsty."

He nibbled at her fingers. "I'll get us a couple of sodas and meet you back here in five. I'm not done with you yet. There are many things I still want to do to you."

She nodded and escaped into the bathroom. There would be no leaving under the cover of darkness tonight. She'd wake up with this man and face whatever future they had together, short or long.

Chapter Seventeen

Logan filled the coffee cup and readied himself for the next hour or so. George Bryson was here this morning to answer some questions. Per the request of his attorney, he'd been smuggled in the back door so the town wouldn't know he was being questioned. Logan wanted this interview in more official surroundings to let George know this was serious police business. Now that Logan had more information about the business dealings of Bill Bryson he had a better understanding of what to ask about. The fact that George was his uncle wasn't going to be a factor in the events this morning.

Not that Logan thought George was a killer. He didn't have the guts to take a life from what Logan had seen. Bill had the stones in the family. George was a pale shadow of his brother.

Logan settled into the chair on the opposite side of the table as George and glanced up at the camera behind the other man. Ava was watching along with Drake in Logan's office. She'd given him a list of questions she thought were important and damn if they didn't almost match his own word for word. Everything about her was impressive.

She was smart, sexy, and a hell of a cook. At least she could make eggs and bacon as well as her mother. Logan had found that out this morning when he'd followed his nose to the kitchen. He'd found breakfast being dished out onto a plate and his stomach had growled in appreciation. She'd made some apology about the cheese being American and not Pepper Jack like her mother used, but he hadn't cared. This was the first time he could remember since his mother was alive that someone had made him breakfast.

Unfortunately they hadn't been able to linger over their meal too long. Drake had called and let him know that George's attorney had agreed to the interview and it was scheduled for eleven in the morning. It hadn't given Logan as much time as he'd wanted to prepare but that was probably intentional by the lawyer.

George sat next to the family attorney, Deke Kennedy, the same man who had delivered the news of Logan's parentage. He wished it was someone else as it made him feel like he was at a disadvantage, wondering if there were other secrets this man knew that Logan didn't.

"Thanks for coming in this morning, George. I appreciate it." Logan ignored the attorney as was his custom when interviewing someone. The questions weren't for him anyway.

George fidgeted in his chair and nodded. "Anything I can do to help, Logan. I want my brother's killer brought to justice."

"Then we agree on that point. We received the ballistics back on the bullet and Bill was shot by the vigilante that's been murdering suspected criminals in this area. Since Bill wasn't suspected of a crime, can you think of a reason the vigilante would want him dead?"

That tidbit of information hadn't been made public. Logan used it right off the bat to unbalance George. Hopefully he could keep him that way.

George turned white and he reached for the handkerchief in his jacket pocket, mopping at his brow. "The vigilante? I've read about him in the papers."

"I assumed you had. Why would he want to kill a fine, up-standing citizen like Bill Bryson?"

Logan watched as several expressions flitted across George's face – confusion, fear, and then finally denial. "I can't imagine why. Bill was a good man who was always doing things for the community. He cared about people. Every Christmas and Thanksgiving he would give a turkey to every employee of Bryson Development. He paid bonus wages when projects were brought in early. Hell, he sponsored a little league team for over thirty years."

Sipping at his coffee, Logan looked over the rim. George was perspiring openly now and he dabbed at his forehead with the hanky.

"He wasn't popular with everyone though, was he?" Logan challenged. "I mean, his business rivals hated him. He bribed local officials to change zoning laws and then used underhanded methods to drive his competition out of business."

No sense beating around the bush. He already had George off kilter; he might as well knock him completely over. George flushed and cleared his throat.

"I'm not sure what you're talking about."

George's tone was about an octave higher than before. Logan pressed forward.

"Come off it," Logan scoffed. "Bill's reputation as an asshole was well-known among his rivals. People hated him. Maybe even you. He kept you out of Bryson Development, after all."

George shifted in his chair, his neck turning red. "Now wait a minute," he protested. "Bill didn't keep me out of the company. I wanted my own business."

"He kept you out because you drink and gamble. Face it – you lived in your brother's shadow. He was the brilliant business man. Not you," Logan countered, leaning forward in his chair. George was feeling the heat and he ran his finger around the neckline of his shirt.

"That's not true. I always wanted to be independent." George's shoulders slumped and he leaned over and whispered something in his attorney's ear. Deke Kennedy nodded and then glared at Logan.

"My brother and I," George began, "haven't always seen eye to eye on everything. It was better for both of us if we had interests of our own."

Logan pulled a piece of paper from the folder in front of him and slid it across the table. "Can you tell me what the twice yearly payments of one hundred thousand dollars were for and why they stopped suddenly?"

The attorney suddenly stood and placed his hand on George's shoulder. "This interview is at an end. You're fishing, Logan. You've got nothing against my client."

"That's true," Logan agreed. "But he knows things about Bill's business that could be pertinent. You might also."

Kennedy simply smiled and snapped his briefcase shut. "Whatever I know is protected by attorney-client privilege."

"Privilege died with Bill Bryson." Logan smiled right back. He loved the cat and mouse games of interrogation. He was, after all, a patient man.

"He was your father, Logan." George stood, his expression entreating. "How can you say these things about him? He was your father," he repeated.

"Privilege still exists with the rest of the Bryson family," Kennedy replied. "A family you are now part of, Logan. You should remember that."

"Being a member of the Bryson family is more important than finding his killer," Logan mocked. "I must remember that."

"Family should come before anything." George's expression was somber. "That's how I've lived my life. Bill did too."

"We're done here, George." The attorney took a step toward the door. "If you have any more questions for George you can submit them in writing to my office."

"I have several more," Logan replied, a smile playing on his lips. He'd definitely received a reaction this morning. "I'll email them today. They're all about Bill's business dealings." Logan directed the last statement to George who looked distinctly ill at ease. He knew more than he was telling.

Logan didn't bother to stand as the two men filed out. He sat there for a long time replaying the conversation over and over in his mind. One thing was clear. George was covering up the truth.

"He was lying." Ava stood in the doorway of his office. "I couldn't see his face but I could tell by how tense his back and shoulders were that he wasn't telling the truth. Do you think he's afraid?"

Logan shook his head and stood. "I think he thinks he's doing the right thing. He seemed genuinely surprised the vigilante killed his brother, but did you notice he didn't go into denial that Bill could have done something to catch the killer's interest?"

"He should have," Ava agreed. "If my sister had been shot by a vigilante I would be arguing she'd never done a thing to deserve it and it must all be a big mistake."

"Well, good old George didn't do that. He started talking about turkeys and little league." Logan stroked his chin. "I think we've only scratched the surface here. Let's get into the attic tonight and go through those old files. Maybe Frank has something there that will help us."

Ava tilted her head. "What makes you think there's anything up there?"

"Because there has to be a reason he hid those boxes. Frank was completely disorganized and totally ignored anything to do with police procedure. Shit, I had to put fucking rules in place when I took over."

"And you hate rules." Ava was peering up at him from under her lashes as they both remembered last night's conversation. His chest tightened as he momentarily relived their moments of passion. Making love to Ava was like nothing else he'd ever experienced.

"I do. But he took the time to retrieve those files and carry them all the way up into the attic. The more I think about that the more it has to mean something."

"I hope it does. We're at another dead end." Ava sighed and crossed her arms over her chest. "We know Bill wasn't above using some unsavory techniques to win. But is it motive for murder?"

"There has to be more." Frustration made Logan rub his aching temple. The more they learned, the less they seemed to know. One mystery solved simply led to a new one. "He must have done something really terrible to catch the vigilante's attention. We have to find out what it is."

They stepped out into the hallway and the throbbing in his head tripled. Wade, Lyle, and Aaron were standing there, apparently waiting for Logan. Wade stepped forward.

"You've been avoiding our calls," he said. "We all need to talk. A lot has happened but we're family. We should be there for each other. Let's have lunch at the diner."

Feeling trapped, Logan tried to think of any reason he shouldn't go, but failed to come up with anything that didn't sound lame. He simply didn't want to deal with this right now. It didn't appear that he was going to be allowed to ignore it any longer.

He threw his arm around Ava's shoulders, knowing he was about to announce their relationship to the entire town. "Okay, but Ava comes too. I don't have any secrets from her."

Logan knew he'd succeeded in shocking the three men but to their credit they covered it quickly. Wade nodded. "If that's what you want. We just want to talk. That's all."

Ava glanced over at him as they headed out of the station. Logan nodded to Drake who had been patiently waiting in the corridor. He would take care of anything that cropped up while Logan was gone.

"Why am I going?" Ava murmured under her breath. "Don't you think you should do this alone?"

"That's the last thing I should do right now, good girl." Logan kept his voice low. "I've got too many of my own emotions. I can't deal with theirs. Not today."

She nodded as if she understood and they stepped out into the midday sunshine. He'd keep it low key and friendly at lunch. He wouldn't be railroaded into a family relationship he wasn't ready for, or even sure he wanted.

"I'm sorry, Mom. It's not working out with me staying here. I don't want you to have to lie to Dad about where I am."

Ava was in her room pulling clothes from the closet and drawers and shoving them into a suitcase. After the world's most awkward lunch with Logan, Wade, Lyle, and Aaron, she was really wishing she drank more. Admitting they'd seen George sneak out the back entrance, the three brothers had quizzed Logan about what their uncle had said. She had to hand it to him. His expression had remained completely neutral and he'd refused to discuss the interview. The brothers had been frustrated but understanding.

Now Ava could only hope her mother would be the same.

"Where will you go?" Carol Hayworth had her hands on her hips. "I can handle your father. I've been doing it for years."

For only a split second did Ava consider lying to her mother. When she'd told Logan she was heading home to make an appearance so her mother wouldn't be worried and they could come up with a suitable cover story, Logan had snorted and told her to pack her bag and move in with him. She hadn't been sure he was serious but it became quickly clear that he was.

"If we only have a few weeks, good girl, I want to spend as much time with you as possible. Let's just not make a big deal out of it, okay?" he'd said.

It was hard not to build it into more than it was but she was pretty sure no woman had ever lived with him before. It was…something.

"I'm staying with Logan," Ava stated, almost daring her mother to say something. Carol Hayworth's brows flew up in surprise before schooling her features.

"Do you think that's a good idea? Logan's a good man but I can see you're falling for him. You're going to end up with a broken heart. He's not the forever kind."

Her mother's voice was gentle and Ava knew she was only trying to help. "I'm not going into the details of our relationship but he's made a commitment of sorts to me. While I'm here in town anyway. It's good enough."

Her lips twisted, Carol shook her head. "It won't be in the end, sweetheart. I know you say you don't want to get married, and that's fine. But I do think you want a man to love you. I think you want that very much."

Ava looked away and zipped her suitcase closed. "I do want that. Logan has feelings for me."

"Is it love?" her mother asked softly. "Do you love him?"

Ava wasn't ready to put a name to how she felt. "It's too soon for that."

"If Logan is the one, well, there isn't anything I could say that would keep you from going. Your father is going to have trouble with this but I'll deal with him."

Ava finally looked up. "I'm sorry you have to do that. I know Dad is going to be livid."

"That is an understatement." Her mother chuckled. "I'll fix his favorite for dinner and make sure he has two beers after work instead of one."

"You know how to handle him, I guess."

Her mother waved away the praise. "I did exactly the same thing when I told him you were going away to college. Then I did it again when I told him you weren't moving back to Corville after graduation."

"I guess I've been nothing but trouble," Ava conceded. She'd never fully appreciated how much her mother had had to go to bat for her in the past.

"You're a daughter any parent would be proud of, sweetheart."

Before Ava could respond they heard footsteps coming up the stairs. Mary stuck her head in the bedroom, an inquiring look on her face.

"Good. You're here. I've been looking for you." Mary stepped into the room, ignoring her own mother. Her foot was tapping on the floor and her arms were crossed over her chest. "I just talked to Lyle. He said you were at lunch with him and Logan."

Nothing good could come from this conversation.

"I was. Is that a problem?" Mary had strange ideas of what was proper and what wasn't. Ava wasn't in the mood for a lecture at the moment.

"Logan wouldn't tell Lyle or his brothers what Uncle George said. I bet he told you. We want to know."

Mary had that crappy arrogant expression on her face that Ava hated. Mary Ellen Hayworth Bryson had way too much self-esteem. She expected everyone to do things her way.

"I don't know anything so your trip has been wasted." Ava wasn't about to tell them she'd watched the interrogation on a monitor and had been sworn in as an honorary deputy. She picked up her suitcase from the bed and set it on the floor, extending the handle. "I have things to do so if you'll excuse me."

Ava started to pull her suitcase on wheels toward the door but Mary stepped in front of her.

"You must have some theories about who the killer is. You said you were helping Logan. He must have said something. Does Logan think it's Uncle George?"

Logan had already told her he didn't think it was George. But he did think George knew things about Bill Bryson's business that could lead them to the killer. He'd said that much at lunch to the brothers.

"He already told Lyle and the others that he didn't suspect George."

"Do you suspect George? Who do you think did it?" Mary asked, her gaze intent. Ava sighed in frustration. Most of the time Mary didn't want to talk to Ava. Now she couldn't get out of the house because her sister wouldn't let this go.

"I don't really have any suspects." It was clear that George hadn't told anyone that Bill's killer was also the vigilante. "I'll call you tomorrow, Mom."

Ava went around her sister just managing to squeeze her suitcase through without hitting the wall or Mary's legs. Mary followed her as Ava headed down the stairs.

"Do you think it's someone in the family?" Mary persisted as Ava paused at the bottom of the stairs.

Tired of being questioned, Ava shrugged. "It could be anyone. Anyone on the streets you see every day. Or it could be someone you've never met in your life."

"Why would someone kill a person they'd never met?" Mary scowled, obviously frustrated with Ava's stonewalling.

"Every heard of a serial killer?" Ava asked. "They kill people they've never met all the time."

"Do you think a serial killer shot Bill?"

Ava dragged her suitcase into the foyer, Mary on her heels. "As I said, it could be anyone. Hell, I once wrote a book where a family member killed a bunch of random strangers to cover up the murder of his brother. It put the cops off the scent. I also wrote a book about a business rival killing off his competition one by one. Now I need to get going."

Ava looked pointedly at Mary who was standing in front of the door. Her sister stepped aside. "So you think the person who killed Bill will shoot a bunch of other people to cover it up?"

Ava wanted to smack her sister. "That's what you got from what I said? I was simply telling you there are a multitude of reasons someone can be murdered either by a loved one or an acquaintance. Don't put words in my mouth."

Mary turned to her mother who was watching the play by play with an amused smile on her lips. "Mom, Ava is being difficult."

Carol Hayworth nodded. "She is. You are too. You keep asking the same question over and over because you don't like her answer. She says she doesn't have a suspect."

"I don't believe that," Mary wailed indignantly. "She must."

"You're calling your sister a liar then?" her mother asked calmly.

"Well, no," Mary sputtered. "Not exactly."

"What exactly are you calling me?" Ava asked. "I really and truly, cross my heart, don't have any suspects."

Mary's shoulders slumped, a glum expression on her face. "I was just trying to help my husband."

Ava liked her sister much better when she acted like a normal human being. She patted Mary on the back and tried to give her an encouraging smile.

"If it makes you feel any better, I don't think Lyle had anything to do with his father's murder."

Mary nodded. "Thank you. It does, actually. He would never do anything like that. He's a gentle man."

A patient man too to put up with her sister's bossiness and obstinate temperament. If he hadn't killed Mary by now, then he probably wasn't going to murder anyone else.

"He is," Ava agreed. "I really do need to get going. I have a lot of work to do on my new book."

Ava rolled the suitcase down the driveway and stowed it in her trunk. She and Logan needed to solve this murder before it started tearing the Bryson family apart. Possibly even this town.

A thought flitted through her mind as she drove away. As long as it stayed unsolved she had a reason to stay in town and with Logan.

Well, crap.

Chapter Eighteen

Logan dropped the last filthy box onto the living room floor. A cloud of dust rose making Ava sneeze and cough. She wrinkled her nose as the scent of mildew and plain old grime assailed her nostrils. This was going to be a nasty job.

"Here," Logan held out some rubber gloves. "I have a pair for both of us. This is going to be dirty work."

"I'm not sure the spaghetti was worth it," she said dubiously. "It was good but this is kind of disgusting. What if there are bugs in there and they jump out when I reach in?"

Ava shuddered at the mere thought. She hated creepy crawlies of any kind. Logan had made a wonderful dinner of spaghetti with a rich meat sauce and crusty garlic bread but now she realized it had all been a bribe. She was cheaply paid labor who could be bought off with a home cooked meal.

"I shook the boxes and nothing came out." Logan's lips twitched as if he was trying not to laugh.

"You lying sack of crap. You so did not shake those boxes, did you?" She narrowed her eyes and tried to look mean but he just threw his head back and laughed.

"Honey, bugs would probably be scared to death of you. I know I am." He patted her on top of the head. Hating it when he patronized her, she knocked at his hand and stuck out her tongue. "If you do a good job, we can have ice cream later."

"We darn well are going to have ice cream later," Ava grumbled. "A big bowl. With chocolate sauce."

"I don't have any chocolate sauce." Logan had a mile-wide grin.

"Then you'll get in the car and go get some," Ava retorted, throwing a large cushion down onto the floor and sitting on it crisscross.

"Yes, ma'am." Logan didn't look in the least contrite. If anything he looked downright delighted. "Shall I get whipped cream too?"

He leered when he asked the question and she rolled her eyes. "I'm not going to be in any mood when I'm covered from head to toe in hundred year old dust and mold."

"It starts already." Logan sighed dramatically.

"What starts?" Ava tentatively reached into the box and pulled out a stack of files sending another cloud of dirt into the air. She choked and coughed, glad to see Logan did the same.

"You move in and next thing you know you're making excuses about sex," Logan declared. He was trying to look serious but she could tell he was picking at her again, trying to get a rise.

"Excuse me?" Ava sniffed. "I am not making any excuses. I only hope you can perform after working all day and then tonight too."

She watched as his astonished expression turned to pure male arrogance. "Don't you worry about a thing," he drawled. "I've got the stamina to please my woman, demanding as she is."

She turned back to the files so he wouldn't see her hot cheeks. Whenever he talked like that she got all warm and flustered. He shouldn't be so sexy…or annoying.

"Where do we start?" she asked, hoping to change the subject. Logan grinned, knowing what she was trying to do.

"Anywhere I guess. We'll end up looking through all the files anyway."

He was right. Luckily there were only two boxes. Still it would probably take hours to go through them all. Maybe she should put on a pot of coffee.

Logan settled on another pillow next to her and she flipped open the first folder, scanning the contents. It was a complaint regarding painted graffiti on the outside of a local business – Stenson Construction – dated 1989. The owner, Garth Stenson, had made a complaint about writing on his building. The report stated that Sheriff Frank Jesse had taken the statement and concluded it was teenagers.

Ava looked at the pictures that were stuffed into the folder. They'd faded with age but she could make out the words clearly painted in bright red on the cream colored exterior wall.

"Some things never change." Ava shoved the pictures back into the folder. "I guess there will always be troubled youth in this world."

Logan's eyebrow arched. "Troubled youth? Do you mean like me?"

"I wasn't referring to that," she denied. "You had a good reason for what you did."

"But other kids don't," he concluded. "You know better than that, good girl."

"I know." Ava sighed. "I didn't mean it the way it sounded."

Logan set his file aside and beckoned for the folder with his fingers. "What are you looking at?"

"Vandalism. Some teenagers spray painted a business." She put the three photos in his outstretched palm. Logan studied them and then looked up.

"Why do you say it's teenagers?"

"Because that's what the police report said." She handed that over.

Logan continued looking at the pictures and then the report before shaking his head. "Teenagers didn't do this."

"How do you know?" Ava frowned and looked over his shoulder. She wished she could see through his eyes. He had that inscrutable cop-look expression again.

"How many teenagers who go around painting graffiti use the words *unscrupulous* and *traitorous* in everyday language? In fact, how many teenagers have an opinion about a man who sells real estate? Did teenagers in 1989 buy and sell a lot of homes? No, this was done by an adult. Teenagers would have used a bunch of misspelled four-letter words."

He held up the picture for her closer inspection. "So Sheriff Jesse was wrong?"

Logan tossed the photos into the folder. "He was. What else is in that file?"

They scanned through the documents and it was more reports of vandalism, including broken glass and slashed tires. "Whatever happened to the Stenson agency? They're not on Main Street now."

Logan shook his head. "They went out of business I believe. I know the Stenson family moved out of town at one point."

"You think Bill Bryson did these things to get rid of competition?" If she was thinking it, she was pretty sure Logan was too.

"It's kind of a coincidence. Let's keep digging and see if we find more of them. I have a feeling I was right. Frank hid these files for a reason."

Ava set the file aside and reached for the next folder. She was eager to find out more. Something had been going on in Corville when Sheriff Frank Jesse was in charge and it was time to get to the bottom of it.

✧ ✧ ✧ ✧

Logan and Ava had only gone through about ten files but it was easy to see that Sheriff Frank Jesse had been corrupt. Whether he'd actually taken bribes from Bill Bryson to cover up his dirty dealings Logan didn't know, but it was clear Frank had turned a blind eye, covering up the evidence.

"Are you okay?" Ava was looking at him with sympathy. "This can't be easy for you."

Logan tossed another folder aside. "Yes and no. The fact is I'm not really surprised. I think there has been a part of me that's known Frank wasn't this great lawman for a long time. God knows when I took over the entire department was a fucking mess and the deputies did whatever they damn well pleased. It took me months to clean it up."

"I kind of assumed he was like a father to you." Ava plucked at her T-shirt.

"Never like a parent. Hell, more like a drill sergeant," Logan snorted. Frank Jesse had been a hard man. The fact that Logan never asked him for anything was probably what had made the two men quasi friends. Frank had always respected hard work and Logan had never let him down there.

"He left the ranch to you," Ava persisted.

Logan shrugged. "He didn't have any family and he knew I didn't either. I think he knew I would take care of the place, and

I have. I've renovated the home and barn and rented out the pasture land. It's a going concern and is firmly in the black. That's more than I could say when Frank was in charge."

He leaned forward wanting to make sure this point was clear. "Listen good girl, I liked Frank. He taught me a lot about being a lawman. He treated me decently and didn't give me a lot of shit about how I lived my life. The fact that he didn't do the things he taught me to do as a sheriff, well, that's on him. I have a feeling before we're done here we're going to find out a whole hell of a lot more that we don't like. It's not going to do me any good to sit around and wonder how I never knew this about him. Frank was a law unto himself and he sure as shit didn't spend a lot of time explaining his actions. To anyone."

Ava waved her hand over the still mountainous pile of files. "I think you're probably right. He was obviously trying to hide this. It's strange that he hid it in his own home though. A house he left to you. You would think he'd have known that you would find this eventually. Do you think on some level he wanted you to find out?"

Logan laughed at Ava's pop psychology. Women always wanted men to be more complex than they really were. "I doubt it. At the end, Frank was sick and his memory was bad. I doubt he even remembered that he hid the files. Don't look for conspiracies where there are none."

Logan's phone vibrated and he pulled it from his pocket, glancing at the screen.

Tanner.

"Hey, what's up?"

"Presley," Tanner answered. "More specifically, she's in labor. Has been for a few hours and Seth is getting mighty nervous. He called me since I've been through it a couple of times but I think it would be good if we could all be there for him. You know, in support."

Seth had been anxious through Presley's entire pregnancy, fussing about the littlest thing. Logan could only imagine what Seth was like now that the moment had arrived. He was probably driving his wife crazy.

"I'll be there. If I leave now I should make it within an hour and a half or so."

"Thanks. Reed is on his way and so is Evan Davis."

It wasn't surprising to hear the Marshal who had introduced Presley and Seth was going to be there. He was good friends with Seth, and Presley was very fond of the man. "What about Griffin and Jared?"

Tanner snorted. "I called Griffin and got a message that he's off on one of his fishing trips. Dare is in charge."

Deputy Darrell "Dare" Turner was Griffin's senior deputy and a damn good cop. He was also the grouchiest son of a gun Logan had ever met. It was as if he had a handful of burrs in his boxer shorts. Day and night. Logan had never seen the man with a smile on his face.

"Griffin loves his fishing. What's Jared's excuse?"

"He's on duty with one of his men out sick. Sounded harassed as hell. He's having a hard time keeping lawmen from what he's been saying."

That was because Jared was a perfectionist. Few people could live up to his expectations.

"I'll be out the door in five. See you then."

Logan hung up and gave Ava a guilty look. He was going to leave her with all this work.

"You have to go, don't you?"

Logan grimaced. It wasn't fair but what could he say? "Presley, Seth's wife, is in labor. I don't have time to explain much of it, but suffice it to say Seth is a nervous wreck."

Instead of being angry, her expression softened. "First one?"

"Yes. Tanner thought it would be a good idea for some of us to go and support them."

"I'd like to meet these people someday."

He'd like that too. More than he wanted to admit.

"I hate to leave you with all this work."

Actually a part of him was relieved. He hated looking through old files for a needle in a haystack.

"No, you don't. You can't stand paperwork. I've got your number, Logan Wright."

Ava was openly laughing at him. She certainly did know him well.

"Let's just say I feel guilty leaving you with all this work."

"That I believe. Get out of here and congratulate your friends. I hope everything goes well."

Logan needed no second bidding. He grabbed his keys and leather jacket, kissed Ava goodbye, and hopped on his cycle. It would be a great time of the night for a ride. Just him and the road.

After Logan left, Ava had gone back to work on the files. It wasn't the most glamorous of tasks but the files needed to be reviewed, and she knew Logan hated the more mundane tasks of investigation. He'd run out of the house almost without kissing her goodbye.

As she reviewed each file, each report, the picture of Bill Bryson was becoming clearer.

The picture was frightening.

Reports drew a portrait of a ruthless business man who bullied competitors and even his own family. Ava was truly shaken, her stomach in knots, as she read report after report of domestic violence between Bill and his wife Margaret. Hospital reports and photographs showed a woman beaten and cowed by a violent man who cared little for his spouse's welfare.

Ava finally had to take a break from reading the files, sick to her stomach with disgust. It was just as well Logan hadn't been brought up in that home. Heaven only knew how he might have turned out.

The thought made her even more queasy. Her sister had married into that family. Although Lyle looked and acted like a reasonable, gentle, even shy man, who knew what lay beneath. Certainly Bill Bryson's secrets had been kept well by Frank Jesse.

Ava went into the kitchen and pulled a soda from the refrigerator. She needed a breather from reviewing the disturbing material but her brain was already whirling with questions. Had the three boys known of their father's violent nature? Had he also beaten them? Was that why he'd been murdered?

She padded back into the living room and settled on the cushion, opening another file. The name of Logan's mother jumped off the page almost stopping her heart. Perhaps this was a report regarding Jackie Wright's disappearance?

Several photos of Logan's home showed all of his mother's belongings still there. Ava shuffled through the papers and found a statement from a woman – Helen Main – who claimed to be a close friend of Jackie's and had seen her the day she disappeared. Ava wanted to scream with frustration as most of the statement had been blacked out with a thick marker. Whatever Helen had said, someone, probably Frank Jesse, didn't want anyone to know. She'd signed the statement at the bottom and dated it.

They needed to talk to Helen Main. If she was still alive and could be found. Logan, whether he admitted it or not, desperately needed closure as to why his mother had left. Good or bad, if she could answer Logan's questions, it would go a long way toward healing the open wound in his heart.

Ava started to organize the statements, photos, and police reports into some sort of order. When Logan finally returned home, she wanted to have this laid out clearly for him. That also meant finishing the unopened folders still in the second box. She had a mountain of work to do but it could be hours before Logan was back. She dug into the work with renewed energy. They were onto something here that was important. She could feel it in her bones. Something in these files was the key to Bill Bryson's murder.

"What did you say to Logan?" Wade asked his Uncle George. "You must have said something."

They were sitting in George's living room enjoying a fine single malt scotch and discussing George's interview. Wade wanted to know what had been said. After all, George had been the family secret keeper for years, especially about Bill Bryson.

"I told him nothing," George blustered, his face already red from the whiskey. "I reminded him that he was a Bryson now and needed to act like it. He doesn't understand what he's digging into."

But Wade understood.

Maybe not every single secret but he knew the important ones. He sure as hell didn't blame Logan Wright for not wanting to sully his hands with the Bryson family. Logan lived an honest, upstanding life, fighting for goodness and justice.

The Brysons?

They lied, cheated, and stole to get whatever they wanted. It wasn't a legacy that Wade cherished. He'd decided long ago to create his own.

"Logan's a good cop," Wade replied, watching George's expression closely. "He's dedicated to finding Dad's killer."

"He thinks someone did it because of your father's business dealings," George finally admitted after taking a gulp of the amber colored liquid.

"Is that what you think?" Wade asked, standing and walking over to look out of the window. The sun was down, there wasn't much moon to speak of, and the land around the house was pitch black. Wade had counted on that.

"It's possible," his uncle answered meekly. George had always been a milquetoast while Bill Bryson had been the lion. Of course in the end it didn't matter. Both had to answer for their crimes.

"Dad didn't care what he did or who he hurt. He didn't give a damn about right and wrong. He angered a lot of people in his life."

Wade's only regret was that it had taken so long for him to realize just what Bill Bryson truly was.

George stood and paced back and forth. Wade watched him in the reflection on the window. "Your father did what he thought was best for the family. Family always came first." George sounded slightly desperate. "Your father loved you, Wade."

Wade didn't turn around. "That doesn't make what he did right. Or what you're doing now. You should have come clean, George. You should have told the truth."

"I'm protecting this family," George protested, his pacing ceased. "I'm the head of the family now and I'll do everything I can to preserve it."

Wade reached slowly under his suit jacket, his back still to his uncle, and wrapped his fingers around the cold handle of the gun, snug in the shoulder holster. Justice must be done.

"No, George. I'm the head of the family. I know what's best."

Chapter Nineteen

Tanner was standing in the hospital waiting room talking to Evan Davis and drinking a tall coffee. Logan slapped the two men on the back and headed straight for the soda machine. It was going to be a long night. He'd need the caffeine.

"Where's Reed?" Logan asked. "Dear God, he's not in there with them is he?"

Tanner laughed, coffee almost coming out of his nose. "Are you kidding? Reed probably won't even witness the birth of his own kids, let alone Seth's. Seth's mom and dad are in there with him. Reed just got caught up doing a few things. He sent me a text a while ago that he was on his way."

Logan popped open the can of soda and took a long drink. "For a man that was shot several times, you look pretty good, Evan. How are you feeling?"

Evan lifted one shoulder. "Not bad. I can predict the weather now by how badly my leg hurts."

"Could have been worse," Tanner said. "You had your vest and it saved your life."

"It did but I'm not sure what for." Evan scowled, a deep vee appearing between his brows. "All I fucking do every day is push paper from one side of my desk to the other. That isn't what I signed on for."

"You'll be back on active duty before you know it," Logan assured him.

"Maybe." The Marshal's mouth was turned down. Logan didn't blame Evan one bit for being bitter. He'd had a great career with the Marshal Service and then got injured in the line of duty. If he couldn't do the job, the government would have no qualms about giving him a medal and an administrative role, relegating him away from the action. That would be worse than death for a guy like Davis.

Seth burst through a nearby doorway. "She's ready to push. It shouldn't be long now."

Wearing a green set of scrubs, the man's face was covered with a mile-wide grin.

All three men cheered the news and Seth ducked back behind the door. Logan turned to Tanner, a grimace on his face. "I'm afraid to ask but what does it mean when he says she's ready to push? Hasn't she been pushing all along? What have they been doing in there all this time?"

"Women don't push until they're fully dilated. The contractions dilate the cervix to ten centimeters." Logan groaned in sympathetic pain. That had to hurt. Holy fuck. "Once they're dilated they can start pushing the baby out. Hopefully it won't take too long."

Evan looked a little pale himself. "How long is too long?"

Tanner chuckled at their uneasiness. "Abby pushed out both our kids in less than half an hour each. It could take much less time or more. It depends on how hard Presley pushes and how big the baby is."

Logan looked down at his soda can. "I think I need a drink. This is barbaric. Why don't they just put them out for this?"

Just thinking about Ava being in that kind of pain made Logan want to wrap her in cotton wool and keep her safe from anything and everything.

"Because women like to have a baby the natural way." The three men heard Reed Mitchell's mocking voice behind them. Standing there with a giant teddy bear, he looked like he always did. Totally calm and assured.

"What do you know about having a baby?" Logan laughed. "Did you rob a toy store on the way here?"

Reed set the bear on a chair in the waiting room. "I have sisters, asshole. And no, I didn't rob a toy store on my way. I bought this months ago when Seth told us."

Evan looked down at the bear and gave Reed a smirk. "Cute. Did you name him Uncle Reed?"

"His name is Teddy. Teddy Bear," Reed replied with just a hint of a smile. "Now what did I miss?"

"She's pushing." Tanner answered. "It won't be long now."

It wasn't long. Within a half hour, Seth emerged. Red-faced and sweaty, he was beaming with the news. A boy. Seven pounds, six ounces. Ten fingers and toes. One set of healthy lungs. Logan could hear the infant's lusty cries from the hallway.

Seth disappeared back into the room, this time with the large bear in tow, before joining them again much later. The baby was being checked out, and Presley was being attended to by a nurse.

"I've got five minutes," Seth declared. "Then I have to get back to my family."

It had only been a year ago that Logan and Seth would go out on double dates or play poker on a Friday night. Now he had a wife and son. A family.

Tanner was planning a wedding with Madison. They might have kids as well. Certainly Tanner wasn't going to be up for a hunting trip this fall. A guy getaway was out of the question. He'd want to spend every moment with his wife-to be.

What was happening to them?

Logan tugged at the top buttons of his shirt, suddenly feeling too warm. "I need some air," he stated, heading straight for the exit. "I'll be right back."

He hit the elevator and then the front entrance before walking out into the night. Breathing deeply, he let the cool air dry the sweat that had formed on the back of his neck. He needed to get his shit together. A little warm domesticity shouldn't shake him up like this. He'd been a groomsman in Lyle's wedding and it hadn't bothered him.

A flash of Ava in that ugly pink dress had a smile tugging at the corners of Logan's mouth. Even then she'd been more beautiful than any other woman in the room. She carried herself with such grace and intelligence. She sure as fuck didn't put up with any of his crap.

He dragged in some more air before turning back to the entrance. Enough of this self-indulgent bullshit. It was time to get back to his friends. He wasn't afraid of a little familial bliss.

It was almost four in the morning when Logan pulled up into his driveway. He was tired, his body dragging up the steps to his home. A lone light shone through the windows. He couldn't remember the last time he'd come home to a house that wasn't empty. Just knowing Ava was there, even asleep, made a difference.

Seth's new baby had been incredibly tiny with a thatch of blond hair on his head and blue eyes that peered out into his new world. It was hard to believe that Logan's friend was going to be responsible for another human life for the next eighteen years or so. Luckily he would have Presley to help him.

Pushing open the door, he tried to enter the house as quietly as he could, not wanting to wake Ava. Hopefully she'd taken his advice and not waited up for him. He'd slide into bed next to her and try and catch a few hours sleep before the day started all over again.

He walked into the living room and stopped short as he spied Ava sprawled on the floor, a smudge of grime on her cheek and her head on a cushion. He felt his fatigue fall away and marveled at how easily she fitted into his life. As if she'd been made just for him.

She was so incredibly beautiful. At this moment, she looked peaceful and innocent, her features in graceful repose, her hair a halo of curls around her face.

How she'd managed to stay so untouched by the underbelly of life and still write about the darker aspects of the world, he'd never know. Maybe it was simply who she was. She certainly saw the good inside of him, even when he didn't see it himself.

He knelt down and fingered a stray lock of hair, like silk between his fingers. He hadn't meant to wake her but her lashes fluttered and her eyelids slowly opened. Her lips curved into a smile and joy filled her eyes as she awoke. He felt the now familiar tightening in his chest, so acute it bordered on pain. She'd become everything in such a short time.

"Logan," she whispered. "You're home."

He was home and it had nothing to do with the four walls that surrounded him.

"I am." He ran his finger down her soft as satin cheek. "You're sleeping in the living room."

She levered up onto her elbow, pushing her hair back from her face. "I am. I guess I fell asleep a few hours ago." She seemed to shake herself awake and then grabbed his hand. "I have so much to tell you. You won't believe what I've learned. Did your friend have the baby? Is everything okay?"

"A boy. No name yet. Apparently they're arguing about whether to call him Elvis."

Rubbing her eyes, she sat up straight. "I think I'm missing an inside joke but I'm too tired to care. I need to wake up to be able to show you everything I found."

So much for getting a few hours of sleep. If Ava had found something he wanted to hear it.

"Let's get some coffee going and we'll talk." Logan held out his hand and helped her to her feet before heading into the kitchen. He stopped as he saw the stack of paper and folders. Photos were stuck onto his whiteboard. He winced when he saw the photos of Wade's mother, her face black and blue.

"Fuck, I had no idea." He pulled one from the board and inspected it more closely, a ball forming in his stomach. The Bryson family was a disaster, and he shared their DNA. "Bill?"

He turned to Ava for confirmation and she nodded. "I think you're right about that coffee. Do you want me to start a pot?"

"I want to put an IV line straight into my veins." Logan scraped at his dry, scratchy eyes and yawned. "But I'll settle for a big cup. Black."

Ava pushed at his shoulder. "Go splash some water on your face."

He hesitated, not wanting to make his fatigue any more important than her own. She waved him away and started opening cabinets. "I got a few hours. I bet you've been up all night. Go."

This time he didn't argue and headed to the bathroom. By the time he got back, the coffee was brewing and she'd pulled a cheesecake he bought yesterday at the store from the refrigerator.

"I see you found the dessert." Logan sat down at the island and began studying the whiteboard.

"Is this what we were supposed to have after dinner last night?" she asked, pulling down two large mugs from a shelf.

"Until you started talking about ice cream, anyway." Logan flashed her a tired smile. "I'm afraid I didn't pick up any chocolate sauce on the way home."

"I'll let it pass this time. Are you ready?" Ava reached for the stack of papers on the island. "You're not going to like this. I warn you now."

"I haven't liked anything we've found so far so why ruin a perfect record? Let's do this and get it over with."

Ava stepped to the whiteboard and began to review the years of abuse Margaret Bryson suffered at the hands of her husband. Logan's expression grew more grave with each picture and police report. By the time she'd shown him all the photos, his lips were pressed together and his eyes had taken on a hard, cold quality.

"Jesus H. Christ. Did Frank do any fucking thing at all while he was sheriff?"

Swallowing hard, Ava pulled a file from the island. "There's more."

"Of course there is." Logan laughed but the sound came out painfully.

Ava opened the folder and took out a few photos, handing them to Logan. "These are from the scene of Margaret's death, which was ruled accidental. The official report was that she fell from a third floor balcony in her home. Bill Bryson's statement was that he was at work at the time."

Logan's lips twisted. "Let me guess. He wasn't. What a charming family."

"I don't think of you as a Bryson." Ava shook her head. Logan was too much his own man to ever identify himself with a family name like the Bryson boys did.

"Me neither." Logan sat up straighter. "So where was Bill if he wasn't at work?"

"That's the mystery. According to one of his employees, he was at the office. According to his own son, Bill was on the balcony with his mother. Wade says his father pushed her."

Ava watched as the enormity of what she said sunk in. Logan scrubbed his fingers through his hair. "Shit. Shit. Shit. Bill killed his wife? Son of a bitch."

Logan's hands tightened on his coffee cup, the knuckles white with tension. Ava couldn't even imagine what it must be like to hear your father was a monster of sorts.

He reached for the reports and she stayed quiet as he read the statements one by one. He finally tossed them aside with a look of disgust.

"Suddenly not having a father is looking pretty good. It's amazing Wade, Lyle, and Aaron turned out as well as they did."

Ava could only hope so. Her sister had married into this family.

"Did Wade ever mention what he saw to you?" Ava asked.

Logan shook his head and stood up, refilling his coffee cup. "No, and that's what's weird. If you saw someone murder your mother, wouldn't that stick with you? Even mess you up a little? Wade never said anything close to that. The few times he's mentioned his mother he always referred to it as an accident."

"How old would he have been when she died? Maybe his father convinced him that he didn't see what he really saw, if you know what I mean?"

"I do." Logan nodded grimly. "Daddy dearest messes with a kid's mind. Of course the kid doesn't want to believe his dad's a killer so he lets himself be convinced. Fuck. I hope Frank is turning over in his grave right about now. If he were here, I'd kick his ass before arresting him for corruption and a bunch of other charges I could name."

Ava wasn't sure Logan was in the right frame of mind but she couldn't keep the news from him. It was too important.

"There's more."

Ava held her breath as Logan's brows shot up. "More? About Bill?"

Licking her suddenly dry lips, she scraped together all her nerve. This was going to hit Logan hard. "About your mother." She handed him the folder she'd set aside. "Frank Jesse took a statement about the day your mother disappeared from a Helen Main."

Logan's skin had gone pale and he'd taken a step back as if he'd taken a blow to the chest. "I remember her. She was a nice lady. She took me in after Mom left. What did it say?"

"That's the thing. Someone took a black marker to it."

Ava pointed to the redacted statement and Logan's hand crumpled the corner of the paper with his death-like grip.

"Someone," he bit out, his eyes narrowed to slits. "Frank. If he weren't dead, I'd kill him."

His voice was low and deadly and Ava's heart tightened in sympathy. Logan had received so few breaks in life and it looked like the people he'd trusted most had been part of the reason.

"We need to talk to her, Logan. She may know something. You can ask her about your mother's relationship with Bill Bryson."

Logan was looking off into the distance and she could tell his mind was somewhere else. She placed her hand on his arm. "Logan?"

Wherever he had traveled to, he was back now. There was a determination to his jaw and a fire in his eyes.

"Yes, we need to talk to her. I'll do some research and see if I can find her. Helen moved out of Corville right after I enlisted."

"Can I help?" she asked softly. While the day had been successful as far as finding leads for Bill's murder, personally it had to be a hard one for this man she'd come to care for so deeply.

"You already have, good girl. Why don't we lie down for a few hours and get some sleep? We have a lot of work to do tomorrow."

Neither of them slept much. Ava dozed on and off and only once when she looked over had she found Logan asleep. The rest of the time that faraway look was back in his eyes. She fought the urge to brush it away and bring him back to the present. He needed to make peace with what had happened so she let him wander on his journey, hoping he could finally make some sense of it.

She wrapped her arms around him, resting her head on his chest, hoping her touch could bring him some peace and comfort. Until he truly dealt with his past, he would never be able to plan a future. And she knew that was something she wanted. Call her stupid or naive, Ava wanted to be with him more than just a few weeks.

Chapter Twenty

George Bryson's housekeeper's face was ashen, her entire body shaking, when Logan arrived at George's house. A ringing phone had woken Logan from a fitful sleep. He hadn't been allowed much time to mull what Ava had found. He was needed at George Bryson's home. The housekeeper, Alice Greeley, had found him in a pool of blood on the living room carpet early this morning.

The ambulance and Drake pulled up just as Logan did, and he stepped aside to let the EMTs into the house first. He had little hope but there was a minuscule chance George Bryson was clinging to life inside.

The EMTs would fuck up his crime scene but the housekeeper had already walked in it. Better to save the victim than preserve a pristine crime scene. Shit, they didn't really exist anyway. Not in Logan's experience. Cops had to do the best they could with what they were given.

Logan put his hand on Alice's shoulder. "Wait here for me. I need to talk to you, but I have to see what's going on in the house first. Drake is going to stay here with you."

Alice nodded and sniffled, her eyes watery. Logan steeled himself for the bloody scene and crossed the threshold, following the sounds from the living room. Two EMTs were leaning over the body, one shaking his head and packing away the equipment he'd pulled out.

Logan scraped a hand down his face. He was fucking tired of dead bodies in his town. One of the EMTs came around the couch and up to Logan.

"We called it. He's been dead for awhile is my guess. Rigor has already set in so it's been hours. ME will know more. Al's calling him now. We'll get out of your way until you're ready for us to transport him to the morgue."

Both men filed out leaving Logan staring at the dead body of George Bryson.

The man was lying on his back on an area rug that at one time might have been multi-colored but was now almost black with soaked in blood. His chest had sunk in and a pool of blood had congealed on what had been a crisp white dress shirt. The most haunting aspect was George's eyes – wide open and fixed as if his assailant had caught him by surprise. Logan was sure George hadn't expected to be shot. An empty highball glass lay on its side about a foot from George's outstretched hand. Forensics would tell Logan if the adjacent brown stain was whiskey and if George was drunk.

Nothing else in the room was out of place. Even the throw pillows on the couch had been artfully arranged. Whatever had happened, no one had been sitting there. There was no sign of a struggle indicating George Bryson had known his killer. Maybe he had trusted him. Or her.

Not liking the direction his thoughts were moving, Logan walked back outside, the air rapidly warming at this time of year. Alice was sitting on the swing located on the front porch while Drake leaned against the house. Logan beckoned to his deputy who joined him just outside the doorway.

"Check the perimeter," Logan directed Drake. "See if there are any signs of forced entry, footprints. You know the drill."

Drake nodded while Logan walked over and sat next to the shaking housekeeper. Logan felt like ten kinds of shit making this woman relive what she'd seen but he didn't have a choice. Pulling a small notebook and pen from his pocket, he took a deep breath.

"I need to ask you some questions."

Alice nodded, a tissue mopping at her eyes. "I understand, Sheriff."

Sometimes his job sucked.

"What time did you arrive?"

Alice sniffled but her shoulders straightened as if bracing herself. "About seven. Since Mr. Bryson's divorce, he likes me to come early and start the coffee and breakfast."

George had recently divorced his third wife. From what Logan knew, all three of them had a motive to kill George. There'd been no love lost when they'd split.

"Was the front door unlocked when you got here?" Logan asked already knowing the answer. People in Corville didn't lock their doors.

"It was wide open. I walked in and found Mr. Bryson lying on the floor." Alice's voice broke. "I couldn't tell if he was dead or not, but there was a lot of blood."

Logan scribbled down the details as Alice recounted her story.

"What then? Did you touch the body?"

Alice's eyes went wide with fear. "I couldn't. I just couldn't touch him. I called 911 immediately. The operator had me hold on the phone until someone showed up."

That was standard procedure, especially as the killer could have been in the house.

"I'd hoped he was still alive." Alice was shaking her head and new tears were running down her cheeks. "He was a nice man. He treated me well."

The way the blood had congealed and darkened on George's chest indicated he'd been dead for some time.

Logan continued to question the distraught woman but it was clear she'd been too shocked to notice much of anything but the dead body on the floor. The killer had probably been long gone anyway so she wouldn't have seen anyone run from the house.

Logan stood up and patted Alice on the shoulder. "If you remember anything else, I want you to call me. Day or night, understand?"

She nodded and another of his deputies escorted her to her car. The deputy knew to follow her to make sure she got home safe. Drake must have finished his investigation of the perimeter because he was standing in front of Logan with a grim expression.

"Nothing?" Logan asked.

"Nothing," Drake replied, a muscle ticking beside his mouth. "No footprints, no broken glass, not a damn thing. Do you think it's the vigilante?"

Fighting the overwhelming feeling of frustration, Logan shrugged. "Ballistics will tell the story. I think we have to deal with the idea that if it is, the Bryson family knows the vigilante. Whoever did this didn't break into the house. Bill's killer didn't either. They were welcome."

Drake stroked his chin. "Friends. Or family. But why kill all those other people? Did he kill them for the same reason?"

"Or to cover up what they did to Bill and George?" Logan finished the unspoken thought. "I don't know. But we're getting close. I can feel it."

Ava was watching the monitor again in Logan's office. This time she could see the faces of Lyle, Wade, Aaron, and Deke Kennedy, their lawyer. Logan had his back to her but she could hear the tension in his voice.

He'd wanted to question each one of the brothers separately but Deke wouldn't allow it, saying that it was all together or none. Logan had given in but she wouldn't call it gracefully. He'd cursed a blue streak when he'd told her about the ground rules the attorney had set down. Deke also said he reserved the right to stop the interview at any time. So much for wanting Logan to enter the Bryson family fold. Battle lines had clearly been drawn and Logan was on the opposite side of his half-brothers.

So far that didn't seem to bother him but he'd been rather stoic this entire time even as secret after secret had been revealed. If it had been her, she would probably have retreated to her fantasy world with a large box of dark chocolate and a bottle of wine. He might be doing fine now but eventually he would need to deal with everything.

But today wasn't that day.

Logan opened the folder he'd retrieved from the kitchen island spreading the photos of a battered and bruised Margaret Bryson on the table in front of the brothers.

"Did you know about this?" Logan asked.

Aaron's mouth fell open and he reached for one of the pictures. "Dear God. Where did you get these?"

"Police files. Seems your father liked to use your mother as a punching bag. I'll ask again, did you know about this?" Logan's tone was hard and unforgiving.

Lyle shook his head, his complexion pale. "No. No way. I can't believe this. There has to be some mistake."

Lyle's voice was hoarse. He truly may not have known. He'd been quite young when Margaret died.

Logan fingered one of the pictures then pointed to the black and blue marks on Margaret's face. "Does this look like a mistake? Does it?"

His voice grated and Wade stood up, his expression angry. "Leave him alone. We didn't know, okay? How could we possibly know something like this?"

Wade's voice had gone up an octave but Logan didn't reply. Instead he reached for another file. Ava tensed as he pulled out the police report from when Margaret Bryson had died. "Sit down."

Wade hesitated but his attorney put his hand on his shoulder and pushed him back down, murmuring in his ear. Wade sat back in his chair.

"I can't believe you're saying I knew this, Logan. Goddamn, you're one of my best friends in the world. Do you think I knew Dad did this?"

Logan didn't answer for a long time and then finally slid the paper across the table so it was in front of Wade. "According to this statement you said your father pushed your mother off that balcony. Are you saying you lied?"

Lyle and Aaron jumped up in shock, both of them talking at once so Ava couldn't tell exactly what they were saying. Logan let the three brothers go at it until Wade cut them off.

"Logan's pulling some police trick. I never said that." He turned back to Logan. "I never said anything of the sort. It's cruel of you to say that. When did you become like this, Logan? You're a real son of a bitch, you know that?"

Ava wished she could see Logan's face but she only saw the imperceptible tension in his body. If she hadn't spent the last several days in close proximity to him she never would have noticed.

"I became like this when dead bodies started showing up in my town." Logan pointed to the chairs. "Sit down."

His voice was low and deadly, and Lyle and Aaron sank into the chairs, their expressions wary. It was clear this had turned into an adversarial conversation. There was no pretense of brotherly love or even friendly camaraderie.

Logan pushed the statement over to Lyle and Aaron so they could peruse it. "So you're saying this statement was made up? It isn't true?"

Wade shook his head, his face growing red. "I don't know where you got that but it isn't true. I never saw that."

Ava searched Wade's features for even a flicker of deceit but found none. He seemed to truly believe what he was saying.

"I suppose that signature at the bottom is a forgery as well?" When Wade didn't respond, Logan moved on. "Do you know of any reason someone would want to kill your uncle?"

Wade looked at his brothers and then at his lawyer. "From what Dad said, Uncle George liked gambling. Maybe he owed somebody money."

"That's possible. I'll be getting a subpoena for your uncle's personal accounts. Do you know what I'll find?"

Wade shrugged, his eyes looking everywhere but at Logan. "I don't know. I didn't get involved with Uncle George's personal finances."

Logan continued to pepper the three brothers with questions but they continued to plead ignorance of anything. They apparently thought their father was a saint and the only issue their uncle had was a proclivity to bet on slow horses.

"One more question." Logan paused. "Do you think George killed your father?"

Lyle and Aaron shook their heads vigorously, but Wade finally turned to Logan and looked him right in the eye.

"Yes, I think he did."

Ava helped Logan unload the groceries they'd picked up at a small general store into the cute little log cabin. Several hours from Corville, the house was tucked into the mountains north of Lincoln. Logan had found Helen Main but she currently wasn't answering her phone. They'd left a message and hopefully she'd get back to them soon. In the meantime they would stay in this cabin Logan had borrowed from one of his sheriff friends, Jared Monroe.

The cabin wasn't large but it was warm and cozy. The air was colder this high up in the mountains but the home had been built to last. The main room was half a kitchen and half a living room with a fireplace on one end. The furniture was old but clean and comfortable indicating this Jared person either cared for the cabin himself or hired someone to do it for him.

Every surface in the kitchen and bathroom were spotless and the sheets on the bed appeared to be fresh. Ava could happily hole up here for weeks and write.

She sat the bag onto the kitchen counter with a huff. "You barely said a word on the drive up here. I'm starting to worry about you."

Logan began to unload the bags into the refrigerator. "I didn't have much to say. I've been mulling everything over in my mind."

"And?" she asked, stowing the dry pasta in one of the cabinets. "Have you come to any conclusions?"

"Sure have," Logan grinned. "Thinking gives me a headache. What about you? Have you figured anything out?"

"I think Wade believes what he said," she admitted.

"About his dad or about George?" Logan tossed the bags into the trash and popped open a beer.

"About his dad. But that thing about George? That was just weird."

"I agree. I think Wade knows more than he's letting on."

"Is that why you asked him?" Ava had been shocked when the question had come out of Logan's mouth. She'd been even more surprised when Wade had answered in the affirmative.

"Wade's the oldest son. He was thirteen when his mother died. I can see the younger ones not knowing what was going on in their home, but Wade? I don't think so. I vaguely remember he was very protective of his mother. I didn't think anything of it at the time but now I firmly believe he knew his father was beating up on his mother."

Logan sank down into one of the kitchen chairs and Ava sat opposite him. "When you say protective..." Ava prompted.

"He kept Lyle and Aaron from being around her at times. I distinctly remember Lyle scraped his knee and he was going to run to his mother. Wade grabbed him by the shirt and pulled him into the kitchen, determined to put a band aid on it himself. I just thought he didn't want his little brother to be a cry baby. Now I see he may have known his mother was covered in bruises."

Logan's tone was bitter and she couldn't blame him a bit. Seeing his friends and half-brothers protect their father and uncle couldn't be easy, although he still didn't appear to have fully processed everything that had happened. He was too calm. Too matter of fact.

He should be pissed as hell.

She couldn't stop herself from asking the question. "Do you think one of them is the killer?"

It sounded farfetched and ludicrous but if they knew what their father was like it was a motive. He may have killed their mother. Had George Bryson known what his brother was like and eventually killed him? If so, why had he waited? What had set him off that night?

Logan was staring off into space, gone somewhere again, but he finally turned to her and nodded. "I think it's a possibility. I have no evidence, of course. That's why I have Jared working on their credit cards. Maybe one of them made a purchase that will give us a clue."

"What are you hoping for? That one of them bought a gun?"

"I'd love it but that would be too easy," Logan snorted. "I was just thinking one of them might have used their card close to a vigilante crime scene. If I can place them near one of those murders, I can tie them to Bill's."

She screwed up her courage and placed her hand on his. "I'm still worried about you. You aren't dealing with everything we've learned in the last few days."

A flicker of irritation crossed Logan's face but he hid it quickly, his expression bland. "I don't know what you mean, good girl."

"You know exactly what I mean. Everything that we've uncovered should be making you angry. You barely reacted to Frank Jesse's actions. Plus the fact that your father turned out to be a wife beater. Don't you care about that at all?"

Logan's beautiful blue eyes turned cold. "Leave it, Ava. I'll deal with things in my own time. Until then, just leave it alone."

His words cut her to the quick but she valiantly tried to hide the hurt. He was in much more pain than she was whether he'd admit it or not.

"Fine." She got up from the table and opened the refrigerator. "How about a steak and baked potato for dinner? I'm getting hungry."

As quick as he'd turned icy, he was back to his former self. "That sounds great. I could eat a horse. I'll go outside and cut some wood so we can have a fire tonight. It gets cold up in these mountains when the sun goes down."

The sun was already dipping close to the horizon. Ava shooed him out of the kitchen. "Off with you. I'll call you when dinner is ready."

Logan laughed and headed out of the door leaving her to start dinner and contemplate everything that had happened. She feared their conversation with Helen Main would only uncover more trauma for Logan that he wouldn't be able to handle. So far he'd played it cool, but Ava knew it couldn't last.

He was a powder keg just waiting for the right spark.

Chapter Twenty-One

Logan patted his stomach and stretched out his legs. He and Ava had finished dinner and were lying in front of the fire. He knew he'd been a jerk earlier and had been trying to make it up to her. He simply wasn't ready to deal with the eight hundred pound elephant in the room. Eventually he wouldn't have any choice, of course. He was living on borrowed time.

"Was everything okay?" Ava looked worried, her brows pinched together.

Picking up her dainty feet, he started massaging the instep. He stripped off her socks to find her toes were painted a delicate shade of pink. Was everything about her sexy? She groaned as he found a particularly sensitive spot.

"Dinner was great. No complaints." The food had been cooked perfectly but he would have told her it was fabulous even if it tasted like paste. She'd stuck by him through all this shit and the least he could do was not be an asshole to her.

"Oh, that feels amazing." Her teeth sunk into her full bottom lip and her head fell back into the cushion. "So good." The last part came out as a groan of pleasure.

Chuckling to himself, Logan continued to work on the pliant flesh. Ava's lids fluttered closed in ecstasy as he dug into the pads of her foot. Suddenly her eyes snapped open and she jerked her leg back.

"Did I hurt you?" He didn't think he had but she'd pulled away from him like she'd been shocked with a cattle prod.

"You've had a bad day," she said. "A bad couple of days."

"Welcome to my life," he replied sardonically. "What does that have to do with your foot massage?"

"I'm supposed to rub your shoulders when you have a bad day." Ava sat up and began to move around him. He wasn't sure he heard her correctly.

"What? I don't understand."

"We have a deal. You have a bad day. I rub your shoulders. Why don't you take off your shirt?"

There was nothing he wanted more except for maybe taking his pants off too, but he was still numb with disbelief. Was she really stopping her own massage just to give him one? He'd never had anyone who gave a shit about his day that much.

He shook his head, trying to move her back into position. "Don't worry about it, good girl. I was giving you a foot rub. I know you liked it."

She gave him a look that said he was dumb as a stump. "Of course I liked it. Who wouldn't? But I promised to rub your shoulders so take off your shirt."

He didn't argue but instead pulled his T-shirt over his head and tossed it on the couch. Her hands were soft and warm as they stroked his skin, his body waking up instantly. His mind, however, wasn't letting go of conscious thought that easily.

She'd kept her promise.

The words tumbled through his head over and over. She'd been the first woman who hadn't wanted anything from him, and now she was the first woman who had put him first. He still couldn't quite believe it, but he wasn't going to question it now.

Her hands kneaded at the tight muscles and he let himself relax as his tension dissolved. It felt good. More than good, really. As good as his shoulder felt, his heart felt even better. She really cared about him. Honest to God.

A part of him wanted to tell her how he felt but the fearful part of him clapped his mouth shut tight. He didn't really know what he felt after all. Having never felt anything for a woman in his life, this could be a mirage or maybe temporary insanity. It didn't mean it was…you know…

Shit—he couldn't even think it, let alone say it.

He grabbed her hand and pulled her to her feet, paying no attention to her protests. He reached behind her and flicked on the radio.

"Dance with me, good girl."

Her smile lit up her whole face, and he twisted the dial until he found a station playing bouncy tunes from the 80s. After all these years, he still didn't know what Wang Chung meant but it was a good song to dance to. He and Ava twirled around the floor, giggling like teenagers. He dirty danced his woman until she was looking up at him with a seductive expression. His cock was hard and aching in his jeans and Ava's nipples were poking holes in his chest.

It was time to move this party into the bedroom. Logan Wright style.

He bent over and pressed his shoulder into her abdomen, lifting her into a fireman hold. She squealed and beat him on the back with her fists but she was laughing the entire time. Clearly she didn't truly want him to stop, but he smacked at her bottom a few times just in fun. She shrieked and wriggled in his arms but it was a half-hearted attempt to get away.

Tonight he'd be with the one woman who could make everything all better.

It simply wasn't fair for one man to be that incredibly sexy.

Logan was shucking off his jeans, boxers, and socks, and Ava sucked in her breath as his beautiful body was revealed. He looked like something that should be on display sculpted in marble. All hard muscle, his body radiated leashed power, and she reached out to trace his ridged abs with her greedy fingers.

Groaning at her exploration, Logan grinned and captured her hands before pinning them behind her back. She giggled at the restraint knowing he would never hurt her. In fact it was exciting to be helpless like this as his lips traveled up the sensitive column of her neck, over her jaw, and rubbing against the corner of her mouth.

His tongue snaked out and ran along her bottom lip and she mewled with frustration until he fused their mouths together. As always his kiss took her breath away and she strained to get closer to him, loving his clean masculine scent and the heat of his body.

"My good girl is frustrated." Logan chuckled and she could feel the reverberation in his chest. "What does she want?"

She twisted but his firm and gentle grip held her easily. She was at his mercy at the moment.

"I want you," she said breathlessly. "Now."

His lips played with hers but never allowed full contact. "So demanding. I think I need you to be more specific. Tell me exactly what you want."

Logan might be the only man in the universe she could do these things with but she wasn't sure she could just out and out ask for it. She shook her head and tried to hide her flushed cheeks.

"Uh uh uh, good girl." One hand released her wrists and lifted her chin so she had to look into the blue depths of his gaze while the other still restrained her hands behind her back. "If you say it, honey, you'll get whatever you want. I swear."

There was a world of promises in those eyes. Promises she desperately wanted to believe. Did she dare put words to fantasies she'd only dreamed about?

"I swear, good girl. Anything you want. It's all about you tonight. Trust me," he urged, his voice deep and compelling. She wanted to trust in him. Believe in him. She licked her dry lips and forced the words past her suddenly thick tongue.

"I want you to dominate me. I want you to be everything."

Logan's eyebrows shot up but then a grin slowly crossed his face. "I think I'd like that. I think I'd like to be everything to you." Logan let her go and stood up. "Strip, Ava."

"Have you ever—" She broke off, unsure how to ask the question but Logan seemed to understand.

"I've played some bedroom games before," he answered softly. "Tonight you don't want to think about the case or what we've discovered, am I right?"

She nodded with relief, glad he understood. She wanted both of them to think of nothing else but each other tonight. Tomorrow would come soon enough and they'd have to face everything.

"I want the same thing." His soft blue eyes locked with hers. "I want to lose myself in your body. I want to own you so you'll never look at another man ever again. Strip, Ava."

His voice was hypnotic and compelling, and she reached for the buttons on her blouse, popping them open one by one. He'd said he didn't want her to ever look at another man ever again.

Ever was a long time. She wasn't sure he was in it for that long, but she was. Logan was her man and she was his woman. Tonight for sure. Tomorrow hopefully. She wasn't going to leave until he told her he was done. She'd stick around and make him happy. Anything could happen. Maybe Logan might fall in love with her. Stranger things had happened.

Ava tossed her shirt aside and worked on her jeans, sliding them down her legs. She felt Logan's heated gaze on her body and her insides turned to liquid. He made her feel sexy and wanted in a way no one ever had. She quickly stripped her bra and panties and let him inspect her bare body, squirming slightly inside. As beautiful as he made her feel there was still that last remnant of the good girl she'd been making her uncomfortable.

Reaching out, he ran his fingers through her hair. "Mine. All of this is mine."

God, yes.

Cool air ran across her heated flesh and her nipples peaked as he ran a finger around one and then the other. "So pretty. All pink and tight for me. Play with your nipples, good girl. I want to watch you."

If she did that she sure couldn't be called a good girl anymore. She probably couldn't anyway as she'd admitted to enjoying the spanking he'd given her. Those weren't exactly the actions of a goody two-shoes.

"Now, Ava. Or you get punished for not obeying."

Her gaze flew to his stern features. He appeared to be completely serious although not angry or mean. Her thoughts went back and forth as to whether she wanted to obey or be punished. The last time had been pleasurable, and she wanted to feel it again.

"You'd spank me?"

She held her breath waiting for his answer. A corner of his mouth tipped up in amusement.

"Punishments will take a form of my choosing. It might be a spanking. It could be something else. Are you going to obey me?"

The possibilities of "something else" made her dizzy with anticipation. Cream was gathering between her legs and her breathing was growing shallow. Apparently she'd waited too long. Logan pushed her back onto the mattress and lifted her arms over her head. She felt something soft wrap around her wrists and she tugged on them but got nowhere. He'd tied her hands to the headboard. A moment of panic flew through her, accelerating her heart as she pulled at the restraints. Logan placed a calming hand on her abdomen.

"Calm down, good girl. If you want me to let you go, I will. But I think you'll like this punishment."

His tone was gentle and soothing and she stopped thrashing on the bed. He was completely calm and in control and she knew he'd untie her in a second if she wanted to be. She lifted her arms and craned her neck so she was looking back.

"How did you know the restraints were there?" she asked suspiciously. "Did you set this up in advance?"

Logan's rich laughter filled the quiet room. "I'd love to be that devious but sadly I'm not. Jared has a…thing for tying up his women. When you defied me, I thought you might like a taste of domination. If it's not your thing I can untie you."

He reached for the soft restraints but she shook her head. "No. Wait. This is a…punishment?"

She was already getting turned on from being tied up. It didn't feel much like discipline.

"It is. You'll see why if we continue."

"Your friend does this all the time?" She stalled for time by asking another question. A thought occurred to her. "How the heck did you know?"

Logan raised his hands in surrender. "I found the velvet ties last time I stayed here and gave him a rash of shit about it until he admitted it. He has to be in charge in bed or something like that."

Ava rolled her eyes. "Yeah, and you don't care either way. Admit it—you like to be in charge too."

"I don't need a woman to be tied up but I do like getting my way. I thought we'd covered that last time. Now what's it going to be? Tied up or not?"

He was looking at her expectantly and she knew what her answer was. She'd only been delaying the inevitable.

"Tied up," she conceded. "I hope I don't regret this."

"Trust me, good girl."

He's the only man in the world she would ever trust to do something like this. She'd had a boyfriend who had once suggested it and Ava had ended that relationship quickly. He'd come across as a guy who would tie her up and then do something that would be all about him. Logan would make sure she enjoyed this, punishment or not.

He insinuated himself between her legs and leaned over her torso. Letting his lips brush her quivering flesh here and there, he drove her slowly out of her mind with the teasing pleasure. His lips encircled an already hard nipple and she arched her back as he suckled it hard, his teeth giving her just the edge of pain.

She could feel his hard cock press into the softness of her belly so she lifted her hips and ground against him. He sucked in a breath and his dick throbbed against her.

"Witch. Naughty little witch," he murmured against her, letting his tongue slide to the delicate underside of her breast.

He repeated his ministrations on the other side while the cool air caressed her overheated skin. She tugged at the restraints and instantly understood what the punishment was now.

She needed to touch him.

His gorgeous body beckoned and she couldn't do anything about it. Her wrists were firmly attached to the headboard and she wasn't getting out until he let her.

"Logan…" she moaned in desperation.

"Easy, honey. It's all about you. I've got everything you need."

Truer words were never spoken. Before she could reply he kissed and nibbled his way down the curve of her stomach, pressing her thighs further apart. His hot breath caressed her already sensitive clit and her body tightened, poised and ready for what came next.

His tongue lashing at the swollen button, he explored every nook and cranny of her slit making her thrash her head back and forth, calling his name. Thick fingers slid inside her soaked pussy and she groaned as it sent off a trail of sparks through her body. She was on the edge of the cliff, ready to go over.

"So tight, baby. You feel so good." Logan's voice sounded like a shovel scraping a dirt road. She shivered as his tongue circled her clit, her entire being ready to fly.

When his mouth closed over it and he sucked and licked gently, she couldn't hold back the tide of pleasure he evoked. No one had warned her how an orgasm felt with someone she loved. It was all encompassing, owning every tiny particle of her.

Just as he had promised.

There wasn't a square inch of her that wasn't under his loving control. The only question was…

Was it love for him?

She didn't have time to ponder the thought. He'd rolled on a condom and thrust himself inside her sending another wave of delight straight to her toes. Now accustomed to his size and girth, her body welcomed his invasion, tightening on his cock until he groaned with pleasure.

They moved together as sinuously as they danced. It was as if a symphony was playing that only they could hear. The sounds of their ragged breathing and gasps of pleasure mingled with the silent music their bodies made.

A scream built up in Ava's throat as each stroke of his cock brought her closer to climax. His features were tense, the corded muscles of his neck tight. He nipped at her lips and whispered hot, naughty things in her ear. She was soaring in the sky when she could take no more, exploding one more time.

Wrapping her legs tighter around his waist, he thrust one more time, biting out a few choice expletives. Her cunt tightened around him and he threw his head back with a groan. Each wave of pleasure made the last seem tame in comparison until they finally ebbed, giving her some respite.

She watched in rapt attention as Logan came as well. Pain, pleasure, disbelief, and then contentment all crossed his features one at a time until he slumped on top of her. He was a delicious weight and he pulled away too soon. She tried to protest but he kissed her until her words died.

His fingers fumbled with the fastenings on the velvet ties but with a few tugs her hands were free. She clutched at his shoulders and brought him back down to her, wanting to prolong the closeness for as long as she could. He let her for a few minutes more but eventually pulled away, kissing her reluctantly.

"I've got to take care of a few things, good girl. I'll be right back."

She was instantly cold as he left the bed and she grabbed the covers, tugging them to her chin. When he returned they curled up together, neither speaking. What they'd experienced had been too strong for words.

She giggled as he nibbled on her chin, whispering sweet words in her ear. His cock was already hard again and it pressed insistently against the globes of her ass. Logan was insatiable.

She turned into his arms, enjoying the luxury of running her hands over the smooth, tanned skin.

"Again," she whispered huskily.

Ava couldn't get enough of this man. This man she loved.

Chapter Twenty-Two

Logan was having a wonderful dream. Fighting the morning sun penetrating his eyelids, he sank deeper into the pleasure of the warm mouth and tongue that were currently sucking and licking at his morning wood. If he woke up, it would surely be over, and he could lie here all day immersed in this heaven.

Warm fingers caressed his balls and his lids popped open, the heavy blanket of sleep lifting quickly. One glance told him this was no dream. Ava was giving him the wakeup call of his life. Already his balls were pulled tightly to his body in readiness to spill his seed deep into her throat.

Something she might not thank him for. In fact, it might get him kicked out of bed.

He ran his fingers through her silky curls, all in disarray around her pretty face. "That's enough, good girl. That's not where I want to come."

She came off his cock with a pop and ran her tongue slowly and deliberately from balls to tip. He had to swallow his groan of pleasure and steel the rising tide inside of him. He wanted more than a quick orgasm this morning.

"Are you sure?" she asked huskily. Her tongue tickled the sensitive underside of his dick and he sat up in the bed, pulling away from her talented tongue.

"I'm sure." The problem was he didn't sound too fucking sure. He sounded like he wanted a blowjob. Badly. He wasn't against the idea but he wanted to fuck her more. He didn't think he'd ever get enough of being inside her snug pussy.

Pushing aside thoughts of the future he snagged a condom from the bedside table and rolled it on. Ava's fingers tangled with his as she tried to help but all she really managed to do was ramp up his arousal until he ached.

"Naughty," he taunted, rolling her over on her stomach and giving her bottom a smack. "Such a bad girl."

If she'd done anything but giggle or wriggle her butt he would have stopped, but damned if she didn't do both plus look over her shoulder and stick out her tongue. A few more smacks and her bottom was a lovely shade of pink and her pussy was nice and wet. He slid his finger in between her legs and chuckled.

"It's a definite yes that you enjoy getting spanked."

She laughed and gave him a pretend pout. "How can going down on you be naughty?"

He pressed a finger inside of her, loving how her muscles immediately tightened on him, sucking him in. "I could have come in your mouth, honey. I doubt you would have enjoyed that."

He added another digit and she moaned her approval. "I don't care. I've never done that before. It would have been hot," she panted, rubbing herself against the sheets. He had other plans for her. He pulled her to her knees and pushed her thighs apart.

"You say that now, but the reality might not be what you think. Maybe we can try it sometime."

He entered her in one hard stroke and her head fell back, her lips parted in a small cry of pleasure.

"Yes," she groaned. "Sometime. Oh God, fuck me, Logan."

There was something about her generously curved figure and open appreciation of the pleasure they shared that got to him every time. Even now the view of her rosy bottom, her hourglass figure, and her full breasts hanging down had him fighting to hold onto some shred of control.

He reached around and plucked at the rosy tips already hard under his fingers and she swayed her ass in response, giving his cock a caress from her tight cunt. Holy fuck this felt so damn good. He pulled out and thrust back in, almost seeing stars, the sensations were so intense.

With every stroke she pressed back against him, their movements becoming more frenzied as the dam of pleasure built higher and higher. He slid his hand onto her clit and rubbed circles around the swollen nub.

Her body tensed and she screamed his name as her orgasm ripped through her. Her pussy clamped down on his cock and he gritted his teeth, unable to hold back his own climax. It seemed to tear its way from his lower back, through his balls, and out his dick. He was barely able to speak when it finally ended, and he kissed her delicate spine in a show of reverence.

Making love with Ava wasn't just sex. It was a transformative event. What he did with those feelings he didn't know. He wasn't fit for a long term thing. She'd grow tired of his baggage eventually, preferring a man who didn't have his issues.

But he could give her this – the gift of pleasure. He was positive no man ever had. It was something they shared, just the two of them.

He pulled from her body, both of them shuddering in sensitivity. He padded into the bathroom and returned to hear his phone going off. Rummaging in his pants pocket, the relaxation he'd felt only seconds earlier fled.

Helen Main.

He swiped his thumb across the screen and lifted it to his ear. Ava had sat up in bed and was looking at him with a questioning expression.

"Logan Wright. Is this Helen Main?"

"It is. Logan, is that really you?" The woman's voice was familiar and brought back a rush of memories good and bad. Why hadn't he foreseen that would happen? He wasn't sure he was prepared for it. He had to ignore all the emotions that were threatening his equilibrium.

"It is. I'm glad I was able to track you down, Helen. I need to talk to you."

There was a long silence before Helen answered. "I've missed you, Logan. I knew this day would come eventually. Hoped and dreaded it, all at the same time. When can I see you?"

Logan flicked a glance at Ava who was hanging on every word, at least of his side of the conversation. "We can be there in about an hour. Is that okay?"

"I'll be here. If you have my number, I assume you have the address," she replied. "I'll make breakfast."

"You don't have to—"

"Hush now. I always liked cooking for you, Logan." Images of Logan, his mother, and Helen in the kitchen crowded his brain making it hard to talk. "Get here as soon as you can."

Helen hung up and he stared at his phone. He hadn't fucking thought this through. He wasn't ready to hear why his mom abandoned him. It would be like reliving it all over again and once was fucking enough.

He tossed his phone down on the bedside table determined not to give in to the feelings of weakness. If he could live through it as a boy, he could take it as a grown man. He wouldn't let this control him.

"We need to shower and dress. Helen is waiting for us." Logan turned on his heel and headed into the bathroom. Ava had been looking at him with something akin to fear. She understood the stakes today almost as well as he did.

He wouldn't let her see him as anything else but strong. No matter what Helen Main had to say.

Helen Main's home was a lovely ranch style painted a soft cream with dark green shutters. Ava got out of the car and took a deep breath knowing the next few minutes were going to be some of the most difficult of Logan's life. So much was at stake here she almost second-guessed her decision to show him the redacted statement from the files. If she hadn't they wouldn't be here exposing him to more pain.

And she wanted to protect him.

That was what love was, she supposed. She'd rather feel pain worse than she could ever imagine than let Logan feel even a fraction. But there was no going back in time. They were here and she would stand by his side no matter what they heard today. He'd need her and she wouldn't let him down.

As they neared the front door it flew open and an older woman with pretty features and graying hair stepped out onto to the front porch. Small and delicate, her blue eyes had already begun to fill with tears and she held out her arms in welcome.

"Logan! Come here and give me a hug."

For a moment Logan seemed to hesitate but then he let the tiny woman enfold him in her arms. A few tears slid down her cheeks and she clung to him, her expression at once both joyous and sad. Logan cleared his throat a few times, obviously emotional at the reunion.

Helen finally stepped back and gave Ava her attention. "You've brought a friend." The woman extended her hand with a smile. "I'm Helen Main, dear. An old family friend."

"Ava Hayworth." Ava shook Helen's hand and the woman smiled in welcome.

Helen clasped her hands in delight. "It's so nice to meet a friend of Logan's." Helen waved them into the house. "Please come in. I've made some breakfast. I hope you're hungry."

They followed Helen, Logan giving Ava a wary glance. He was obviously as worried as she was about what they were going to hear this morning.

Helen's breakfast bar was stacked with large plates of bacon, scrambled eggs, and pancakes. Despite the tension in the air, Ava's stomach grumbled with hunger.

"Please have a seat and help yourselves. Juice? Coffee?"

Both Ava and Logan answered affirmatively to the offer of coffee and began filling their plates. Helen sat down with them at the bar and began pouring maple syrup over her pancakes.

"You always were a heartbreaker, Logan. Goodness, you had every female in Corville in love with you."

As far as Ava could tell, nothing had changed except that she was now added to those ranks.

"Not every one, Helen," Logan said dryly. "I'm sure there were more than a few who had no interest."

"Name two," Helen retorted. "You had to beat them off with a stick if I remember right."

The back of Logan's neck had turned a dull red. "Where are Katie and Todd?"

Helen laughed. "Grown. Katie's a schoolteacher and married with two children. Todd owns an extermination business and is divorced with a son. They weren't that much younger than you." She turned to Ava. "Katie and Todd are my children from my first marriage. They worshipped the ground Logan walked on. He was older and therefore idol-worthy."

"I remember," Logan said slowly, his gaze far away. "Katie always wanted to be a teacher."

"She did," Helen agreed. "I also have two more children from my second marriage. But they're grown as well. Two fine girls."

They ate in silence for a few minutes, no one wanting to rock the tenuous boat they were on. Helen stood up and went to the coffee pot, refilling their mugs. Her expression closed, her lips pressed together. The smiling woman who had met them at the door was suddenly filled with tension.

"Has Sheriff Jesse retired yet?"

Logan nodded. "He's passed on, actually. I'm sheriff of Corville now."

If Ava wasn't mistaken, Helen took a deep breath of relief. Her entire body language seemed to change back, becoming more relaxed.

"May God have mercy on his soul." Helen returned the pot to the warmer. "He was a hard man."

"Bill Bryson is dead also. Shot in the head a few weeks ago." Logan appeared to be watching Helen's reaction closely. She didn't disappoint. Clutching the counter, her face went white with shock.

"Bill is dead?" She sat carefully on the chair. "May God have mercy on his soul as well."

Logan put down his fork and pushed his plate away. The pleasantries were done. His jaw was tight and clearly he was a man on a mission. "I need to know the truth, Helen. I need to know what happened. I've learned some but it only created more questions. I hope you can answer them."

Helen nodded and wrapped her hands around her coffee cup. "I'll tell you what I know and what I think. Those are two separate things. I can't prove any of it. Not really."

"I might be able to," Logan replied. "Tell me about Bill and my mother. I know he's my father."

Helen's eyes shone with tears. "Your mother never wanted you to know, Logan. I don't know how many times Bill would show up at the apartment and try and convince your mother to tell you. I lost count. But she never would, and it only got worse as you grew up. Bill could see you were head and shoulders above his other sons. He blamed Margaret but it was him that raised them to simply be yes-men. He hated them in his way, and admired what you were becoming. He wanted it, coveted it, so he tried bullying your mother. She wasn't afraid of him and always sent him away. In the end it may have been a fatal mistake."

"Was that what was in your statement to the sheriff?" Ava asked. "Something about Bill?"

Helen's lip curled in distaste. "Frank Jesse was bought and paid for by Bill Bryson. Bill was the one that got him the job and then continued to keep him on the payroll. I made a statement the day your mother disappeared, Logan. Like any good friend would do. I always assume Frank burned it. It certainly didn't do any good. He declared your mother's disappearance a missing person's case." She shook her head. "She never in a million years would have left you willingly. Never. You were the light of her life. She loved you more than anything in the world. Never doubt that."

Logan's body next to hers had gone stiff. She could feel the emotional tension radiating from him and she placed her hand on his thigh trying to soothe him just a little. He was so focused on Helen Ava's gesture didn't even seem to register.

"She left me." Logan's voice was flat, daring this woman to argue with him.

"No." Helen shook her head. "I don't believe that and neither should you. She never would have left you voluntarily."

"Maybe you could tell us what your statement contained? It had been redacted so we couldn't tell what you'd said." Ava asked gently.

Helen took a sip of her coffee before beginning. "It was a Friday. Logan, Katie, and Todd were at school. Both Jackie and I worked at the local diner waiting tables. We had so much in common," Helen explained. "We were both divorced, single mothers living paycheck to paycheck. Jackie got me the job at the diner and it was a good one. I made good tips there and with my child support we did okay."

"Anyway, we both had worked the lunch shift but were back home before the kids got out of school. Bill Bryson came by that day. It wasn't the first time. The walls were thin and I could hear them arguing. Bill wanted to tell Logan and Jackie wouldn't hear of it. She considered Bill to be a mistake she'd made when she and John were having problems. But, she always considered John to be your real father. He'd been there for you when you were young."

"He left too," Logan replied bitterly. "I don't seem to inspire parental devotion."

Helen straightened in her chair, her eyes stormy. "I should smack your face for that, Logan Wright. Your mother couldn't have been more devoted to you. As for John, well, he fell in love with another woman. And yes, he left." Helen shook her finger at Logan. "But it had nothing to do with you. That was on Jackie. She had terrible taste in men. Just awful. Give her a room of ninety-nine good men and one bad apple, and she'd find the rotten one. She tried to raise you to be a better man than Bill was."

Logan scraped his fingers through his hair, an exasperated look on his face. "I'm sorry, but I feel like I've been in the dark most of my life. I think I have a reason to be angry about it."

"You do, but you can't let it ruin your life. You can't let Bill Bryson win," Helen urged.

"What else happened that day?" Ava asked, trying to move the conversation back to where it had started. Things could easily escalate if they weren't careful.

"The arguing was loud and it seemed to go on forever. I finally couldn't take it anymore and pounded on the door to see if Jackie was alright. She opened the door and Bill was there, his face red with anger. She assured me everything was okay and she would call me if she needed anything. That was the last time I saw her." Helen's voice caught. "It did get quiet. When you came home, Logan, she wasn't there so you checked at our apartment. Of course she wasn't with me. To this day I think Bill Bryson did something to her. Lured her away and hurt her in some way. I tried to tell Frank Jesse but he was only concerned with covering up for Bill."

The older woman's tone was filled with anger. She'd had seventeen years to think about what had happened that day and it was clear to see it still haunted her.

Logan swallowed and he seemed to sway with the shock of what he'd heard. She squeezed his thigh and he turned to look at her, his brilliant blue eyes dull with pain. There wasn't much she could say to take away the hurt there.

He turned back to Helen. "Why didn't you ever tell me?"

This time tears did spill over. "I wanted to but you were so young to bear that burden. Frank made it clear to me that if I pushed the issue he would make it his mission to ruin my life. He hinted I could lose my job, or worse, end up in jail on some trumped up charge. I would have lost my kids. I couldn't take that chance. Please try to understand," Helen pleaded. "I tried to care for you when Jackie disappeared. I did my best, and then you went into the Army. I knew you'd be safe there, away from Frank and Bill."

"Frank sent me there," Logan said, clearly shaken. His face was ashen and he practically vibrated with tension.

"Yes," Helen agreed. "He wanted you out of the way where you wouldn't ask questions. His promise of a deputy job was just to get you under his thumb."

Logan stood and walked over to the sliding glass doors that overlooked the backyard. "We think Bill Bryson killed Margaret Bryson, and that George killed Bill."

"I wish I could say I was surprised but the whole town suspected Bill abused Margaret. She would disappear for days and then when we would see her again, her makeup was applied with a heavy hand. She was terrified of Bill and would jump whenever he came into a room. I didn't know her well but she seemed like she was afraid of her own shadow. As for George, I doubt he'd have the backbone to kill anyone, honestly. He was weak and cowardly. His only mission in life was to follow Bill around like a puppy."

"Did George know about what Bill did?" Ava asked.

"I expect he did." Helen shrugged. "He was with Bill once when he visited Jackie."

"Were you ever going to tell me my mother didn't abandon me?" Ava could hear the tightly leashed fury in Logan's tone. His back was ramrod straight. Every line of body spoke of a man holding onto his control by a thread.

"I told you every day," Helen exclaimed. "All the time. I always told you that your mother never would have left you, Logan."

Logan whirled around his expression full of anguish. "Did he kill her, Helen? If he did, where is she? Where's my mother's body?"

Helen looked sick to her stomach. "I do, indeed, believe that Bill is the reason your mother disappeared. As for where she might be, I don't know. They did have a meeting place out by the lake. He may have taken her there. I just don't know."

It was surreal to hear them talking about the location of Jackie Wright's body. Logan's chest was rising and falling rapidly and Helen didn't look much better. She'd grabbed a tissue and was dabbing at her eyes. This journey into the past had been painful for all involved.

"We need to go." Logan paced the kitchen liked a caged lion. "I'll call you when I find something out."

Helen placed her hand on his arm, a pleading expression on her face. "I don't want to lose you this time. When I left town at Frank's urging, I lost track of you. I don't want that to happen again."

"It won't." Logan shook his head, his features softening. "I promise I'll keep in touch. I want to hear about everything that's happened in the last seventeen years."

"Me too," Helen agreed softly. "I can see you've grown into such a fine man. Jackie would be proud."

A spasm of pain crossed Logan's face. "I hope so. That's all I've ever wanted."

Ava felt her own throat close up with emotion. The veneer of cool calmness that Logan had cultivated for years had been stripped away leaving him raw and exposed. She wanted to heal the wounds that had been festering too long but didn't even know where to begin. How did you heal a heart and soul that had been battered and then abandoned?

Logan hugged Helen and moved toward the door. Ava quickly said her goodbyes and followed him to the truck. It had all come to a head and something had to give. Soon.

Chapter Twenty-Three

Logan simply hadn't been able to take it any longer. Not being able to stand the sympathetic expression on Ava's face, he'd headed out for a walk after he'd dropped her at the cabin. He wasn't fit company for anyone at the moment.

She'd tried to comfort him but he wasn't ready for a sympathetic hand on his forehead yet. He needed to move, to breathe. He needed space around him to be able to make sense of all the secrets and truths that had been laid before him these last several days.

He walked for a long time, pushing his body hard, the brisk mountain air clearing not only his lungs but his head. By the time he reached a ridge that overlooked an expansive valley, he was exhausted and sweaty. But he wasn't just tired from physical exertion, he was tired of being emotionally pummeled at every turn.

He wasn't a goddamn victim, had always railed against that. He hated the pussy whining of those that felt their childhood shaped their entire life. Now here he was faced with the decision to let the past define his future or reject the baggage that people had burdened him with. It simply wasn't in his nature to look backwards although he was being forced to at the moment. The present was what truly mattered.

Sitting down on a large rock, he let one overriding fact finally sink into his consciousness.

His mother hadn't left him.

He could go over and over the evil things Bill Bryson had done but the fact was Logan had seen worse in the Middle East. What had happened to Margaret Bryson and his mother was far more personal but bad people were what Logan dealt with for a living. He'd ceased to be shocked by acts of depraved violence years ago.

His mother hadn't left him.

The words were burned into his brain and the familiar but wieldy albatross of being unlovable, unwanted, slowly fell away. He'd been dragging it around for a long time and now that it was gone it felt strange not to carry its weight. He felt lighter but a part of his heart still beat for revenge. If Bill Bryson were still alive Logan would have taken great pleasure in arresting him. Seeing him prosecuted to the fullest extent of the law. Cold cases were notoriously hard to prove but Logan would see justice done for his mother. Somehow he would prove Bill Bryson had been responsible.

Bill Bryson had met a nasty and bloody end but he'd lived his life the same way. Once again Logan couldn't help but wonder how the vigilante chose his victims. How had he known when Logan himself had been ignorant of the facts? And why now?

More and more Logan was moving away from the theory that George had killed his brother. Unless something they didn't know about had been the catalyst, there seemed little motivation for George to do the deed. It also left little reason for anyone else. Unless one of his victims had risen from the grave, and Logan didn't believe in ghosts.

His mother hadn't left him.

He kept coming back to that. It was the one bright thing that had come from all this fucking mess. And it was a mess. A lot of people were going to be hurt before Logan was done here. He couldn't feel guilty about it. He'd carried the stigma of his mother's defection for too long to feel badly about others having some heartache when they had to face the truth about their loved ones. Bill Bryson hadn't been anyone to look up to and Logan would take great pleasure in making sure everyone in Corville and beyond knew that.

His mother hadn't left him.

She'd loved him, and hadn't he lost track of that all these years? She'd said it every day even when he'd grown too old for her hugs and kisses as he went off to school. She'd looked at him with love and adoration in her blue eyes that exactly matched his. He could recognize the emotion now that he'd seen the same in Ava's eyes.

Ava.

He couldn't deny the love he felt for her any longer. He'd wanted to believe she hadn't gotten to him, but here he was. Aching with love for a woman who didn't even live in Corville. He wanted to reach out for a future with her but he'd avoided thinking about building a life with someone for so long, he wasn't even sure how to begin. Always before he'd thought love would be snatched out of his greedy fingers. It would take courage to go after what he wanted.

Deep down he'd always felt there was something seriously wrong with him if his own mother left him. He'd believed this defect would keep a woman, the right woman, from staying with him. Eventually she'd see all his faults and leave. Everyone left, after all.

His father. His mother. Even Helen had left.

But there wasn't anything wrong with him. At least nothing fatal. He wasn't so much Bill Bryson's son as he was his mother's. She'd been the guiding hand in his childhood. Logan would hold onto her and reject the Bryson name and money. From the looks of things, it hadn't brought anyone happiness or peace.

Ava was right. There was nothing more pathetic than an aging playboy trying to hold onto the past. A past that wasn't even that good. It had been pleasurable but with each passing day it had made him emptier inside. Isn't that why he'd let Ava help him with this case? His heart and soul had been crying out for someone real. Ava was as real as it came.

He sat there for a long time working through the facts and innuendo. One thing shone clear. He wouldn't let his slim chance of happiness slip through his fingers. He could see the truth now for what is was. It was his job to accept it and move on. If he didn't it was his own damn fault.

Levering up from the rock, he headed straight back to the cabin. He had a lot to say to Ava if she was ready to hear it.

Ava had just about worn a hole in the kitchen linoleum pacing back and forth. She'd attempted to read a book and then had sat outside with a cup of coffee but Logan still wasn't back. She understood he needed time to process everything but as the sun started to set Ava's concern was growing. He wasn't the type to do anything desperate but his expression when he'd walked out of the house had scared her. Pale, his mouth in a grim line, he'd looked as if he'd never smile again. Her heart ached for this amazing man who had experienced so much pain in his life. It was no wonder he kept everyone at arm's length.

She poured herself another cup of coffee and leaned back against the kitchen counter. The fact was she didn't know which Logan would return to the cabin. Would it be the laidback, devil may care ladies' man or the softer, loving and open man she'd spent time with these last few weeks? She feared the former and could only hope for the latter.

The sound of his boots on the front porch made her heart accelerate in her chest. The moment of reckoning was upon her. Logan would either be on the way to putting the past behind him or he would be destroyed.

The door swung open and one look at his slumped shoulders and grave countenance made any hope she'd had dissolve. Even a strong man like Logan couldn't be expected to weather something like this. It was asking too much. She was always doing that, always hoping people could be something they really weren't. She wouldn't do that with him. Accepting who and what he was? It was the only gift she could give him now.

"Is there enough coffee for me?"

Ava nodded and hurried to fill a mug. He sounded normal enough but instead of coming to put his arms around her he simply sat heavily at the table. She slid the cup in front of him and he sipped at it, not speaking or looking at her. Finally when she didn't think she could stand the silence any longer, he spoke.

"I did a lot of thinking out there."

Her fingers tightened around the edge of the counter but she forced herself to let go and sit in the chair opposite him.

"Did you come to any conclusions?" Ava could hear the fear in her tone but she had no way to cover it up. All her defenses had been stripped away today.

Logan nodded, leaning forward on his elbows, the mug cupped between his hands. "I did, actually. When I went out there my mind was all confused. I couldn't think straight. But one thing was crystal clear." He looked her right in the eye. "My mother didn't leave me. She loved me. Somewhere during all these years I lost that fact. Looking back I don't see how I could have ever believed she didn't love me. She said it every day and with every action. Every decision she made was about me. I remember that now."

A tidal wave of relief shook Ava to the core. He'd seen some good in all this. He'd taken all that life had thrown at him and found the kernel of truth and happiness he could cling on to. "I'm glad, Logan." She smiled, trying to hold back her own tears. "You're easy to love."

A corner of his mouth tipped up. "I'm glad you think that, but I haven't always believed it. The fact is I'd forgotten so many things about my childhood and my mother. When we talked to Helen today it all came rushing back. And I knew one thing. I was loved."

A sob caught in her throat. "Of course she loved you."

"It's not a given, you know. In my line of work I've seen some parents do some awful things to their kids. But Mom wasn't one of them."

Wiping a tear away, Ava fought the urge to tell him how much she loved him. It wasn't the time or place to think about what she wanted. This was about Logan and he didn't need the added burden of her emotions along with all of his own.

"What happens now?" Terrified to ask the question, she still couldn't stop the words from leaving her mouth.

Logan took a deep breath and set his coffee on the table. "As I said, I made some decisions out there. The first is that I have no desire to be a Bryson. I'm my mother's son and I'm happy with that. So I plan to sell anything I've inherited from Bill Bryson back to Lyle, Wade, and Aaron. I want no part of it."

"I think that's a good plan." Ava had to swallow the lump of emotion threatening to close her throat.

"The second thing is that I'm going to sell the ranch that Frank left me. I don't want a daily reminder of what he did to this town or to me personally. An adjoining ranch once made an offer to buy it so I'll see if they're still interested."

Logan seemed to be divesting himself of his life in Corville one step at a time.

"And then?" Would he tell her he was leaving town? Starting all over?

"Then I start the search for my mother. I need the closure of giving her a proper burial, Ava. She's been disrespected enough." Suddenly Logan the lawman was back, his shoulders straight, his expression dark. "I want to settle the cases on Mom's and Margaret Bryson's deaths officially by re-opening them and including all the statements that were hidden. I can't prove it with forensics but I can close the files with an official conclusion that Bill Bryson was the murderer."

Ava reached across the table and tentatively placed her hand on Logan's. She needed the connection to him, wanted to draw the pain from his body and take it into her own.

"Sounds like you did a whole lot of thinking out there. What about the vigilante?" Ava's voice was still thick with tears.

Logan shook his head and stood, her hand falling away from his. "My gut is telling me that George didn't do it."

"Then who did? Someone who knew the Bryson family and wanted to avenge something they'd done?"

"I'm looking at every angle. Including the family. Jared should call soon with their credit card information."

"What if you don't find anything?"

"Then it's back to square one," he said crisply.

"Not really square one. We have motive now," she observed.

"Square two then. Bill, and maybe George, get added to a long list of murders where the motivation is clear but the opportunity is not."

"We'll have to go back to the beginning. See who had opportunity at the wedding and cross-check for opportunity for the other murders."

"I've had Drake working on that since we found out Bill was killed by the vigilante. He's been through more than half of the guest list."

Ava knew it would be tedious, time-consuming police work. The kind they didn't show on television.

"So do we head back to Corville tonight?" The sun was low on the horizon and it was a long drive.

Logan gave her a lopsided grin. "We aren't done with our talk yet, good girl. No, we'll head back in the morning."

"What else is there to talk about?" Ava asked tremulously.

"Us."

"Us?" She didn't know whether to run and hide or stay put exactly where she was.

"Us," he replied his face relaxing into a smile. "We need to talk about the future."

"Do we have a future?" she asked carefully. "I mean after this case is solved."

"I think we do. You love me, good girl. I recognize the look in your eyes. My mother had the same look. Minus the lust, of course."

She didn't like the way she felt exposed. It was like she was sitting butt-naked in front of him. And not in a good way.

She chewed on her lip. "So what if I do? It doesn't mean anything."

"It sure as shit means something," he said incredulously. "No one has ever loved me since Mom died."

"I'm sure someone has," she argued. "Christina loves you. There are probably dozens more."

"Christina loves what she thinks I am." Logan shook his head. "You love the real me. You even sing with me in the shower."

He'd promised to never bring up that day they'd sung "You're The One That I Want" under the steamy spray. She couldn't carry a tune in a bucket.

"I can't believe you brought that up," she said crossly. "You promised."

"You sing pretty good. I also promised I'd never fall in love and I broke that one. I guess I can't be trusted."

He was the most trustworthy person she'd ever met. Wait…what did he just say?

"Say that again," she demanded.

"I love you, good girl." His expression had gone all soft and gooey and there was tenderness in his eyes she wanted desperately to believe in. If he thought she could sing, he must be in love.

"When? How long?" She practically choked on the words.

"It wasn't a moment. It just kind of snuck up on me gradually. Under the radar, so to speak. I'm not sure I can make you happy, but I damn sure know no one else is going to get to try. Besides, I know you love me back. I can see it. I'm greedy for it. I can't tell you how much I want it."

"How long have you known I love you?" She was deliberately stalling and he seemed to recognize the fact. His lips twisted into a knowing look.

"I just realized it today when I remembered my mother. I guess I'd blocked the memories that didn't jive with my reality. I see everything so clearly now."

She placed her hands flat on the table as if to steady herself. "I won't ask you for any commitments. I won't tie you down with a lot of promises about the future. When you want to walk out the door I won't stop you or anything."

He walked over and pulled her out of the chair, tipping her chin up so she had to look at him.

"Stop offering me things I don't want. I'm in this for the long haul. I didn't think I was capable of it, but I know different now. I'm in love with you, good girl. The real forever kind. You've got me twisted into knots. I love your brains and your heart. I love your passion and your gentleness. I just love everything about you." He pressed his lips to hers lightly and her heart started to pound, as her head started to believe. "I know you like getting tied up. Is it so hard to believe I like being tied down?"

She slapped at his arm but a smile curved her lips. "Stop teasing. It's not nice." She sighed, blissful as she basked in his admiration and love. "Say it again. I don't think I'll ever get tired of hearing it."

"That's good because I intend to say it all the time. I love you. I've never said that to any woman before, Ava. I'm going to need to hear you say it every day. Will you do that for me?"

"How can you doubt how much I love you?" she asked, holding him extra tight. "But I'll say it at least twice a day if it will make you feel better."

"That should do it." Logan nodded in satisfaction. "There's no way any doubts could seep in if you do that."

A terrible thought occurred to her.

"What about our geographic situation? I live in Portland."

"I'm well aware. Don't put up barriers, honey. We'll figure it out, and we have a lifetime to do just that."

The certainty in his voice made her believe in miracles, and the love shining from his eyes pushed away her last doubts.

Logan Wright loved Ava Hayworth.

If anyone had told her at that fateful wedding reception that she would be planning a future with a rakish playboy she would have laughed until she cried. But something deep and profound had changed this man's mind about himself and she could only be grateful and happy.

"What happens now?" she asked, laying her head on his chest so she could hear his steadily beating heart. It made it all seem so real, so grounded.

Logan swung her up into his arms and headed straight for the bedroom. "Now we make love. Tomorrow we keep working on the case. I like working with you, good girl."

She had no objections to that turn of events. He dumped her onto the bed and began to pull off his clothes, revealing his drool-worthy body to her hungry gaze.

She didn't know what she'd done to deserve this man. Maybe she'd eaten all her vegetables or helped an old lady cross the street. Whatever it was, she thanked the heavens above and began tugging off her own clothes.

It was time to get down and dirty with the man she loved.

Chapter Twenty-Four

Logan had known Ava loved him but he hadn't expected it to feel quite this good. He'd been expecting there to be some trepidation or fear but if anything he felt free and unencumbered. The shackles of his past were gone and he wanted to put them firmly behind him. Looking back was a waste of time for the most part and he'd spent too much doing just that.

Lying on his back, he pulled her on top so she was straddling him. Her silky skin brushed his leaving a trail of heat wherever she touched him. He reached up and cupped her generous breasts with his hands, teasing the nipples with his thumbs. Her thighs tightened on him in response.

"You are a bad boy," she gasped when he pinched the taut peaks with his fingers. He chuckled at her predicament. She might be on top but he was in the driver's seat. His favorite place to be.

"Then how come you're getting the spanking?" he teased, giving her a quick smack on her round bottom. Her breath quickened and her eyes sparkled. He did it a few more times before tangling his fingers in her golden brown curls and pulling her down for a kiss.

He took his time, exploring the warm cavern of her mouth, not wanting to rush this moment. His cock ached to be inside her but it would have to wait. He lifted his head and pulled on a curl, watching it spring back into place. An image of a round faced toddler with those same curls and blue eyes flashed in front of him.

A thought like that should have sent him running for the nearest exit but he wasn't even tempted. Instead he folded that picture away in a file titled "Someday Soon", tucking it away for the right moment. Their love was too new to ask Ava to consider something so life changing. Already he was going to have to ask her to move to Corville. If she wasn't willing, he'd quit his job and move to Portland. But it would be nice if they could settle here. He loved the wide open spaces, plus Ava had her parents and sister. It wasn't a bad place to raise a family.

Her palms skated down his torso and she slid until she was perched on her knees between his legs. Dipping her head, she snaked her tongue around the head of his cock. A bolt of electricity shot from his balls to his toes dragging a groan from his lips. She gave him a saucy smile.

"Like that? I can do it again."

"Again," he growled. "Don't think you're in control just because you're on top."

She caressed his balls sending shocks of pleasure through his body. "I think I have your undivided attention."

Scrunching the sheets up in his fists, his breath hissed out as she engulfed the head of his cock with her mouth. She flitted her tongue on the underside as her head bobbed and he had to grit his teeth together to keep from cursing.

"Where did you learn to suck cock like that?" he asked, barely able to breathe.

She giggled and her cheeks turned a pretty pink. "From my friend Kaylee's books. She writes erotic romance and we critique each other's work." She fluttered her eyelashes. "I aim to please."

He reached down and hauled her up his body by her arms. He couldn't take any more torture.

"You please very well but I don't want to come yet."

Ava leaned over and grabbed a condom from the nightstand. "I know exactly what you want."

Logan sat up – this was going too fast. "Easy, honey. I'm not ready to saddle up and ride."

"I've never tried riding a bucking bronco." Ava kissed his chin and let her tongue trace his bottom lip. "Will you throw me off?"

He wouldn't hurt her for the world but a hard and fast ride wasn't how two people should seal their love.

"We should do this soft and slow. No broncos."

Ava ran her hands up and around his neck. "Why? I love it no matter how you give it to me."

"Dammit, Ava, I'm trying to be romantic," he huffed. This woman was going to be the death of him.

"You are romantic," she assured him, leaning forward to whisper in his ear. "Now fuck me like you mean it. I'm ready for you, bad boy."

There hadn't been nearly enough foreplay but it was impossible to deny her when she was in this mood. He plucked the condom package from her fingers and tore it open with his teeth. He had to stifle a moan when her fingers joined his to help roll it on.

Clutching her hips, he positioned her on top of him. If she wanted to ride a bronco, he'd damn well give her what she wanted.

"Do it," she said huskily.

He entered her in one mighty stroke. The sensation of being balls deep in her hot tight pussy almost sent him over the edge immediately. He gritted his teeth and dug his heels into the mattress as they started out at a canter. Her hips were grinding against him, undulating in a rhythm designed to drive them both out of their minds.

The movements sped up, their breathing becoming increasingly ragged. A fine sheet of sweat covered their bodies and the air was perfumed with the musk of their arousal. Only the sounds of their gasps and moans could be heard.

He tried to hold on as long as he could but the pleasure was too great. He reached between them and ran his thumb over her swollen clit. She screamed his name and threw her head back. Her body arched, thrusting her breasts out as she leaned back and braced herself on his thighs.

His own orgasm was wrenched from his soul, shattering him into a million pieces. Making love with Ava was more. More beautiful. More pleasurable. More satisfying. Everything that had come before had simply been a rehearsal for the real thing.

She collapsed on his chest and he wrapped his arms around her, stroking her back, while their hearts still raced out of control. Eventually he pulled away, missing her warmth immediately. He tucked her under the covers so she would stay comfortable.

"I'll be right back."

He quickly took care of things and headed back into the bedroom. Ava was a lump under the covers, the blankets pulled up to her chin.

"Room for me?" He yanked at the comforter and she giggled, scooting over. He curled his body around hers and nuzzled her neck.

"I love you, good girl."

"I love you, bad boy."

"Are you going to make me dinner?" He loved to tease her.

"Since I've promised to make breakfast, I think you should make dinner."

She'd kept that promise since the day she made it. He really should let her off the hook.

"You don't always have to make breakfast. I'll make breakfast sometimes too."

"I'm not going to argue." Ava yawned. "How about we take a nap and then we both make dinner?"

He nodded and let himself relax for the first time in a long time. There was much to be done but it felt good having made some decisions about his life. The most important decision was lying right next to him.

Logan's voice pulled Ava from a deep sleep. They'd gone to bed late last night after a good meal and a deep conversation about the case. They'd vowed to go back to the beginning and go through the guest list for anyone who might have had an opportunity to know about the Bryson family sins.

She rubbed her eyes and tried to focus on what Logan was saying. He was sitting upright on the bed with his cell to his ear, a serious expression on his face.

"Thanks, Jared. I appreciate all the work you did. I know I dumped a lot on you."

Logan hung up the phone and tossed it on the mattress. She waited for him to speak but whatever Jared had said had him lost in his own world.

"Did Jared find anything?"

Logan nodded, rubbing his chin. "He found a gas purchase just a few blocks from one of the vigilante murders in Reed's town. It was in the window of the possible time of death. He also found a restaurant receipt for lunch the day of one of the murders in Griffin's town. It's hours before the actual time of death but it could still be significant." He leaned back on the headboard, his hand covering his eyes. "He decided to look further and found two of the three brothers have a .38 registered to them. That's the same caliber that the vigilante uses."

Realizing the seriousness of what Logan was saying, Ava took a deep breath. "All three of them? Then which one is it?"

Her heart beat fast in her chest and a strong sense of foreboding took over. She couldn't see Logan's face but she knew it wasn't good.

"Christ, all three of them might be working together. Wade and Aaron have the credit receipts and Wade and Lyle both have guns registered." Logan's voice was hushed as if saying it out loud somehow made it truer.

Ava's heart plummeted to her stomach. She hadn't realized how much she'd been hoping Logan's friend wouldn't find anything on the Bryson brothers.

"They must have known about their father. Wade saw him kill his mother, after all. All of them would have had opportunity at the wedding," Ava reasoned. "Can they shoot a gun?"

Logan pulled his hand away from his eyes. "Yes. Their dad taught them. I remember when Wade got his first rifle. I got one too from my dad that year for Christmas."

She rubbed his thigh through the sheet. "I'm sorry, Logan."

His eyes were bleak, his mouth a grim line. "So am I. Although we don't know for sure. This will give us enough for search warrants. I want that gun for a ballistics match."

Logan was holding out hope still and she prayed he was right. There wasn't much left to say. They showered and dressed, eating a quick breakfast before packing the truck and getting on the road. They deliberately kept to neutral topics, talking about when they would visit Helen again and what kind of house Logan should buy when he sold the current one.

By the time they arrived back in Corville, Ava's nerves were stretched thin. She wanted to scream in frustration. When she was this close to the end of a book she got the same way. She would write day and night, eschewing eating and sleeping until she wrote *The End*.

There was no such option this time. The wheels of justice grind slowly and Logan would need to get a warrant before anything else could happen. There wasn't anything she could do to speed this process up in the least.

Her phone buzzed in her purse and she pulled it out with a sigh. "Hi Mom. What's up?"

"I've been trying your phone for the last few hours, sweetheart. Are you okay?"

"I'm fine. We must have been in some dead spots on the drive back, that's all."

It felt strange to be talking about such mundane matters as cell phone coverage when a huge issue hung over their heads like this.

"I called to tell you that George Bryson's funeral is tomorrow morning at ten with a get together at the estate afterward. You'll be there in support of your sister, won't you?"

"Of course I will. Do you want me to pick you up for the funeral?"

"We'll meet you there. Your father is taking the morning off of work. But you can give me a ride home afterward so he can go back to the office."

"No problem. Listen Mom, we just got back into town and haven't even unloaded the car. I really need to go."

Ava wasn't sure she could keep up the facade any longer. She wanted to blurt out to her mother that things were going to go from bad to worse.

"I'll let you go then. See you tomorrow morning. Love you."

Her mother rung off and Ava dropped her phone back in her purse.

"George's funeral is tomorrow morning with a get together at the estate afterward."

She wasn't sure Logan would want to even go under the circumstances. It would be difficult enough not to show any of her thoughts and suspicions.

"That's perfect. I'll execute the search warrants while everyone is at the funeral. It will be easier and quicker if no one is at home."

"Can you do that?" she asked.

"It's actually preferable because it's safer for the officers. We just leave a copy of the warrant on the table."

Ava twisted her purse strap. "Do you want me to not go to the funeral? I can call my mom back."

"No, I need you to go," Logan answered. "I don't want to tip anyone off as to what is going to happen. I'll meet you at the estate after we've finished to pay my respects. It will be as good a time as any to tell them I'm selling out my share."

Ava wasn't sure if it would make the brothers happy or upset. At this point, it probably didn't matter one way or the other.

"I'll go. But I'll be worried the entire time."

Logan smiled and pulled her in for a kiss. "I'd be disappointed if you weren't. Now let me get the car unpacked. I have to head into town and see the judge. Relax and work on that new book, honey. I'll be home in a couple of hours."

Ava tried to write after he left but she couldn't concentrate. The evidence kept swirling around in her brain making her forehead pound. She finally gave up and took two aspirin with a big glass of water.

She walked out into the backyard and climbed up into Logan's treehouse. Feeling the need for quiet and serenity, it seemed like the best place. She could hear the singing of birds and the rustle of leaves in the wind but nothing else. Sitting back on to the bed, she tried to imagine how things would be if all or any of the brothers were guilty.

The Bryson family, including her sister, would be torn apart. Ava would have to come to terms with her own culpability in destroying this once prominent family. If she'd been less intrigued by the mystery and Logan less of a lawman, things might have gone very differently.

Her mother's words came back to haunt her. "If wishes were horses…"

Wishing wasn't going to make this go away. The truth was going to come out eventually. They'd set in motion a series of events that was now out of their control. The case had taken on a life of its own.

This morning she'd been enfolded in the warmth of love with Logan. Mere hours later they were facing the cold hard facts about someone they'd known their entire lives.

Life could turn on a dime.

Chapter Twenty-Five

Ava shifted in her seat as the eulogy droned on and on. Carl O'Halloran, president of the Rotary Club, was standing at the podium extolling the virtues of George Bryson. If Carl was to be believed, George had lived his life in a perpetual state of sainthood. She was sure George had done good works but this was ridiculous.

Carol Hayworth leaned close to Ava's ear. "When will Logan get here?"

"Later," Ava whispered back. She'd already answered the same question earlier for her father who was sitting on her other side. Mary was in the front row with Lyle. "He had to work. He'll try and meet us at the estate if he can get away."

Ava's answer seemed to appease her mother at least for the time being. Her dad had been awfully concerned about Logan's whereabouts this morning as if he was daring her to admit that she'd been dumped. She'd told him Logan had to work and left it at that, not in the mood to entertain her father's issues. Bruce Hayworth still couldn't look Ava in the eye as if having sex outside of marriage embarrassed him in some way. He studiously avoided her gaze as if it might turn him into a pillar of salt.

From Ava's spot about three rows back, she could see Wade sitting next to his wife and three children with Lyle and Mary on his other side, and Aaron with his wife and children next to Mary. All three of the brothers looked ghastly with gray skin and trembling lips. With their hunched shoulders they didn't look much like serial killers. But then Ava had never actually met one in the flesh. She'd read about several in her research and they could run the gamut from antisocial misfits to charming sociopaths. Where the brothers fell on the spectrum she didn't know.

The eulogy came to an end and row by row they stood and filed out of the chapel. Ava followed her parents to the exit, breathing in the fresh air. The chapel had been stiflingly hot and crowded. The entire town had come out to bid farewell to another Bryson family member. She quickly scanned the parking lot looking for any sign of Logan.

He'd kissed her goodbye this morning, the search warrant he'd procured last night in hand. There had been a purpose in his step as he'd left the house. He wanted to know the truth. They both did. If any of the Bryson sons was indeed the vigilante, it was time to put a stop to the killing.

Ava's father fished his car keys from his pocket. "I need to get back to work. You'll take your mother home, Ava?"

"Of course, Dad."

He nodded curtly and headed towards his car. She shook her head in frustration. "Is he ever going to get over it?"

Carol Hayworth put her arm around Ava as they walked toward her vehicle. "He's old-fashioned, that's all. He'll get used to it eventually, I suppose. Is there any chance you and Logan will get married? One grandchild and he'll forget all about this, dear."

"Stop," Ava groaned. "It's too soon to be talking marriage. Or babies. It's a pretty big deal that we've made a commitment.

I've never been someone who absolutely needed to get married anyway."

"Are you going to move here? It doesn't make sense for you to live in Portland when Logan is here."

Ava had been coming to this conclusion herself. Logan's job was here. She could work anywhere. As much as she liked Portland, Corville was truly home. She didn't want a long-distance relationship.

"I'm thinking about it," Ava hedged, catching sight of Wade helping his wife into the limousine. Everyone was going to the graveside. "My life is easier to relocate."

Ava's mother followed her daughter's gaze. "The family seems to be holding up well for having a second tragedy so close to the first. Have you and Logan made any headway in finding out who did this? It must be hard on the boys not knowing."

It was hard on everyone, especially Logan. Knowing he might have to arrest his childhood friends for multiple murders had kept him tossing and turning all night. Eventually they'd both got up and sat out on the porch watching the sunrise.

"We've made some progress but there are still some unanswered questions."

She should be a politician. Her mother smiled and pulled open the car door, seemingly satisfied with the vague non-answer.

Ava got into the car and started the engine, fighting the urge to text Logan and find out what was going on. He was busy and she'd know soon enough. It wouldn't be long now.

The smiling housekeeper opened the front door to Wade's house. Logan had sent his other deputies to Lyle and Aaron's homes but he wanted to search this one himself. Wade had the strongest motive for killing his father since he had been an actual witness to his mother's murder.

"Sheriff Wright, what can I do for you?"

"We're here to execute a search warrant, ma'am. Please step outside."

The housekeeper gasped and her face went pale. "I—I need to call Mr. Bryson," she stammered.

Logan had assumed she would. It wouldn't matter either way. There was nothing Wade could do to stop him.

"Do what you need to do but we have a warrant. You'll need to step aside. Alex, please keep her company."

Stepping into the foyer, Logan slapped the search warrant on the round table directly in front of the door and slid a vase of flowers onto the corner to anchor it.

"Everything by the book. Take your time and do it right," Logan stated to his deputies. "Drake, help me with the office. Tony, take the closets. I want that gun."

Drake followed Logan into Wade's large home office overlooking the backyard. Logan pointed to the dark oak cabinets on one side of the room for Drake to look through. Heading straight to the matching desk, Logan began pulling open the drawers shuffling through files, pens, and miscellaneous office supplies. Searches were never fun and this one was at the bottom of his list.

"He's organized, I'll give him that," Drake observed. "He's made good use of a label maker."

"See if there's a shelf marked 'Gun for illicit activities'." It wasn't funny but there was something about the situation that invited gallows humor.

He'd hardly slept a wink last night, keeping poor Ava awake as well. The thought of one or more of his childhood friends being a cold-blooded serial killer hadn't sat well with him. The fact that this friend had systematically hunted right under Logan's nose made him even less happy.

Of course there was always the chance that they were all innocent.

Logan didn't believe in coincidence. He'd always relied on his gut as a cop. It hadn't let him down yet here at home or in the Middle East as a soldier. Although Aaron had been in Griffin's town the day of a murder, it was only one piece of evidence. Logan's gut was currently telling him that Wade's purchase of gas in another town at the time of a vigilante murder was more important. It was compelling enough to get Logan to personally search Wade's home on the day of his uncle's funeral. If Logan was wrong, he would owe Wade a huge apology. If he was right…

It might not be a bad idea to move to Portland with Ava. If Wade, or any of the brothers, were indeed the vigilante, Logan would be blamed for bringing them down. It wouldn't make him popular with the Bryson family nor their friends. Small towns could be funny that way. A scandal like this could rock the very roots of Corville, changing it forever. People didn't like change, so they might not like him by extension.

"Got something." Drake reached deep into the cabinet and pulled out a handgun. "It's a .22. Not what we were looking for."

"Get it bagged anyway. As soon as we're done here, I want you to take it to the state ballistics lab. I need to know if it's a match to any other cases that may be unsolved."

Logan had already received the call this morning that the two bullets pulled from George Bryson's chest matched all the other murders. If Wade was the killer, he'd shot his father and his uncle. Who was next? Lyle, Aaron, himself? Or maybe some other accused criminal? Logan needed to put an end to this once and for all.

Finishing the drawers on the left side of the desk, he pulled open the middle drawer. Sitting down at the desk chair, Logan opened the drawer as far as possible. A couple of pens, a pencil, a ruler, and a pair of scissors were at the front. Nothing.

Logan's phone vibrated in his pocket. Pulling it out, he scowled at the screen.

"Logan. What's up, Dave?"

Deputy Dave Hoskins was currently leading the team searching Lyle Bryson's home.

"We found a .38 in a drawer. Looks recently fired."

Logan rubbed his temples, his frustration growing. Every time he thought he had something figured out, this case would take a twist. Yet he couldn't help feeling a moment of relief that Wade might be innocent.

"Bag it and get it ready to take to the state lab. Then give it to Drake when we get back to the office."

"Got it, boss."

Dave hung up and Logan tried to get his mind back on the search. He couldn't let the discovery of a gun distract him from what he'd come to do. It might not even be the actual murder weapon.

It was time to finally put the vigilante behind bars, but he would need the ballistics before he could make the final determination. One thing he knew for sure, he couldn't face any of the Brysons today at a social gathering. The next time he saw one of them, it would be with an arrest warrant.

Logan pulled his cell from his pocket and sent a text to Ava.

New evidence. I'll tell you about it later. Not going to the funeral.

◇ ◇ ◇ ◇

Wade fucking hated funerals.

A bunch of people he hadn't seen or talked to in years, gathering together to create some grand illusion about someone who was now worm food. The parasitic assholes would suck down the free food and booze before heading out, not to be seen again until the next poor bastard kicked the bucket.

He felt a hand on his shoulder. "It's a good turnout, isn't it?"

His little brother Lyle was standing there, his eyes bloodshot as if he'd been crying.

"It is. George was loved." Lyle nodded in agreement, either not hearing or not understanding Wade's irony. Uncle George was a slime who had sucked at the tit of the Bryson wealth for years. Wade's father had been systematically paying George every year to keep his mouth shut. It was the only thing George had ever done well in his entire life. He'd kept secrets and protected Bill Bryson.

"You should check on Mary. All this has been hard on her." Wade nodded to where Lyle's wife was holding court with the other 'ladies who lunch.' Mary Hayworth Bryson hadn't done a decent day's work in her life. She was perfect for this family.

"You're right, it has. I'm going to make this up to her when this is all over." Lyle made a beeline for his wife and Wade went back to studying the mass of people who had taken over the living room of the estate house. Standing near the long dining room table, he could easily see out into the living room and also into the backyard.

It looked like everyone in town had shown up for the funeral and now the after party. Everyone except Logan. Wade had kept a watchful eye out for him but he was nowhere to be seen. Perhaps Logan had decided he didn't want to be a Bryson.

Anger churned in Wade's gut. Logan didn't understand the lengths Wade had gone to making sure the Bryson family tree was purged of its evil. Bill Bryson had been a son of a bitch, beating his wife, cheating on her, and then finally pushing her off that balcony. He deserved to rot in the fiery depths of hell for all eternity.

It had been a surprise when Logan had questioned Wade about his mother's death. His memories had been hazy about that day for so long, but had come into sharp relief the night of Lyle's wedding. Overhearing his father talk to his uncle about being Logan's father had shaken Wade to the core. He could have handled his father's actions toward him, but what Bill Bryson had done to Logan had been unforgivable. Wade had been left with only one option. His father had to die for his crimes.

Out of the corner of Wade's eye he saw Ava Hayworth chatting with his brother Aaron. A passably attractive brunette, she'd caught Logan's fancy. Everyone in town knew she was helping him try and find the killer. If she was sleeping with Logan, she probably knew about the family dirt. Luckily Aaron and Lyle were also ignorant of the true extent of Bill Bryson's crimes. Wade had done what he could to shelter them. He'd always tried to protect his younger siblings from the ugly side of life.

He took another swallow of bourbon, enjoying the heat as it traveled down his throat and into his stomach. Savoring a fine whiskey was something Uncle George had never mastered. He'd been a sloppy drunk who chased women and lacked self-control. He wouldn't be missed. He'd brought nothing but shame to the family.

Wade's pocket chimed and he ducked into a hallway and pulled out his cell hoping it was Logan with a good excuse as to why he wasn't here with the rest of the family.

"Wade Bryson."

"Oh, Mr. Bryson!" The shaken voice of his housekeeper came through the phone. "The sheriff is here and they're searching the house! I didn't want them to but they had a warrant. Please don't be mad."

Stone cold anger fisted in Wade's chest at the intrusion. There was nothing to find, he'd made sure of that. But this meant Logan was closing in. If Wade were caught it would be all over. Killers, wife beaters, and pedophiles would be free to roam the streets, raping and murdering again and again. He couldn't let that happen.

He gulped down the last of the whiskey and muttered some platitudes to Alice before striding over to where Ava was talking to Aaron. "Ava, do you know where Logan is? We expected him to be here."

Something flickered in her eyes before she could hide it. She knew exactly where Logan was and what he was doing.

"He's working, I'm afraid. He's hoping to be here soon though."

Lying bitch.

"That's too bad," Wade replied smoothly. "He's so dedicated to his job. We're lucky to have him as our sheriff."

Aaron nodded in agreement. "He's the best sheriff this town has ever had."

"Wade! Aaron!" Lyle and Mary were hurrying toward them, their expressions stormy. Lyle was holding his cell in his hand. "Our neighbors just called. The police are at the house with a search warrant. Paul went over to ask them what they were doing and he saw it. Logan has deputies searching my house. He saw them carry out my gun in a plastic bag," Lyle squeaked.

The words tumbled out of Lyle's mouth in a rush. His face had gone completely white and Wade had to put a hand on his brother's shoulder to hold him steady.

A black cloud of rage clouded Wade's vision. It was one thing for Logan to come after him, but his baby brother? Lyle was completely innocent, as was Aaron. Wade knew what he needed to do.

Turning to Ava he asked, "I assume you knew what Logan was doing today?"

Color flooded her features but she lifted her chin in defiance. "Logan doesn't tell me everything."

"I doubt that." He needed to make sure Ava stayed right where she was. He didn't need her gumming up his plan. "Mary, it would appear your sister knew your home was going to be searched today. So much for family loyalty."

Wade had seen Mary's venom on one other occasion and this time was more of the same. Her face was purple with anger, her features twisted into something ugly. Her finger was wagging in front of Ava's face almost jabbing her in the chest. Ava would be busy with Mary for quite awhile.

With everyone's attention on the two women, Wade ducked into the hallway. The persecution of his family stopped today. He wouldn't be swayed from his path of justice. It was Logan's turn to die.

Logan climbed out of his truck and headed up the porch steps. It felt like the weight of the world was on his fucking shoulders. It would be a damn miracle, but he could only hope he had ballistics by tomorrow morning. If it was a match, Logan wouldn't hesitate to arrest Lyle and bring all this shit to an end. If it didn't…then they were back to the goddamn drawing board. They hadn't found anything that would help them in Wade's or Aaron's homes.

Logan flipped open the mailbox and sifted through the envelopes as he unlocked his front door. Typical crap. Advertisements. A power bill. Logan grinned as he read a postcard telling him he'd already won a cruise for two. Sure. And he was George Clooney.

Tossing his keys onto the counter, he called for Ava. "Hey good girl! Are you home yet? Guess what we won?"

Without warning, what felt like a cannon ball hit the back of his skull, jarring his teeth and blurring his vision. Logan grunted as pain radiated through his head and down his spine. He reached instinctively for his gun but his arms felt heavy and uncoordinated. The room swimming before his eyes, his knees gave out, jarring every bone in his body as he slammed into the ground.

Black spots appeared before his eyes, and his last thought was that he prayed Ava wasn't in the house.

Chapter Twenty-Six

Logan tried to lift his eyelids, a huge hammer pounding inside his head. He blinked several times, his vision slowly clearing. Awareness returned and the memory of being ambushed in his own house became sharp. He was sitting in a kitchen chair with his wrists cuffed behind his back. Wade was standing in front of the white board studying its contents.

Son of a fucking bitch.

Logan looked around but Ava was nowhere in sight. Thank God.

"Looking for your girlfriend, brother?" Wade turned around, a mocking smile on his face. "She's very busy calming down her harridan sister who is more than a little upset that you had her home searched."

Wade's expression hardened. "Stay away from Lyle and Aaron. They have nothing to do with this. This is my calling. My legacy."

Logan inwardly shook his head at the clusterfuck this entire situation had become. What a fucking waste of a life. Wade had a family, for God's sake. Had he never given them even a thought? He'd watch his kids grow up on the other side of a glass partition, and that was a best case scenario. As a multiple murderer, Wade could be eligible for the death penalty.

Logan pulled at the handcuffs that encircled his wrists, his brain trying to make sense of everything. Wade had been a good friend. They'd grown apart in the last several years but people did that. With a wife and three kids, Wade hadn't had much free time to hang out, drink, and watch sports.

I never really knew him.

Wade had managed to perpetrate these crimes, and Logan hadn't, until recently, suspected his friend of being capable of such heinous actions. Did that make him stupid or simply loyal?

That was what was truly bothering him. It wasn't that someone he knew was a killer. He'd put people he knew behind bars before. It was that he hadn't known it was Wade. He'd been fooled. Blinded by a friendship that had been steadily fading over the years.

If Logan were honest, he and Wade had grown apart a long time ago. Hadn't it been a surprise to be invited to be in Lyle's wedding? All this was about Logan's pride.

Behind his back, Logan began twisting the chain that attached the two bracelets. If Wade had restrained Logan with his own handcuffs, and he hoped that was the case, getting out of them shouldn't be too difficult. They'd taught him how in the military years ago after all. Brand new cuffs were more difficult, but Logan's had been used over and over. An expensive pair, the metal was harder and more brittle than the cheaper models and would, if locked together just right, break into two pieces.

Logan didn't care if the chain snapped or the weld at the bracelet gave way, he just wanted free. The only thing he needed was enough time to lock up the links before Wade noticed what he was trying to do.

✧ ✧ ✧

Logan knew the truth now.

But he didn't know why. Not truly. Wade wanted to make Logan understand before he killed him. Everything Wade had done had been for good. For justice. Wade had been fighting the age old battle of good versus evil. And he was winning.

Logan swallowed hard, obviously aware he'd been beaten by a better man.

"I didn't want it to be you."

Wade hated to see the disillusionment in his friend's eyes but it couldn't be helped. There would always be innocent casualties in a war.

"You know now."

"Did you do this alone?"

"Lyle and Aaron are innocent. You searched their homes like they were common criminals. That was wrong."

"They didn't know what you were doing?"

Wade laughed and sat down in a chair opposite Logan. "Hardly. They would never approve. But they didn't see the things I saw. That's why I have to do this. You'll try and stop me. This has to be done, Logan. I'm doing what the justice system can't. I'm making things right."

A muscle ticked in Logan's jaw and Wade instantly went on alert. His friend was in cop mode. The blood they shared was inconsequential. "Let's talk about it then. I want to hear your side of the story."

Wade loved Logan like a brother but he was a damn liar. He didn't want to talk about it. He wanted to stop Wade's righteous crusade. He felt a trickle of perspiration run down his back but inside he felt no fear.

"You don't want to hear shit," Wade growled. "You don't understand. Dad and George deserved to die. So did all those other people. I did it to help you. I did it for you, Logan."

Logan's eyes had gone dead and cold. Whatever they'd shared years ago was dead and buried. It would make this easier. Much easier.

"No, Wade. You did it for yourself."

"I did it for you," Wade insisted. "I got criminals the justice system couldn't hold onto. I made things right."

Logan's gut churned with disgust as he listened to Wade's excuses.

"Is that why you killed your father?" Logan asked. Wade's face turned a reddish-purple at the question.

"Our father. Bill Bryson was evil personified. He beat and killed my mother and the justice system did nothing. He lied, cheated, and stole from his competitors. Still nothing was done. The night of the wedding I heard him talking to George about you. He wanted to tell you he was your father. I hadn't known that. He'd wanted to for a long time but felt guilty because he'd killed your mother by accident." Logan's heart plummeted to his stomach. Bill Bryson had indeed murdered Jackie Wright. "He got away with everything his entire life. I couldn't let it go on. So I got justice, Logan. For you. For me. For all of us. He needed to answer for his crimes."

"In a court of law," Logan replied, his voice cold. "Everyone, even Bill, deserves their day in court."

"Courts were useless for him. He would have bought off the judge or the jury. He never would have seen the inside of a jail cell. There are two systems of justice, Logan. One for the poor and one for the rich. Denying it makes you look foolish."

"Is that what you plan to do?" asked Logan, twisting the chain on the handcuffs as quietly as he could. He wouldn't be able to keep Wade talking forever. "Lawyer up and pay off the right people? You've killed dozens, Wade. I don't think it will work."

"Dozens of scum," scoffed Wade. "There isn't a jury in the world that will convict me. They'll see what I did. It was justifiable homicide. I managed to do what the system couldn't. I'll never go to jail. They can arrest me but I'll be out before nightfall."

"Are you sure? If you had stopped killing after the child molester a few months ago? Maybe you would have. Or even after Bill, perhaps. But you killed George, Wade. You got a taste for it, didn't you? You liked it. Enjoyed it. No jury will believe George was a righteous kill."

Wade's cool facade slipped for a moment, and his face twisted into an ugly mask before regaining his composure. Logan was getting to him. "George had to die just as the others did."

"Why? What had he ever done? You shot him because you like killing people. It makes you feel powerful. That's why you did it. Not to help me or anyone else. You did it for you. Are you going to kill me next? I've never committed any crimes."

Beads of perspiration popped out on Wade's forehead. "You're not listening to me."

"I've heard it all before," Logan jeered, playing for every moment he could get. "Every criminal says he's innocent. You're no different than anyone else. You shot George in cold blood."

"I am," Wade insisted. "I am different. I'm a hero. Just like you."

His voice had gone thin and desperate but Logan didn't budge. "You're a scared little man who feels bigger with a gun and a cause."

Wade stood up, a half smile on his lips, his eyes lifeless in his pale face.

"Actually I am different. Everyone in this town thinks you're invincible. I used to think that too. But you're human. You bleed red just like everyone else."

Wade went over to the island and pulled out a large knife from the butcher block.

"I'm a student of crime, Logan. I read all about those drug murders not long ago. That's what this will look like when I'm done with you."

Logan's heart accelerated and sweat pooled at the back of his neck. If he couldn't get out of these cuffs in time he was going to be cut open and gutted like a fish. Not a pretty way to go. He'd never feared death but he sure as hell had a lot to live for now with Ava.

"Don't you want the world to know you did it, Wade? This just makes you look guiltier. You know this isn't justified. You're killing me because you want to. Plain and simple. It makes you feel powerful."

"I am powerful," Wade hissed. "I fight evil and make things right. I won't let you stop me."

Wade stood right in front of Logan's chair, his face contorted with anger and something evil that Logan had only seen a few times in his life. Wade lifted up the knife and brought it down in a wide arc, the blade slicing through Logan's shirt and the flesh of his upper arm.

Logan hissed and gritted his teeth, not wanting to let Wade know how the pain bloomed and burned. A red stain had formed and was growing larger on the fabric of Logan's uniform shirt.

"Only about fifty or so more of these to go, Logan. A tough son of a bitch like you is going to take a long time to die."

Logan could feel the blood dripping down his arm, the cool liquid a contrast to his sweat-covered skin. He rotated his right wrist one last time and felt the chain lock tightly. Knowing this was the moment, Logan pressed the metal bracelets together tightly, feeling the links in the chain give way with a snap. The rings were still wrapped around him but his hands were no longer tethered together.

He would have to thank Frank Jesse for sending him into the military. Otherwise he never would have known how to do that. He took a deep breath and waited for the right moment.

Ava fumed as she pulled into Logan's long driveway. Her sister was a complete and total bitch and Ava didn't care if she ever spoke to her again. Mary clearly blamed Ava for anything and everything, and she was tired of being Mary's whipping bitch. She'd finally cut her sister off and stomped out of the Bryson estate. She wanted to talk to Logan and hear what he'd found. Happily his truck was in front of the house.

Bounding up the steps, she pushed open the front door and headed straight for the kitchen. Logan was probably sitting at the island working on whatever he'd found today.

She went through the foyer and stopped dead in her tracks. Fear kept her from moving, her limbs frozen and her breath shallow. Logan was sitting in a chair with a couple of large bloodstains on his shirt. Wade was brandishing a horrific knife, his own clothes splattered with a few blood drops.

She must have gasped or maybe even screamed because Wade whirled around, the knife still in his hand. He roared and started heading straight for her, his teeth bared in some kind of animal rage. Finally able to move, she turned to run but before she could make it to the front door she heard a crash. Logan had tackled Wade to the floor.

Wade growled in frustration as the two men rolled around, each trying to subdue the other. Logan threw a punch to Wade's jaw, just as he brought his knee up into Logan's gut. The two men grappled until Wade was sitting on top of Logan. Wade tried to bring the knife down into Logan's chest but it was a battle of strength at this point. Normally Logan would win easily but injured was another story.

Giving an eardrum rattling battle cry, Logan managed to dislodge Wade, sending him sprawling onto the area rug. Ava watched as Wade's features twisted, his chest heaving with his exertion. He awkwardly tried to stand but his legs didn't appear to have the strength to hold him.

Logan levered up onto his knees and grabbed Wade's wrist, knocking the knife to the floor. It skittered across the hardwood and came to rest several feet away. Still holding Wade's arm, Logan pulled back his right hand and punched his foe in the nose, blood spurting everywhere, the crunching of bones making Ava shudder.

Whatever fight Wade had in him was now gone. All the rage that had been driving him seemed to leak out at that point. His body went limp and he whimpered in pain, curling up in a ball.

Ava hadn't realized she'd been holding her breath but she finally sucked in a lungful of air, her head spinning from lack of oxygen. Relief and disbelief warred inside of her.

Wade was the killer.

Logan sat back on his heels, his breathing ragged, and finally turned to her.

"Call 911. Then go into the bedroom and get my spare cuffs from the bedside table."

That snapped her to attention. She quickly dialed 911, giving them the particulars then ran to get the handcuffs. He also had a handgun, a set of brass knuckles, and a Taser nestled right next to his supply of condoms. They really needed to have a talk.

Logan slapped them on Wade who was still lying on the floor with tears streaming down his cheeks. Ava found some dishtowels and wrapped them around Logan's arms where he'd been cut hoping to stem the flow. They didn't look deep but he would probably need some stitches.

She and Logan sat back against the wall in exhaustion as they listened to the sirens growing louder. Tires squealed on the concrete driveway and Deputy Drake came in the door taking in the scene.

"Put him in the car," Logan directed. "Read him his rights."

"Looks like we need to get you handled first, Logan."

Logan shook his head. "Deal with him. I'll be fine."

EMTs suddenly filled the doorway. "Wherever you go, I go," Ava said, determined she would stay with Logan even if they took him to the hospital.

"Honey, I wouldn't have it any other way."

Statements were made. Wade was carted off to jail, and Logan was stitched up by the paramedics. It seemed like hours before the last person pulled out of the driveway and Logan and Ava were alone once again.

Ava carefully wrapped her arms around Logan. She didn't want to hurt him but she needed to be close to him right now. She was trembling as the adrenaline drained from her body.

"You scared the hell out of me." She was smiling and crying at the same time. She'd been terrified walking in on that scene. She should have known better. Wade was no match for Sheriff Logan Wright.

She ran her hands up and down his chest, loving this man more than anything in the world. "When I walked in here I swear my heart stopped beating for a few seconds."

He leaned down to kiss her gently and the events of the day fell away. "So did mine, good girl. I still had some hope, even as I came home today, that he wouldn't be guilty." Logan shook his head sadly. "He is. And delusional by the sound of it. He thought he was doing the world a service."

"He wanted to be just like you." Ava laid her hand on Logan's jaw feeling the roughness of his beard. She'd heard Logan's statement about why Wade became a vigilante. "I can't say as I blame him. You're my hero, that's for sure."

A dull red stained his cheeks. "I'm just a cop." He looked up and seemed to notice the house was empty. "I need to call my sheriff friends. They'll be wanting to hear all about this."

"Ten minutes. Then I'm putting you to bed with a pain pill."

Logan chuckled but didn't object. Whether he admitted it or not, he needed more than scrambled eggs and a shoulder rub. He needed her to care for him. He'd fight her all the way but this was one argument she was determined to win.

"Fifteen and I'll obey your every command."

She knew better than to believe him. He was ornery and stubborn, and he was going to make her crazy. She'd love every minute of it.

When he was feeling better, she'd tell him her decision. As she'd watched for a few horrible seconds while Wade try to stab Logan, she'd known she could never be without this man. There and then, she'd decided to sell her condo and move to Corville. She wanted every single day and then some.

"Make your call. I'll be right here waiting. Always."

"We have to be at the wedding in an hour," Ava scolded. "We can't be late."

"The church is ten minutes away," Logan smiled. "We have plenty of time."

Ava draped his blue silk tie over his shoulder. "Stop playing with your treehouse drawings and finish getting dressed. It's a sad day when I get ready faster than you do."

For the last six months, Logan had been poring over the plans for a new treehouse. The ranch had sold quickly and they'd purchased this lovely two-story home in a newer neighborhood with large three acre lots. The property they'd chosen had several trees that were good candidates for the elaborate structure that Logan had been dreaming up with his sheriff buddies. It would be a palace in the clouds.

Ava's condo was also sold and they'd gone back to Portland for a short trip to pack her belongings and say goodbye to her friends. None of them had blamed her for marrying Logan and moving back home. If anything, they'd been in awe of what one of them called "sex on legs".

"I've been busy. Besides, weddings are for women. Honeymoons are for men," Logan teased. "At least our honeymoon was."

Logan slipped the tie around his neck and began executing a perfect Windsor knot. He really was a Renaissance man.

"I think we both enjoyed the honeymoon." Ava hopped on one foot while she pulled on a black high-heeled pump. "We tolerated the wedding."

"Are you sure?" Logan paused, a scowl on his face. "Do you regret not having a big wedding like Christina and Jack? Did I cheat you out of that rushing you to the altar?"

He *had* rushed her to the altar. Indecently so. Her mother had even delicately questioned her if perhaps a bundle of joy was on the way. Her father hadn't said a word about the haste but he was now able to look her in the eye when he spoke. It was progress.

Of course Mary hadn't attended the small wedding. She wasn't speaking to Ava and her parents were firmly caught in the middle of this emotional tug of war. Mary was determined to play the victim and in her mind Ava was a terrible, no good sister for helping uncover Wade's crimes.

Wade's attorney had him pleading insanity and he was currently awaiting trial. The state had already announced its plan to seek the death penalty due to the sheer number of victims, some of them very probably innocent of what they'd been accused of.

"Not in the least." Ava shuddered delicately. "I've never dreamed about a big white wedding. It was nice just having a few friends and family at the church and then a little dinner party at my parents' afterwards."

Helen had even been able to join them. Ava was determined to make sure Logan and Helen never lost touch again.

The woman had been right about the location of Logan's mother's remains. After an extensive search they'd found her by the lake where she used to meet Bill Bryson. After DNA had confirmed her identity, they'd buried her in a lovely grave at the top of a hill. Since then Logan seemed to be more at peace than she'd ever seen him. The demons that had driven him were finally gone.

"I just want you to be happy." Logan's handsome face was perfectly serious.

He showed her that every day of their lives. He'd even offered to move to Portland for her but she'd known she was doing the right thing returning to Corville. Her mother, especially now with all the family strife, needed her.

"It was your idea to even get married," Ava teased. "I would have lived with you in sin."

"You're too much of a good girl to live in sin. Besides, I wanted you firmly tied to me. For life."

"After what we did on our honeymoon, I don't think you can call me a good girl anymore." She tugged at his tie. "Speaking of being tied down…what are you doing later after the reception, bad boy?"

His eyebrow rose. "I have to wait that long? I'll never survive."

Sliding her arms around his waist, she smiled up at her husband. She loved him more every day. "We can't duck out early. We have our whole lives to play bedroom games. Christina and Jack only get married once. Although I do think weddings make you frisky. You were like this after Tanner and Madison's wedding."

Logan lifted her up out of her shoes and laid a smoking hot kiss on her lips. She marveled at how he could still make her dizzy with desire as if it was the first time. "I'm like this every night or haven't you noticed?" She had noticed, as a matter of fact, but she sure wasn't complaining. "The wedding didn't have a damn thing to do about it. I love you."

He said it every day, just as he had promised. They took turns making breakfast and rubbing each other's shoulders. In a few short months, they'd built a true partnership.

"I love you too. Can we go now?"

Logan laughed and tapped her on the nose. "Anything you want, good girl."

It wouldn't always be this easy. They were both strong people with definite ideas of how things should be done. They'd already butted heads a few times. But even when they disagreed, the love and respect they felt for each other never wavered.

Neither of them had been looking for love and forever, but they'd found it in each other. They'd faced the secrets of the past and found a truth all their own.

Deep abiding love.

Epilogue

Logan pulled into the parking lot of the roadhouse and swung out of the truck. It was the first decent spring day of the year and he sure as shit didn't want to spend it indoors. As soon as this meeting was over he was heading straight home so he and Ava could take a ride out on the bike. Between work and the weather they hadn't ridden for months.

Getting used to "writer Ava" had been something of an adjustment. She would stay up until all hours, barely eating and sleeping when she was close to finishing her book. He'd been compelled to step in and make sure she took care of herself and at first she'd been more than a little steamed. Once she realized he was doing it out of love things had been better. She still got snippy with him but she didn't hold a grudge. Logan was learning when to back off as well. She'd get this wild-eyed expression when she was writing and he knew now to throw chocolate and step out of the room.

"My month just isn't complete until I see your ugly asses," Logan said with a grin. "How did I get so lucky?"

Pulling out a chair, he sat down and reached for one of the soda cans in the middle of the table. Everyone but Reed appeared to be there and before Logan could even ask about him he was flying in the front door, a harassed look on his face.

"Sorry I'm late. Shit, I need a vacation."

"You never take a vacation." Tanner slid a soda down to Reed. "When was the last time you had some time off, anyway?"

Reed shrugged and popped open the can. "I don't remember. I never know what to do on my days off. What do you do?"

"Come here and meet with you guys," Jared laughed. "Logan was just telling us how much he loves us. It made me feel all warm inside."

Logan flipped Jared the bird across the table. "Fuck you, asshole."

Griffin pounded on the table. "Can I call this meeting to order?"

"Let's get to it," Seth agreed, looking happy and relaxed now that the baby was sleeping through the night. Bennett Elvis Reilly was growing by leaps and bounds and turning into the cutest kid Logan had ever seen. He had Seth's coloring and Presley's outgoing personality. The boy would probably grow up to be president.

Tanner leaned back in his chair. "It's been a quiet month for me. In fact we've had nothing but quiet months since the vigilante was caught. Logan, can you give us an update on the case?"

All eyes swung to him and Logan took a drink of his soda before answering. He'd had months to get used to talking about it but it still didn't come easily. "They're still pursuing the insanity plea although I've heard rumblings it's just the starting point for negotiations to get the death penalty off the table."

"I can believe he's insane." Reed's brows were pulled down. "It isn't normal to kill people with delusions of being some kind of hero."

"He's not insane," Griffin snorted. "Crazy like a fox maybe. He hid his crimes. He knew he'd done wrong. I do feel sorry for him. He watched his father murder his mother. That has to fuck with you. I can see why he felt the justice system let him down. But he's not crazy."

That was a lot of words at one time for Griffin. He was compact in his speaking.

"After talking with him, I don't think he's insane either," conceded Logan. "I think he knew what he was doing. He just needed to feel justified."

Tanner scratched his chin. "Have you heard any more about the unsolved murders in Denver when Wade was attending school there?"

Logan shook his head. "No. They're looking into him as a possible suspect. Not that it will matter even if they get the evidence and an extradition order. He'll never see the light of day."

Bryson Development had been sold to a large corporate entity to help pay Wade's legal bills which were going to be ungodly huge. Logan had taken his share and donated it to the only battered women's shelter in the county. He certainly hadn't wanted anything to do with that blood money. Lyle and Aaron were planning to move their families out of town due to the intense publicity. They couldn't go anywhere without people whispering behind their backs.

Ava would lose her sister but it was probably for the best, at least for now. Mary had been playing her parents off of one another and it wasn't healthy for anyone.

Seth slapped Logan on the back. "You did good, buddy. With hardly any help from us. I kind of felt left out."

"You had Presley and Bennett to worry about. You can help next time."

"Kind of ironic that it ended up being you," Seth mused.

"Did you think I wouldn't bring him in if I caught him?" From the look on Seth's face that was exactly what his friend thought. "I wish you had been there. All of you. This was a joint effort. I couldn't have done this without you."

Reed threw back his head and laughed. "You couldn't have done it without Ava. She's a damn good investigator. Good looking too."

Reed was just trying to yank Logan's chain. He'd taken a lot of shit these past months about being roped and tied. "Ava has officially retired. No more police work."

"Does she know that?" Tanner chuckled, a smile playing on his lips. "She seemed pretty gung ho last time I saw her."

"Retired," Logan said flatly. "I'm serious about this. I don't want her to get hurt."

The rest of the time passed quickly as they traded information about some minor drug dealing before the meeting broke up. Logan had made it to his truck when a hand came down on his shoulder.

"You did good," Reed said. "Just for the record. I always knew you'd bring the vigilante in."

"Never doubted me for a second, huh?" Logan's lips twisted into a smile.

"Not at all," Reed assured him. "You're a good lawman. Maybe one of the best. You always knew you'd bring him in."

Logan had known it. Not once had it ever crossed his mind to turn the other way.

"It's over now." Logan unlocked his truck and pulled the door open. "I don't know about you but I'm looking forward to things getting back to normal around here."

Reed nodded to where Griffin was climbing into his truck. "No one more so than Griff. He likes it quiet and boring in his little town."

Reed and Logan waved to Griffin as he grinned and backed out of the parking lot pulling close to where they were standing.

"Either of you in the mood to go fishing? I'm headed out to the lake." Griffin jerked his thumb toward the bed of the truck. "I've got plenty of supplies."

Shaking his head, Logan declined. "Sounds like fun, but I'll have to take a rain check. I'm on duty today. But you should take this guy." Logan slapped Reed on the back and his friend groaned.

"Aw, shit. Fishing with Griffin? Do I have to?" Reed was just busting Griffin's balls, and the man didn't appear to take any offense.

"Some fresh air will do you good. You can follow me in your truck." Griffin gunned the engine of the massive vehicle.

"You need to learn to relax. Who better to teach you than the Grand Master himself?" Logan teased.

Reed flipped him the bird but didn't argue as he climbed into his own truck, pulling it behind Griffin's. As they sped down the road, Logan didn't feel an ounce of regret that he wasn't going with them. He had something much better to go home to.

Pointing the truck toward Corville, Logan knew he'd found the right balance between dedication to the job and building a life and family. He would always put the woman he loved first. It had taken him awhile to get here but now that he was, he couldn't imagine living any other way. He was a husband and hopefully someday a father. Ava was his family. She'd kept her promises.

THE END

Cowboy Command
Cowboy Justice Association
Book One

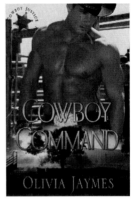

Sometimes you have to die to be born.

One minute Katie is eating lunch with her sister, the next she barely escapes a car bomb meant to kill her. If that wasn't enough, someone sets fire to her home and burns it to the ground. Luckily, Federal agents are going to give her a new identity until she can testify against the man who wants her dead. They change her name to Presley, her hair color to brown, and her shorts and sandals to jeans and cowboy boots. She's not thrilled about being sent to a small town in Montana to hide, but she wants to stay alive.

Sheriff Seth Reilly is doing a favor for an old Army buddy. He's promised to watch over a woman whose life is in danger, but he didn't plan on her being so young and beautiful. He's tempted, but she's a bundle of trouble. Seth likes his women calm and sedate. Presley is the kind of woman who would keep him up at night and make him crazy. Too bad he's starting to enjoy it.

Passion flares between Seth and Presley, heating up the cold Montana nights. Knowing they only have a short time together, they vow not to fall in love. But when danger finds Presley, Seth will risk everything to keep her safe until she can testify. Will Presley get her old life back or start a new life with Seth instead?

Justice Healed
Cowboy Justice Association
Book Two

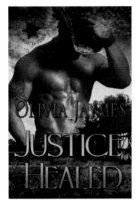

You can't go home again, but if you do, pretend you want to be there.

Dr. Madison Shay has left Chicago and moved back to her small town roots to take over her father's medical practice. She's not the skinny, gawky red haired, four-eyed girl any longer but it sure feels that way. She still remembers the painful teasing from her classmates and always feeling like she didn't belong. She wants this time to be different but deep down she knows she'll never be part of the cool crowd.

Sheriff Tanner Marks might have been the captain of the football team years ago but things aren't as rosy now. He has a son who hates him, and an ex-wife who is about to marry a man Tanner thinks might be a criminal. He doesn't really have time in his life for a woman. Considering the things he's done in his past, he's not sure he deserves one either. He can't help but feel envious of his friend, Seth Reilly, though. He found the love of a good woman. Is it too much to ask that fate send him someone as well?

Madison and Tanner aren't looking for love but it feels like the town has other plans. They keep finding themselves thrown together and it's not unpleasant in the least. In fact, they're starting to enjoy themselves. There just might be a future for them after all.

When a drug war between two cartels breaks out, their little town is caught in the crossfire. Tanner will call in every favor he can, from the five cowboy cops he trusts most in the world, to keep his town and the woman he loves safe. He's going to show the bad guys what cowboy justice really means.

Cowboy Truth
Cowboy Justice Association
Book Three

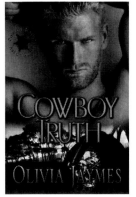

People will do desperate things to keep the truth dead and buried.

Sheriff Logan Wright might be the sexiest bad boy Ava Hayworth has ever seen but she's not interested in the least. He can have every other woman in town and probably already has. All she wants is to help him solve the murder of a prominent local citizen by a mysterious vigilante serial killer. A fling with a smokin' hot cowboy cop isn't in her plans.

Logan doesn't need a mystery writer who thinks she's a detective, trailing after him while he tries to do his job. She's smart and cute, but he doesn't want her to get hurt. By him or the investigation. He enjoys the pleasures of women – many women – and that's not going to change.

But as painful secrets are revealed, Logan begins to depend on Ava for more than just friendship. She's the first woman he's known who has kept her promises. It shakes him to his very core, challenging long held beliefs.

Everything Logan wants, but never thought he could have, is within his grasp. With the help of Ava and his friends, he's going to have to fight the past if he wants any kind of a future.

About the Author

Olivia Jaymes is a wife, mother, lover of sexy romance, and caffeine addict. She lives with her husband and son in central Florida and spends her days with handsome alpha males and spunky heroines.

She is currently working on a series of full length novels called The Cowboy Justice Association. It's a contemporary erotic romance series about six lawmen in southern Montana who work to keep the peace but can't seem to find it in their own lives.

Visit Olivia Jaymes at: www.OliviaJaymes.com

Made in United States
North Haven, CT
14 July 2025

70672057R00185